# MOLTEN IRON

## BEN NAAS

A NOVEL

NEXT DIMENSION PUBLISHING, LLC

Published by Next Dimension Publishing, LLC

Cover designed by Xavier Comas and Rafa Andres Pio

Interior designed by Ben Naas

Manufactured in the United States of America

ISBN: 979-8-9851158-2-6

ISBN (E-book): 979-8-9851158-3-3

This one is for the people at Better Blend. Thank you for being more than a company, introducing me to my best friends, and completely changing my life. You guys will always be my biggest supporters.

# Table of Contents

# Dossier

## The Knights
### Camelot
**Nathan Stromberg (Merlin)** - American
The "ruler" of Camelot
**Savannah Hamlin (Sir Guinevere)** - American
The Ember Knight
**Isabella Knowles (Sir Tristan)** - English
The Alchemy Knight
**Immanuel Kasongo (Sir Ector)** - Congolese
The Space Knight
**Masaru Kato (Sir Kay)** - Japanese
The Death Knight
**Sabine Hochleutner (Sir Bedivere)** - German
The Sun Knight; killed by Pierre.

### Fernando's Team
**Fernando Santos (Sir Bors)** - Argentinian
The Time Knight
**Bihn Nguyen** - Vietnamese
Santo's personal bodyguard.
**Bors the Younger** - Gallic
Maid 1
**Tessa Snyder** - Canadian
Maid 2
**Ilcaeus** - Daegaryn
Santos's ace in the sleeve

## The Others

**Rajeev Patel (Sir Galahad)** - Qatari

The Iron Knight

**Eoin McGowan (Sir Lancelot)** - Irish

The Sea Knight; former member of
Camelot

**Elise Laurent (Sir Gareth)** - French

The Life Knight

**Pierre Castillon (Sir Gawain)** - French

The Earth Knight

## The Powerless

**James Cox** - American

Savannah's therapist and only friend

**Dmitri Smirnov** - Russian

Rajeev's employer

**Yasmin Patel** - Qatari

Rajeev's wife who has brain cancer

**Tej Vayida** – Indian

Agent that is used as scapegoat for
Santos

## The Daegaryns and Their Dji

**Azarox** - Fire

**Balthasar** - Superstrength

**Catharsis** - "Literal silver tongue"

**Eryon** - Camouflage

**Glanderos** – Intangibility

**Diomedes** – Heat and x-ray vision

**Kalynst** – superspeed

Father and uncle killed by Merlin

# Prologue

**A man, dressed** all in black, approached his companion, meditating in the dry, Colorado heat. However, the sky had been growing darker by the second, foreshadowing the first rain in months, a heavy one at that. There was a slight limp in his step and his right foot left a deeper mark in the ground than the other as he reached his friend, a large Irishman with a bushy, fiery beard that clung to most of his face and tree trunk of a neck as if to replace the lack of hair on top of his head.

"It's ready," the giant said in a gravelly voice, juxtaposing his hearty Irish accent. His head remained facing his lap, where a longsword lay across. "Where's Elise?"

"Here!" a youthful voice flowering with French called. The man turned around to see a beautiful young girl of the age of fourteen with mocha skin, riding to them on the back of an elk, a quiver slung over her shoulder. How she always was able to sneak up on them on that thing, he would never know.

"Were you seen?" he asked with a similar inflection as her.

"No, Pierre," she smiled prettily. "I was hidden in the

herd."

"And the guards?"

"Asleep. Or at least all that were in my range. The snipers are probably still awake and alert." She scratched the elk behind the ear. "Don't you trust me?"

"Of course, I do. It's just . . ."

"We're about to break into the most secure prison in the world," she said, grinning as if it's just a game.

She's too young to know of the vulnerabilities of the Knights of Merlin as that *connard* had called them. He just needed to glance down at the pillar of hard Colorado soil attached to his knee—the current replacement for the leg that was taken from him—as a reminder.

A raindrop landed on his cheek, another on his arm. He looked up at the sky filled with thick, dark clouds.

"It's time," the Irishman voiced, then stood, showing them his dark blue eyes, solid with no irises or pupils.

"Where's our ride," Pierre asked of Elise.

She whistled sharply into the air, which was received by the frightening bugle of elks. A volley of dust appeared in the distance. *Our ride.*

By the time the horned beasts reached them, the rain increased in tempo to a steady beat. Soon it would be pouring down, decreasing visibility significantly. They mounted the elk, Elise's eyes then glowing a dull green, the shade of summer woods. With a nod from Pierre to the young French girl, they were off.

It was a quiet ride to the prison, each of the trio concentrating on their respective jobs.

The Rockies appeared to them first as a faint outline against the dark sky, before the Supermax emerged from the haze of the rain—now at a downpour. Pierre loosed the battle axe in its sheath on his back at the sight of the concrete facility.

ADX Florence was the most fortified prison in the entire world, housing some of the most dangerous people, including the Boston bomber: Dzhokhar Tsarnaev, Al-Qaeda cofounder: Mamdouh Mahmud Salim, and the infamous El Chapo. Each prisoner was confined to their 7-by-12-foot cells for twenty-three hours then getting one hour in a slightly bigger cage outside. They were worried about a different type of cell, however, one only known by a handful of higher-ups.

The herd reached the baseball field, where prisoners with a year of good behavior could play a few innings and circled it. They didn't have much time; the snipers in their nests could spot them any minute even with the rain and dust disrupting their view. ADX didn't get their reputation for anything.

Pierre leaped off his elk, landing just behind home base. He raised his arms out as if he was in the middle of worship, his eyes turning an earthy brown as he stared up towards the heavens and the rain pouring from it. Yet, oddly, it was just rain, no wind, nor lightning or thunder to join it. A storm without the rage.

The ground in front of the Frenchman cracked, spreading around the length of the crappy prison field. The infield began to rise, dirt crumbling down the sides.

A sharp crack filled the air. The storm had found its rage, but a large chunk out of the corner of Pierre's head said differently. The earth dropped back down with a heavy thud.

"Shit," the giant cursed, reaching for the sword on his back, and searched blindly in the storm for the sniper.

"I got him, Eoin," Elise shouted at the Irishman.

Closing her eyes, she grabbed an arrow, pointed it out into the monsoon, and released it, where it traveled like a missile toward the target. There was a sharp cry, barely audible with all the rain, and the arrow returned to her, only now it was red. She replaced it, seemingly unfazed.

By now Pierre had recovered, with no sign of the bullet

wound except for the stickiness in his dark hair, which was already getting washed out. Five minutes later, metal gleamed underneath the rising field. In another two minutes, a windowless chamber was fully revealed, and Pierre lowered his arms, eyes returning to their normal baby blue irises.

"You two stay guard," the Frenchman ordered. "I have a feeling we're about to have some company."

Standing in front of the cell, Pierre punched in the code given to them (not exactly willingly). The door unsealed with a dramatic *swish* and swung open. Inside stood a frightened young girl, wearing only a sheer uniform. She couldn't have been much older than eighteen.

"Please help me," she pleaded in a harsh German accent. Her platinum hair was crudely sheared off. "I didn't mean to do it."

*It doesn't matter.* He unsheathed his battle axe from behind him. The blade was made of some dark metal not found on Earth, with runes carved into it, while the shaft was just crafted from common steel. He hefted the ancient weapon—*Gravedigger* Everton called it—to the sound of distant gunshots and heaved it into the smooth, pale flesh of her neck.

# Part 1

---

# The Burden of Power

*For death itself is victory, and a healing unto the soul.*
-Geoffrey of Monmouth<br>The History of the Kings of Britain

# Chapter One

**Her face glowed** in the red light, accentuating auburn hair that stirred softly in the light, Kentucky breeze while bringing out the freckles she had hated so much for the early years of high school when she still cared. Luke Bryan sang about some country tragedy he probably never dealt with, while the '96 Mercury Mystique purred softly under her feet. The woman took a sip from a bottle of Jim Beam, her hand shaking just slightly. In the other hand, she rubbed her thumb over the three on the chip. *A new record.*

Red changed to green, the color of the chip she threw out the window as she pushed the tired car forward though it grumbled at the request. The check engine light had been on for two months. *If I can stay sober for three months, this car can wait for another two*, the woman thought while taking a hit from her Vuse, breathing in the minty vapor.

Trees surrounded her when she pulled into the dark driveway. No neighbors for the next twenty miles, just how she liked it. The Mystique stopped with a squeal in front of the house, five hundred feet from the main road. It was a quaint thing, made of brick and mortar, with one floor, containing only a bedroom, kitchen/laundry room, bathroom, and living room. There was no need for anymore; she lived by herself and planned to keep it that way. And friends . . . she didn't really have any. Not that she wanted the company.

After turning off the ignition and exiting the car, the woman entered through the sole outer door, flipping on the lights and tossing the keys into a tray. Still holding onto the whiskey glass, she dragged herself to the kitchen and transferred a Skyline 5-Way from the fridge to the microwave that badly needed to be cleaned. While she waited, the woman turned on the small TV in the corner. She checked her phone as a news anchor discussed the turmoil going on in Europe.

*"How was work?"* James had texted her.

*"Good,"* the woman quickly replied.

*"Savannah, describe it."* She could almost see him scrunching up his nose as his eyes narrowed. *"What happened? Anything out of the norm? Did you have any irritable customers?"*

*"Normal deli things. Not really. No more than usual."*

Her phone rang. *Shit.* If she ignored it, he would know she was drinking. If she answered it, he would know she was drinking. She sighed and swiped right, might as well rip off the bandage.

"James, I'm really tired," Savannah answered with a strong Alabama twang, straining to sound sober, even though she knew it was pointless.

"You've been drinking, haven't you?"

She didn't reply, instead retrieving her leftovers.

"What happened?"

"This lady said I'd sliced her a third of a pound when she just wanted a quarter and that it was too thick." She sat down at the plastic card table.

"And how did you reply?"

"Why do you want bologna? Is it because it reminds you of your wife?"

"Savannah!"

"What? If you saw her, you'd be thinking the same thing." Savannah took a bite of the 5-Way, chasing it down with the whiskey.

"That's what caused you to break your sobriety?"

"Nah, she got the manager on my ass. He said I had one more chance, or I'm gone."

"Savannah, you have to quit with this. Control your anger."

*But why did he have to smoke a cigarette right in my face?*

"Yeah, I know. I'll do better next time," she said, just trying to end the conversation.

"And you need to stop drinking every time something or someone sets you off."

*What if that's the only way to keep the demon on a leash?*

"Yeah, that embroidery suggestion is really helping."

"I don't need your sarcasm, all right." She could hear his deflated irritation on the other end. "I was just saying to find a hobby. Make some friends. Go on a date. Just do something that keeps your mind occupied."

She pushed the Skyline to the side, no longer hungry.

"I'm trying, James, I really am trying to . . ."

"To what?"

*Live*

"To control my anger, but it's like there's . . . a fire inside me that wants to consume."

"And alcohol only increases the ferocity of a fire."

"I'll see you Wednesday, James."

Hanging up, Savannah reached for the whiskey and hesitated. "Screw it." She took a large swallow. *What does he know about what I'm dealing with? Nobody does.*

Leaving her dinner on the table, she moved into her bedroom. As modest as the rest of the house, it contained a concrete drawer placed next to a tiny closet, both facing a waterbed with room for just one. She undressed, struggling to undo her jeans with her drunken fingers, and threw the clothes into the overflowing bin in the corner. The bathroom adjoined her quarters, and she went there now, starting the shower. As it warmed up, she stared at herself in the mirror, tracing the cursed, purple mark on her left breast that had brought so much pain to her life.

After her shower, she went to her bed still naked, double-checking the fire extinguisher next to it before she sat down. A single framed photo perched on the bedside table, the edges charred. Holding it in one hand, the other drifted unconsciously back to her breast.

Her life was ashes.

# Chapter Two

**No alarm woke** Savannah. It was her day off and time didn't matter to her. Every hour meant the same to her and the only difference between night and day was the amount of light in the sky.

She slowly got dressed and then started a pot of coffee, turning on the TV—the sole source of entertainment in the house—while the water boiled. Some fat news anchor was on, talking about a terrorist attack in Libya, wherever the hell that was. She changed the channel to Comedy Central that showed some sitcom she didn't care enough to follow. She needed to laugh, or at least that's what James told her.

Savannah poured the finished coffee into a mug and mixed in two dollops of International Delight creamer and just a dash of sugar. On TV, a man with glasses and dressed in a mustard dress shirt sliced the face off a CPR manikin and then wore it, quoting from a movie she had seen long ago. No laughter escaped her throat even though she felt it should be funny. Humor did not come easy to her anymore. Especially when it involved the mockery of murder. She turned the TV off and slowly sipped at her coffee. There was nowhere she had to be.

Later she left for the gym in her struggling Mystique, wearing a sweatshirt over a pair of sweatpants. James had said working out was good for the mind. It seemed everything she did was because James had advised her to do it. She was getting too close to him, but life wasn't meant to go at alone.

Or so James said.

Anyway, working out did help her, and she did it about every day. It wasn't a good substitute for drinking. But it was something. And it was better than just sitting around her house all day watching crappy television.

She started out on the treadmill and increased the speed to 7.0 to warm up. Strangely, Savannah was well-conditioned for someone who vaped all the time and only ate fast food. She bumped it up to 9.0, then 10.0, running without breaking a sweat until she hit three miles and finishing in just under twenty minutes. For the remainder of her workout, Savannah hit the machines, never taking off her sweats. An hour later, she left, not bothering to take a shower in the locker rooms.

In her aging Mercury, Tyler Childers's "Feathered Indians" played while Savannah pulled up the DoorDash app and left for her first delivery. The pickup was at some kind of smoothie shop called Better Blend, where a giddy, young man greeted her with the delivery. She drove the product to the "poor part of town"—not many of Pikeville's citizens were even close to being considered rich. The recipient had requested the smoothie to be left at the front porch—a shabby thing—and as Savannah did, she made sure to slip in a ten-dollar bill.

James had told her—she was beginning to wonder if she had any independent thought, though maybe that was for the best—charitable works would be beneficial to her degrading mental health. Savannah hated when people thanked her, knowing she didn't deserve the gratitude. So, she found another way. She only needed money for the basic bills, so she gave the rest away. Maybe it would've been easier for her to just donate online, but it did feel good to know the recipient was right behind the door. And DoorDashing gave her something to do. Life gets boring sometimes.

She would do this until she got tired—stopping only for lunch and dinner—then go home and sleep. Wash. Rinse. Repeat. Same thing, different job. The only escape from the daily routine was her time with James.

Or to escape to the bar.

# Chapter Three

**The constant humming** buzzed in the back of Rajeev Patel's head as he climbed the side of the first of the two Al Fardan towers. He long ago accepted it as his impending insanity. Rajeev usually could block it out but sometimes it would linger, making it very difficult to concentrate. And for the job today, he would need every bit of his mental capacities.

Rajeev wore all black today which included a ski mask, an essential detail when scaling a building filled with vacationing celebrities, successful businessmen, and conspiring politicians. It also helped to hide the fact that he did not use any equipment. All he needed was himself, a human magnet that could attract every type of metal known or unknown to man.

And so, he climbed—though that was a poor word; he walked on the outer wall as easily as on the ground—focusing on the mission before him to keep the humming at bay. It was a senator from India who was here for pleasure rather than business. Damini Joshi was her name, and she would be dead before sunrise. The reason for her demise was not what he was paid for.

He reached the twenty-seventh floor and crossed into the middle of the building, walking between windows until he reached the fourth one closest to the sister tower. Inside, a curtain blocked his view and there was no latch to unlock and open the window. They were fixed.

Rajeev had overlooked that in his research but there was no going back to reassess; Joshi's checkout was for tomorrow morning. He stared at his reflection and an idea came to him. Removing his metal backpack with gloved hands, he took out a bag of razor blades. The blades levitated before him, then ripped through the plastic bag. They circled for a bit in the air then moved to the window where they cut a circle into the glass. Rajeev winched at the sound, loud to his strained ears but hopefully nonexistent to the senator within.

Now, here came the tricky part. He placed a hand on the cut piece of glass, careful not to push it in, and closed his eyes as he sensed within the apartment, searching. It only took a second before he located a small, cylinder-shaped object and slowly moved it toward his hand. A moment later, it pushed the glass into his hand. The thing was a vibrator of all things, and he put it and the glass into his pack, replacing them with a handful of miniature iron rods. Rajeev forced them into the hard-earned hole and when inside, they formed a hand, which he used to pull the curtains to the side.

Finally, he could see his target, fortunately still sleeping soundly under a silk blanket. Without allowing any time for what was left of his morals to affect his decision, he removed a spent bullet—less questions—from a pocket and pushed it hard at her temple. There were no sounds as she died. *Killed by an assassin with a nine-millimeter with a silencer attachment while she slept, the news would say.*

He turned to leave but then a little girl's cry drew him back. The child came into view, calling for her mom. She glanced out the window and a bullet led her to a quick, painless death.

*Also murdered Joshi's young daughter*, the merciless reporter would continue. *What a monster.*

Rajeev walked back down Al Farden.

On the outskirts of Doha, Rajeev walked in the shadows of suburbs that appeared to be asleep yet were anything but. He had been mugged only once here, but after the mangled body was found on the sidewalk outside his duplex, his neighbors tended to avoid him. It was a dangerous place to live, but he was a dangerous person. And just on cue, a gunshot followed by two others sounded a few blocks away as he walked up the steps to his duplex. He ignored them. Not his problem.

"Rajeev," A weak voice called from upstairs when the door with rusty hinges squealed open. "Is that you?"

"Yes, *lav*," He returned. "Why are you still awake? It's . . ." he checked his watch. *Al-ama.* "Four o'clock."

"I couldn't sleep."

Rajeev dropped his pack on the floor and hurried upstairs, the old floorboards creaking loudly as he did. "Is it the pain?"

"It wasn't that bad earlier, I swear."

"*Lav*, you know I could've gotten you more tonight. But I'll be picking up some tomorrow morning."

He opened the door to their bedroom. Yasmin Patel was twenty-one, three years his junior with the most beautiful hazel eyes that shined when she smiled at him through dark sockets. Less than a year ago, she had fainted while making dinner. The doctors had said she had a brain tumor in her cerebellum and gave her six months to live. It has now been eight. Screw the doctors. He could bend steel with a single thought, yet Yasmin was even stronger. What was a brain tumor to the likes of her?

There were two bags on a rack connected to the IV drip but only the one with the chemotherapy drugs contained anything—just a quarter. The medicine for her pain was depleted and it had been getting worse lately. That's why he did what he did.

"It *is* tomorrow morning." She smiled, even though obviously in pain. "And why is it that I feel you have to force pain onto others to relieve my own."

"It's—"

"I know, I know. You just track down criminals for the government. But there's something in your eyes that just seems different lately. Darker and more tired. Like they've aged a great deal in the last year."

"They have aged," Rajeev agreed. "But it's going to get better soon, I promise. The people I work for—the government—are coming close to developing a method to remove pituitary brain tumors. They said that we could be part of the first trial."

It was all a lie of course—the miracle cure, his employer, and the job requirements—but to see her eyes light up for just a bit, it was worth it.

He gave another lie that he was going down to the kitchen to make himself a sandwich and instead sat down to cry through his murderous hands.

# Chapter Four

"**I want the** ham," a fat man in a scooter with more hair sprouting out his nose than on his head demanded.

"And what kind of ham do you want, sir," Savannah inquired, leaning over the deli counter to get close to the nearly deaf man.

He shrugged as if he didn't come here at least once a week.

"We got Private Selection, Boars Head, Bluegrass, honey, black forest, smoked—"

"Huh." He dabbed his nose with a very used handkerchief. Savannah tried not to make a face. "I don't know what any of that shit means. I just want ham."

She put on a thin smile reserved for everyone who decided to interrupt her silence and removed the most expensive ham from the case.

"And how do you want it sliced?"

"Sliced," he answered shrewdly, lifting his butt to do God knows what.

*No, I thought you wanted the entire ham.*

"Of course."

She sliced the ham, letting the cold meat flop onto the wax paper. She threw the pound of cold cuts onto the scale, punching in the PLU with one hand while battling flies with the other.

"I wanted a half-pound," the man pointed out surlily, wiping his nose with the back of his hand.

"Of course." She threw half the pile into the garbage next to the slicer.

"Don't waste it!" he snapped at her.

"I'm sorry. Guaranteed fresh, also means guaranteed waste." She was already bagging the ham. "What else can I get you?"

"Turkey."

Later, Savannah was at a table on the far side of the deli, making trays for an order with pre-sliced meats and cheese. She stopped for a moment, standing up straight to stretch her aching back. Her two coworkers were both hard at work, holding down the counter and serving the growing line of customers. She considered going over to help them, but the order had to get done. And she really did not want to deal with anybody. Solitude was always her preference.

The delicatessen was stuffed into the corner of a Kroger, consisting of three slicers—two for meat and one for cheese—a long, glass counter with a case for the product and three employees who hated their job. There was also a backroom with a cooler and freezer, as well as the office for the deli manager, where he would stay for most of the shift to play *Candy Crush* on the company computer.

"Savannah," one coworker called from a slicer. She had one foot planted onto the bottom, bracing herself as she shaved a buffalo chicken. "Could you help us for a minute?"

Savannah looked out and saw that line had almost reached the bakery next door. "Yeah sure, Connie." She grumbled something else under her breath.

Connie Sears was an older lady, not quite sixty, who was definitely one of the nicest of her elderly coworkers. She had two sons who had both run off on their respective eighteenth birthdays. If the rumors were true, the oldest, Cory, was having a successful career as a pot dealer, while his brother Zack was a little worse off but Cory's best customer. On her days off, she would serve in the local soup kitchens, preaching the goodness of her lord and savior Jesus Christ. She would continue her raving to her less-than-enthused coworkers.

The other one, Conney Knaley, not so much. She was well over sixty and was constantly talking about how she was going to retire soon. But with a handicapped husband—her third and still finalizing the divorce papers on this one—in and out of the hospital with a low-income job, who knew when that would happen.

Savannah changed her gloves and went to work.


Savannah leaned against the railing on the cool autumn night, watching the parking lot slowly empty for the night. The light poles illuminated the sweat glistening from underneath her askew hairnet that covered her reddish hair tied in a bun. Scooter Man wasn't the only snarky customer she had that evening; she needed a break.

The door opened behind her. It was her boss, dressed in his normal Hawaiian shirt, bulging at the gut with the threat of a button to pop off and hit her. It was also buttoned halfway down his chest to expose his ginger hair. Juice from some deli product stained his beard, supporting his self-dub of Meat Daddy.

"Brian," she acknowledged him, taking a hit from her Vuse.

Brian Hansel had worked at this location since it opened in '92, a fact he would discuss with great remembrance, as if he was an experienced general at the end of his career. Though, asking how all those years only got him the position of a deli manager, would subject them to working every Sunday for the next month.

"Another fun day at the deli," he guffawed. Savannah tried not to grimace at the cyst poking through just above his belly button.

"Yes sir," she answered curtly.

"Customers haven't been giving you a hard time, have they?"

"No sir. They're the reason we're here," she recited.

Brian grunted at that and pulled out a cigarette. Savannah made to go back inside.

"You still have another five minutes, don't you?" Brian asked, removing a lighter from his left breast pocket.

"Yes sir, but I don't need it." She had one hand on the door handle.

"Stay, the union will get on my ass if they see my employees taking short breaks." He flicked the Bic. "They would say it's my fault, too. Goddamn pencil pushers."

Savannah nodded her head shyly, wiping clammy hands on her apron. She was on the last straw with her boss, so it was best to just shut up and obey.

He was able to get a flame to unfurl from the lighter. She traced it with fearful, brown eyes, as it danced and invited the Marlboro to its warm embrace. The cigarette kissed it, transferring the fire into itself. The end burned with a faint glow as dark smoke curled up from it. Her eyes glowed the same color as she watched the scene, her own fire blossoming within.

"What's wrong with you, huh?" Brian asked just as the fire consumed the cigarette in the blink of an eye. He cursed as flames licked at his fingertips and he dropped the remains onto the ground, stomping it out as if it was a large spider.

"It's close enough," Savannah said, checking her watch.

"I'm clocking back in."

After the deli closed and they had finished cleaning the slicers, Savannah walked to her car; it was parked in the back of the lot as mandated. Though, unlike a scene in a horror movie, it was lit. No shadowy area for a boogieman to jump out from.

She opened the back door first, tossing in her meat-stained apron, before opening the front door.

"M'lady." She spun around coming face-to-face with a man dressed in a navy-blue robe that seemed like something out of the Middle Ages. A hood shrouded his face. "Does thou hast the mark?"

Savannah dived into the passenger seat, searching for a nine-millimeter that was no longer there. She pulled back and plastered her rear to the Mystique, the aluminum cool in the fall night.

"My apologies, Guinevere." He lifted the hood, revealing a youthful face with long, brown hair that threatened to cover his baby, blue eyes. "I forget myself sometimes. My name is Merlin."

"Where's my gun?" Savannah, her mind still not processing the strange man-child. *He knows about the mark!*

"With powers as great as thine, why does thou needeth a gun?"

"Dude, I work at a deli. My *power* is not murdering my customers."

"But ye do, m'lady, powers that exceed anything thy greatest scientists could even fathom. Powers that could wipe out entire countries. Entire *continents*." He scratched at the pitiful excuse of a beard he was trying to grow. "I saw that little act thee did with that pig's cigarette."

"Have you been stalking me?" she asked, furiously reaching into her pocket for her phone. Savannah pulled it out, but the screen was black and unresponsive. She knew it had at least a thirty percent charge when she left the deli.

"Only since the morrow."

"What does that even mean!" Savannah looked around frantically, but the parking lot was mostly empty. She jumped into the Mystique and slammed the door, stabbing the lock button.

*"Please don't leave, we hast so much to talk about."* His voice seemed to come from almost inside her head.

Savannah ignored the man calling himself a wizard and quickly pulled out of the space. She glanced over at him, but he was gone as if he was never there. Like a ghost.

*"I'm not the only one trying to find thee,"* rattled within her skull as she sped off into the night.

# Chapter Five

**"Very interesting methodology** last night," Dmitri Smirnov said. Rajeev's Russian employer sat behind a desk, mostly barren besides this morning's newspaper, a family-sized bag of Twizzlers, and a handle of vodka "taken proudly from the Motherland and made by my ancestors, hehe." Smirnoff was written on the side of the bottle. He was an older man—in his sixties, perhaps seventies—but didn't show it in his immature mannerisms. A messy handlebar mustache over a white beard stained with his breakfast (or maybe even last night's dinner) didn't help. A large belly completed the Russian Santa Claus recently divorced from the former Mrs. Claus look. "Murdering the little girl, very smart. I can't say I didn't expect it. Dmitri Smirnov can see it in your eyes, a killer. Yes, yes indeed."

"She saw me, so I did what I had to do," Rajeev said solemnly.

They stood inside the QIPCO building, commonly known as the Tornado Tower due to its shape—thick at the bottom then thins in the middle only to again widen at the top. It's not far from Al Fardan. The Russian hadn't left any expense in the design of his office. A leather couch of a sure-ly costly—and perhaps exotic—origin sat off to the side and across from a TV that dominated the majority of one wall. The other walls were covered with paintings of naked men poised in ways to just cover their genitals. Dmitri used his ho-mosexuality—though he did hint at some past mistresses—in ways to make his visitors feel as uncomfortable as possible.

"Yes, yes, yes. Of course, of course," Dmitri smiled at him, and several gold teeth gleamed in the LED lights of the office. "How's your girlfriend—I mean wife, how could I for-get? You married her as some kind of romantic gesture when she was diagnosed, yes? Is she well—oh, of course she's not well, she has fucking tumor in that beautiful head of hers—but how's the pain?"

Rajeev made sure to keep his face devoid of emotion—Dmitri took cruel satisfaction out of anger. "The bag is com-pletely empty. The chemotherapy drugs are almost gone too."

"A pity." The Russian feigned sadness. "Fortunately, you completed the job with an astounding effort."

He opened up a drawer and pushed the two bags of drugs across the stainless-steel desk between them, along with a slim file.

"Now, enough with this small talk, no matter how enjoy-able it has been." Dmitri reached to flip the folder, revealing a check—it would only be enough to get him through the month—and a picture of a young Indian man. "Your next target is a professional cricket player from India. Virat Kohli is his name. He will be—"

"A cricket player, are you serious?" Rajeev's goatee below a sensible mustache twitched as he tried to control his ire. He never questioned the reasons behind his job, but this was insane.

"I will admit, it's a bit of, uh, a personal grievance than . . . oh, whatever. Anyways, he lost me a lot of money," Dmitri poured himself a finger into a crystal glass from the bottle of vodka.

"I can't keep doing this," Rajeev stood and faced the other wall, where two men curled around a third. "At least not for a single bag, I need more. *She* needs more."

"Oh, why the drama, Rajeev?" The Russian flashed him a golden grin and ripped off a piece of the licorice with artificial teeth. "I thought we were friends. But a deal's a deal. One target killed, one pack of morphine. A bag for a bag, hehe."

Rajeev placed—not slammed—his fists on the desk and stared Dmitri hard in those icy eyes of his. "I have powers like that of a god and you sit here and act as if I'm expendable. *I need more medicine.*"

"Oh, how could I forget? You move metal with your mind." He took a small sip of the liquor. "You're like that superhero—er, villain—now what was his name? Oh right, Magneto, because he's a human magnet. Very creative those Marvel writers. Did I ever tell you I used to collect comic books as a boy? Of course, I didn't—why would I tell you those mundane personal details? But anyway, I used to love to read them, and me and my friend would always go down to the corner store with any change we had found between the cushions and—well, there I go, you see, boring you with personal details.

"What were we talking about again? Oh yes, your payment." Dmitri leaned forward in his rolling, office chair, a dark air to his complexion. "No, you are not expendable, Rajeev. But who would hire a criminal who killed his father—who sure drank a lot which made him a bit fiery in spirit but was beloved by all those who knew him? Hey, hey don't give me that look—I despise your respite—I know you didn't actually kill him, truly. A metal light fixture fell on him while he ate dinner, it makes complete sense—it does! I abhor sarcasm.

"His eyes twinkled. "And who's to say you didn't kill your

dear mother, who disappeared one cold, December night."

The storm under Rajeev's thin eyebrows grew even darker at the mention of his mother.

"The government, for one, sure won't hire you—too stuck in their ways for super soldiers or vigilantes. And mercenaries are not exactly listed on Craigslist—do you have that here? Good luck finding someone that will be grateful for your skills in a city that has yet to adapt to the new world."

The Russian sat back in his seat, hands placed behind his balding head. "So, no, Rajeev, Dmitri Smirnov is all you have. And you will take your payment with gratitude and be glad I don't turn you over to my more *dangerous* friends."

Rajeev nodded in somber acceptance and reached for the brief and medicine. But in his other hand, he removed a knife and threw it at the Russian.

It floated just in front of Dmitri, between his taunting eyes.

He only laughed and swallowed the last of the vodka. "You're a killer, my boy, I've seen it, yes I have. But you won't kill me. You need me just as much as I need you."

And with that, Rajeev carefully placed the medicine and file into his pack, slowly moving out of the office with the feeling that he mimicked a child storming away from their father despite his best efforts.

# Chapter Six

**Savannah rolled out** of bed as it squished around under her, last night just a bad dream. The bourbon helped with that. Grimacing from a hangover she stood and got dressed. With no work today, she wore a t-shirt with a pair of jeans—not much different than her deli attire. In the kitchen, she started a pot of coffee. *I'm not the only one trying to find thee.* She shivered even though she was never ever cold and walked to the corner of the room to retrieve a twelve-gauge.

Her hand went to her left breast. *He knows about the mark. How does he know about the mark? Who is he? Who am I?*

Peering down at her right hand with a cringe, she remembered how the bones had moved under the skin after she had broken her finger during a high school basketball practice. It was mended in minutes. And then there were the fires.

*Shit!* A glance at her watch told her she was late for her session with James.

Savannah poured the rest of the coffee into a rambler—barely feeling the piping hot liquid when some spilled on her arm—following it up with cream and sugar before running to her Mercury, making sure to not forget the shotgun. The

Mystique started up on the second try with a dying growl.

The old car rolled into James's driveway twelve minutes after her appointment. She rushed to the door and quickly rapped on the door. As she waited, Savannah fixed her hair—now tied in a loose ponytail—in the reflection of the window to the right of the door. The door swung inward, revealing a man with glasses that gave him more of a Kit Harrington appearance rather than a *Revenge of the Nerds* one. His dark hair was spiked but in a subtle way where it was not oiled up like Ross Geller. This morning he was dressed simply in khakis and a pink collared shirt that hung past his belt.

"Savannah," he welcomed her with a warm smile on his face, playfully checking his watch. "Running a little late, huh?"

"Got stuck behind a damn tractor," she lied, returning the smile.

"And then I'm sure a dragon got in your way after that," the therapist teased, moving to the side to let her go by him. "Coffee?"

"Always." His coffee was much better than the gritty kind she had made at home.

She sat down in the corner of the leather couch.

"Cream and sugar?"

She threw up a thumbs-up and he went to the kitchen. As Savannah waited, she regarded the pictures of his kids, him, and a very beautiful woman. James didn't talk too much about her—*It was a nasty divorce*, he had said early on and left it at that—but his two boys, on the other hand, one couldn't get him to stop bragging about them.

"Two splashes of cream and a spoonful of sugar," James announced when he entered the parlor.

"How long have we been meeting?" She grabbed the mug from him.

"18 months," he answered immediately.

"Then why can you still not remember that it's *one* cream

and *two* sugars?" He had gotten it correct, but she loved to mess with him every now and then.

"Oh," the therapist flushed like he had just spilled the coffee over her rather than just mess up an order that was actually right. "Let me get you a new one."

"It's fine, I guess." Savannah took a long sip to hide her smile.

"It has always amazed me how deeply you can drink from a piping hot coffee."

" 'Cause I ain't a little bitch like you."

He laughed in a high-pitched manner that she had grown to love. "Okay, let's get started. My next appointment arrives in forty-five minutes."

Both quieted down to a serious tone that Savannah had grown to hate.

"When was the last time you drank?" He sat back on the couch, his face transforming from friend to therapist.

"Starting off hot, huh." Savannah sighed. "Monday night when you called." She usually was more open to him but didn't want to explain to him the reason she got wasted last night.

"Where's your chip?"

"Somewhere on 23."

James sighed. "Just like the last one and the one before that, I suppose?"

She remained silent, looking at a picture of him and the boys at Noah's Ark in Williamstown. *Eight and ten*, she thought he had said they were.

"And what about the alcohol?"

"Jim Beam. Devil's Cut. Highly recommend," she said, feeling a little guilty about her snarkiness to a man who has been so kind to her.

"Where is it?

"Somewhere on 23."

"So, I won't find it at your place when I come over for dinner?"

"Are you asking me out?" Their flirting was more of a running joke rather than anything else. But with that being said, they still would eat at her or his place—mostly his for obvious reasons—once in a while. It's nice having a friend.

"You ever think about dating? It could help."

"Do you?" James never talked about his love life other than brief mentions of his ex.

"Touché. But all I need are my kids." He used that excuse a lot. "But we're talking about you, not me." James seemed a little flustered. "What about a pet? Having something that relies upon you can be beneficial."

"Fine, I'll get a puppy. Will that make you happy?"

"C'mon, Savannah. Be serious."

She sat still for a minute before asking, "What if I can't be helped?"

Twenty-five minutes later, Savannah left feeling worse about herself than when she got there as usual. She had a feeling that was not the intended effect of these sessions. There's been close to no improvement since she started a year and a half ago.

She stopped in her tracks right after she closed the door behind her. Leaning against her car was a heavily muscled, black man, with a tattoo of a dragon's head that covered half of the right side of his face, the eyes overlapping with the human ones. Though, something was off about those eyes.

"Who are you? What do you want?" Savannah just managed to keep her voice steady and hard. She got a bad feeling about him. *I'm not the only one trying to find thee.*

The dragon man walked towards her. All he wore was a pair of black pants. Savannah stood her ground; she was in the suburbs at one in the afternoon. There was no need to be frightened. Yet, instinct told her she should. Standing in front of her, he smiled at her, revealing a row of sharpened teeth. Now she got a closer look at his eyes. They were that of a reptile, pupils vertical and irises yellow. This was no human.

She heard a stick crack beside her. It was another one, this one white with a dragon tattoo wrapped around its abdomen. Savannah snapped her head to the left to find a third identical to the second with even the same tattoos.

The black one opened his mouth wider than was thought possible, and orange fire roared from the back of his throat. The pressure of it slammed her back into James's door as it engulfed her in an almost comforting embrace. Her eyes flashed the color of the flames that grew brighter and hotter around her, unknowingly catching the house on fire. Savannah's clothes were nothing but ash by then, but she didn't care. Didn't even notice. She *was* the fire. Gathering the flames around her as easily as moving her arms, she threw them at the man in front of her. The dragon guy just absorbed the fire, seemingly unaffected. Then something heavy knocked her to the ground.

She must have blacked out, because when she came to, one of the twins was lying beside her, blood flowing out of the area where its head used to be. Out in the middle of the yard, a hooded figure fought off the other two with a strange staff, where one blade was on each end, both facing out on opposite sides. *The man last night*, she guessed. *The one who called himself Merlin.* No one else dressed like that.

The black one spit fire onto her stalker. He spun quickly, but the end of his blue robe got singed and quickly went aflame. Merlin ripped it off in a dramatic manner, exposing a toned six-pack and black pants that rose above his waistline. His weapon spun in a blur, but the reptilian men were impossibly faster, dodging his every slash.

As he continued his fight, Savannah remembered James still inside his burning home. She quickly stood, her head pounding from where the dragon man had slugged her and started to the house.

*Mommy. Help me. Mommyyyy!*

She dropped to her knees as the screams penetrated her skull.

*Help! Savannah!*

Tears ran down her cheeks, evaporating before they reached the bottom. She looked up at the inferno, the memories burning her like no fire ever would. *I'm sorry, James. I just . . . can't.*

Suddenly, Merlin flew past her and slammed through the door, splintering the heavy oak door. She twisted her head behind her and found the other white man headless as the first, but the leader was gone. Just a minute later, he returned with James slung over his shoulder. He laid him down next to her and stood back. She slowly turned her head to gaze at her friend. His eyes stared up at the clear sky without seeing it. A sob escaped her, and she buried herself onto James, tears sizzling on his bare, burnt chest.

# Chapter Seven

**Dmitri Smirnov had** found Rajeev when he was at his lowest. Yasmin had just gotten diagnosed with cancer not long after his father died—and he *did* kill the drunken *chelb* with zero guilt. The allegations against his father caused Rajeev to be "let go" from his warehouse job. The Russian then swooped in with a contract, pen, and medicine. Rajeev signed his life away in a heartbeat with the knowledge he'd be using his powers for good.

Rajeev failed to believe those words as he spied on a cricket player from across the coffee shop. Taking a sip from his coffee—disgusting, he never understood how people could just guzzle the stuff down—he typed mostly random nonsense into a Word document. He wore a traditional white robe that reached his toes known as a *thobe* and a headdress with a black rope halo called a *gutra*, while he had followed Kohli from his hotel—different from the one the Joshi was at—keeping twenty feet behind him and staying on the opposite side of the street. Rajeev had almost lost the Indian a couple of times, but he had been doing this for a while now and stuck with him.

Virat Kohli sat with other male Indians similar in age, teammates probably—all wearing casual attire. Rajeev tried to guess why Dmitri would want him dead. Imagining him blowing up a grocery store or maybe killing a friend of a friend of the Russian. Assassinating a terrorist was easier to do than murdering an innocent kid. *He's actually probably older than me,* Rajeev thought. He had to grow up fast at a young age.

Fifteen minutes later, the group got up and left. Rajeev packed up and followed. They only stopped at a petrol station to purchase a twelve-pack of something—not beer since alcohol was only legal with a permit and only sold in select areas—before returning to their hotel room.

He considered hanging around to see if they would go out again but decided he had done enough for today. On his way back, however, he took notice of a man following him. He wasn't doing a great job, wearing a blue T-shirt among a sea of white and black. And size—built like a truck to where the clothes threatened to rip any minute—only made him stand out more.

Rajeev continued on for ten minutes, walking in a random direction away from his home, then ducked into a convenience store. Inside was fortunately empty except for an acne-riddled teenager dressed in a loose tee with a cheap gold chain manning the register. He made the pretense of a browsing customer with nothing else to do and eventually took an energy drink and a bag of candy up to the cashier as his stalker trundled in.

Glancing at the mirror in the upper corner, Rajeev got a better glimpse of the man. He was Middle Eastern but was missing the facial hair common to Qataris. The giant seemed very interested in the rotating sausages.

A security camera in the adjacent corner to the mirror turned after Rajeev glanced at it to point at the magazine rack.

"Just those?" the teen asked in Arabic as he scanned them.

Instead of answering, Rajeev focused on the chain—just iron painted gold—and pulled it down without touching it, bringing the worker's face with it.

He turned away from the unconscious kid and faced his shadow, casually slipping his hand into his pocket over a jumble of coins. The man smiled in an almost genuine fashion and approached Rajeev until he stood right over him—which most people did, but the man must've been over seven feet. Rajeev stood his ground, though; this guy had no idea who he was up against.

"Who are you?" Rajeev asked, no tremble leaving his lips.

"*Balthasar*," the man whispered in a voice that was impossibly loud as it was quiet with strange undertones of something reptilian. It was filled with malice that rose from some dark void where souls were tortured without mercy. It was an evil voice and now Rajeev trembled.

"*Come*," the creature—for it was not of this world and God help the place it came from—continued.

"Why?" Rajeev asked but already felt his feet carry him toward the creature. It was incredibly persuasive with so few words, and he had to forcibly anchor himself to the linoleum floor.

"*You work for us now.*"

"I have another employer, h-he—" Rajeev's stammering came to an end when the thing reached its hand out to him, giving Rajeev a glance at the dragon tattoo on its forearm that he somehow didn't notice. But in his hand was something else much more alarming: an eyeball with an icy blue pupil.

"*You work for us now*," it repeated, casually placing the eye back into its pocket.

"Okay," Rajeev found himself saying, not sure if the creature had enchanted him or if he had just succumbed to fear. Anyhow, Rajeev knew this creature, Balthasar, was not something he could kill and for that he had no other choice.

Prey followed predator out of the store and into the busy streets of Doha.

As if in a trance, Rajeev suddenly found himself standing in an open area behind some dingy buildings. Before he could fully gain his bearings, he was grabbed from behind and rocketed into the sky.

And though Rajeev had never been afraid of height—it was, in fact, an important aspect of his job—he screamed as the city where he spent his whole life grew into view below him.

"What are you doing? Where are you taking me?" Rajeev rambled off at Balthasar, craning his neck to try to get a look at the monster. "My wife is down there. She needs help. Please, she has cancer. A brain tumor. She needs me."

The creature either couldn't hear him over the roaring wind or was ignoring him. Both choices seemed equally likely to Rajeev, and he gave up after a couple of minutes and considered the fact that he was flying. He had expected that he wasn't the only one out there with extraordinary abilities. And with any metal board he could do the same, but he never dared to go this high before. With that being said, Rajeev was sure Balthasar wasn't like him. But he did believe they were somehow connected. Why else would he kidnap him?

*Dmitri.*

Who else could've arranged something like this but the Russian he had threatened yesterday? Is that where the thing was taking him? This wasn't nearly the first time he had gotten angry with Dmitri. So, why now?

For now, all Rajeev could do was be patient and wait for the right opportunity. He knew a brute strength approach could very well result in his death. Observing everything could be essential to his survival and getting back to Yasmin.

*Yasmin,* he thought with alarm. She was all alone with fresh pain and chemotherapy medicine bags, but they would only last so long. She had a phone for emergencies, so perhaps the hospital could take care of her if really needed. There would be a lot of questions—*where did you get the medicine from; where is your husband?*—that would be difficult to answer.

Rajeev tried to block those thoughts out and just pay attention to the scenery below him even though every instinct told him to close his eyes and maybe vomit. He kept his lunch in, though, and noticed they were heading west into Saudi Arabia.

They entered the Middle Eastern country after a brief period over the Persian Gulf, flying above a city not even half the size of Doha, but also the first he had ever seen other than his hometown. Then past that, it was only sand dunes that rolled and waved and stretched towards the horizon like the waters of the Gulf.

The further he was flown, the less this seemed like Dmitri's work. It just didn't make sense.

Sand turned into rocks that grew into mountains and an eternity later, Rajeev sensed metal, a large source of metal different from the deposits underground. It was a city and not just any one. It was Mecca, the destination of the annual Islamic Hajj. He had only seen pictures of it in high school but had many friends who had taken the pilgrimage with their families. His own father never brought it up and he had been too scared to ask. Rajeev thought his father may have feared being struck down by Allah upon entering the holy grounds.

Mecca wasn't nearly as tall as Doha—except for the Makkah Clock Royal Tower which rose much higher than all the buildings in his hometown—but it was wide, maybe even ten times the area.

Before he could get close enough to see the Haram Mosque he had heard so much about, they dropped into a sharp decline. Rajeev let out an involuntary scream and shut his eyes as Balthasar hurled them between two small mountains. The fear of impact was replaced by a feeling of coldness just as light had vanished beyond his eyelids. Rajeev opened them once he finally felt the earth under his feet. They were in a cave and there was light but from the unnatural source of torches that didn't help his vision much. He rubbed his eyes and tried to get them to adjust but even still he could only see at most ten feet in front of him.

*"Welcome to Halgarth,"* a voice just a tone softer than Balthasar's came from the darkness. A woman, the top half of her body as bare as her head was, stepped into the light. Rajeev quickly averted his eyes. Most women in Qatar donned an *abaya* that covered their entire body, and it was illegal to wear much less. Even with Yasmin, he never saw her naked until their unofficial wedding night. It was Islamic tradition to be conservative in dress, and the sight of the woman's bare chest bothered him.

*"Look here. Here!"*

Rajeev jerked his head and tried to stare into her eyes, but he didn't find much sanctuary there. Actually, in the flickering of the flames, they appeared almost lizard-like.

*"It's just skin, fat, muscle, blood, and nerves just like yours. The only difference are ducts that secrete milk, yet your kind holds them up as some kind of forbidden fruit,"* She smiled cruelly, peeling back blood-red lips to reveal sharpened, yellow teeth. *"Would you like a taste of my forbidden fruit, Rajeev?"*

He looked down at her breasts and did find something enticing about them. A dragon's face stared at him from one. They were large and he bet they were firm unlike Yasmin's flat and—

*Stop it.* With Balthasar, it had been fear that controlled him. Here it was something different. There was magic there in her voice. A literal silver tongue. He could feel it tearing at his amygdala and awakening his animal instincts. Vigilance would need to be constantly enforced in his mental.

Eyes back at her face—he was surprised by how beautiful he found her to be even without hair—she was grinning, perhaps reading his mind or more likely just seeing his thoughts on his face. "*I am Catharsis, a daegaryn. Our kind is what your ancestors based their flying lizards after and who butchered our name in their labeling of the beast. But we are not monsters. We are like you. The same element that gave you your powers created us. And against common belief, we were born on this planet too. Daegaryns live for centuries but even we must die. Oh, am I boring you?*"

Rajeev realized where his eyes had settled and brought them back up. "No, no," he found himself saying.

"*I understand, you have had a long, eventful day and need to rest.*" She walked up to him. Slowly and seductively. This close, she towered over him, probably close to a foot taller than him. His eyes level to just above her rosy nipples. "*Where have my manners been? I apologize, love.*"

She bent down and kissed him full on the mouth, and he thought he kissed back. But it wasn't warm or moist. It was cold. Dry. Paralyzing.

Intoxicating.

# Chapter Eight

**Losing a loved** *one is a terrible thing. It's a loss that will be remembered for the entirety of one's life. Losing two in a single lifetime is poor fortune spun by the cruel fates. Losing three will release the tears of God Himself. Losing six, now that's a curse by the Devil. Life for that poor individual will be short and painful. How tragic it is to die of a broken heart.*

"Lady Guinevere, I'm terribly sorry for thy loss." Merlin gave his condolences. Now shirtless and in brighter light, he seemed even younger than she had thought—*twenty at the most*—but numerous scars along his body added years to him.

Merlin had just returned from "hiding the fantastical," grabbing each *thing* by its shoulder and dragging them off with minimal effort into seemingly nothing. Both living and dead just suddenly disappeared. He would reappear a minute later and do the same with the other body. Once more he did this, carrying a head in each hand. Savannah stayed where she was, her brain going a mile a minute as she tried to comprehend what had just happened. *James is dead because of me. If I hadn't been so scared and just gone in, he'd still be alive. What were those things? One of them is still out there. What if he comes back? Where is Merlin going? How is Merlin going there?*

"What?" Savannah asked now. Another question to be answered.

"Thy mark," He stared pointedly at her bare chest. "The burning heart of Lady Guinevere. Thy sigil enchanted upon thy breast for eternity."

She now realized she was naked for the whole world to see but didn't care. Instead, she peered down at what she had thought of as a birthmark for so long. Lately she figured it was something else. And it did actually look like a burning heart now that she considered it. An anatomical one with flames brimming around it.

"Who is Guinevere?" She stroked the sole patch of James' black hair.

"The queen of King Arthur." She could hear the surprise in his voice. "Thee."

"I'm just Savannah." She answered absently. All she wanted to do then was get drunk and forget herself.

"That may be of thy physical vessel, but the soul of Lady Guinevere resideth in thee."

Savannah just remained where she was. James had just died at the hands of some kind of heavily muscled, reptilian men with dragon tattoos that breathed flames. A kid calling himself Merlin says she is a medieval queen. And she has powers that have to do something with fire. Savannah didn't know how to react.

"This we can talk about later." He draped his robe—burnt but intact—around her shoulders and pulled her to her feet. He was surprisingly strong for his size. "But Azarox may return any time with more daegaryns."

He slung the lifeless body of James over his shoulder and marched him into the remains of what was his house.

"What are you doing?" Savannah asked him almost in a

daze.

"The authorities would wondereth how the body ended up in the yard. I'm preventing the asking of unnecessary questions." He continued back into the house.

Two minutes later, he came back and picked up the double-bladed staff he had placed beside her with strict instructions to not touch it. It was very plain looking, the blades made of a metal dark as night while the staff itself was more silver. Strange markings were carved into each blade.

Merlin then paced the front yard, searching for something. She knew how pointless it would be to ask any questions. Merlin paused where he had killed the first thing—daegaryn, *is that what he called them?*—and held his hand out over the patch of blood. Unbelievably, drops of blood rose from the ground then disappeared like the dragon men. Almost like evaporation but in a mystical way.

When he had finished and was moving to the next kill scene, he saw her shocked expression. "I only separated the molecules of the blood from that of the grass," he answered nonchalantly as if it was as simple as that.

With all the evidence removed—seeing her Mercury disappear into thin air was almost more than her mind could take—he joined her where she stood, shivering under borrowed robes even though the day was warm.

"What if someone saw?" Savannah asked, suddenly aware of the neighboring houses even though she never saw a single person walk by or even a passing car actually. Strange for the suburbs.

"They are asleep," he replied without emotion or explanation. "But now we must leave; I cannot hold them forever."

Without waiting for a reply, Merlin grabbed her hand and with the other, he waved in front of them. This time she fully noticed the portal, shimmering from the ground to just above Merlin's head. It was thin, though, not even half a foot wide, and it sucked at them like a magnet. He stepped through, pulling her in behind him, then they were standing in a place she had only seen on TV. Large, heavy rocks surrounded them in a circle, most standing, some fallen, others bridging pairs of the stones.

Savannah looked side-to-side in shock, wondering how much the mind could take before it completely snapped. "Stonehenge," is all she said.

"Indeed, it's incredible how rocks can give such an effect." Merlin agreed, misunderstanding her awe. "Mayhaps it haveth to do with the question of how twenty-five-ton stones were maneuvered in this way. Some historians hast said t'was wicker baskets or ball bearings that men used to roll the boulders. Others suggest it mayhaps been Mother Nature's doing, where glaciers did her heavy lifting. Some even believeth t'was a gift from ancient aliens.

"In reality, I, in my original body, transported the stones with magic from Ireland for King Aureoles as a burial ground for British knights slain in betrayal by Saxon soldiers. Giant's Dance t'was called, named for the giants that built baths with them, ones that healed all illness and injury."

He noticed Savannah just staring off into the distance, barely hearing what he said. "But of course, you hast much on thy mind."

He walked over to a pile of lying rocks. "Like the British and the giants before them, I too hast the ability to change the positions of the stones. To give them power." With a tilt of his head, the two boulders rose and then settled on their feet. A third laid on top of them, creating similar structures to others in the monument. A door.

"After you, m'lady." He gestured towards the conformation.

She hesitated but walked through it. What did she have to lose? There's nobody waiting for her back in Kentucky except

Brian. Also, even with huge, tattooed, fire-breathing men-like monsters after her, no one was more dangerous than she was to others. She had nowhere else to go.

They stepped into a room in front of a queen-sized bed with a canopy and orange-red drapes hanging from it. Behind her was a vanity with a gold-rimmed oval mirror hanging over it. Candles flickered toward her as she stared at her reflection, naked under the wizard's robe. An unnatural wind blew in the windowless bedroom moving the medieval garb to the side, exposing her breast. The mark seemed to almost glow in the candlelight. *A burning heart.* She shuddered and closed the cloak tightly around her.

"Clothes will be in yonder wardrobe," Merlin nodded at the large oak dresser. Then he pointed at one of the wooden doors. "And the privy chamber is over there.

"The restroom," he clarified, noticing her further confusion which was already rightfully plain on her face.

She sat on the edge of the bed—*feather?*—making sure to face away from Merlin and crossing her legs for good measure.

"We will talk of this—" He waved his arm around the room. "—and everything else on the morrow. But for now, get some rest. You will need it come tomorrow."

He left through the other door and Savannah immediately slid between the sheets—*definitely feather.* But it was hours before her brain could slow down enough for her to fall asleep.


The next morning—or at least that's what she thought it was, the lack of windows made things confusing—she sat on the edge of her bed, looking around at her abode. *It was not a dream.* She never truly thought it was, but she hoped. An image of James flashed through her head, face blue while the rest of him red and black. Tears welled up in her eyes, but she angrily wiped them away. James was dead. Her family, the same. And yet she lived, not for lack of trying, however. Bullet to the head, hanging, slit wrists, bleach drank neat. Maybe one of those dragon people will do her job for her. *Screw it,* she needed to go on as she had done her whole, cursed existence.

Savannah stood and went to the "privy chambers" but stopped in her tracks when she saw the "toilet." It was just a bench with a hole in the middle. "Fuck me."

Later, she walked out wearing a low-cut, red dress with fires embroidered upon it in orange. Hideous and extremely uncomfortable, but the wardrobe held nothing else. Straight ahead was a hall leading to a spiral staircase. The faint odor of weed met her at the bottom as she found herself in another hall except this one filled with suits of armor. A black one on her right. A green knight to her left. A third, red as her dress, leered down at her as she passed it. Doors were spread out between them as if they were guarded by the empty suits. Savannah continued, letting the flames of the candles guide her. It was weird that she was so attuned to something she had feared her entire life. *It's all I have left.*

At the end of the hall, she found herself in a massive library, the bookshelves almost scraping the roof.

"Lady Guinevere!" Merlin called beyond the shelves.

Savannah followed the sound of his voice, skimming the books as she did. She was never a bookworm, but even she found it odd that modern authors like Stephen King and Colleen Hoover were present in a castle—or at least that's what she assumed this place was.

The waves of books stretched far, and it took a minute before she found him sitting next to a fire that seemed to flare when she approached. He wore another robe, this one the color of blood, and was reading from a book.

"Please, just call me Savannah," she pleaded, sitting down

across from him in a wooden chair with a plush cushion on the seat.

"If that will please thee," he closed the book around his finger, looking up at her with his usual impassive stare. "Does thou like to read?" Merlin didn't wait for an answer. "Many a book resideth upon these shelves. Some have yet to be written." He held up his book. *The Winds of Winter.* "The first of two currently unpublished novels from the most riveting series by George R.R. Martin. Will not be published until the end of the year 2025." A twitch of a smile threatened to break the tight skin of his face. "Tyrion Lannister fans, however, will not be fond of the ending."

"How'd you even get that?" she immediately questioned before remembering she was in a magical castle with an actual wizard.

"You know nothing, Savannah Hamlin." There was a little glimmer in those blue eyes as he stood up.

"Can you at least tell me where we are?"

"Camelot. Enchanted by myself to lie between realities. That is why there are no windows. There is no outside."

*Between realities, that makes sense.* "Why?"

"Why what?" His face was like stone again. "Why are we in a castle long thought to have not existed? Why do we have powers beyond all imagination? Why did God, who is all-powerful, not kill Satan, knowing what he would do to the human race?"

She just stared into the fire.

"At the turn of the sixth century, a meteor, as large as this castle, struck down in northern Scotland. My ancestor was only a young man then and had traveled from Britain to see what could be made of this meteorite. Immediately, he felt an ancient power emanating from it. With the help of slaves, he got to work harvesting the ore, now known as olmerion. But powerful metal was not the only phenomenon housed within.

The daegaryn that attacked thee earlier came from the same astral home as the meteorite and many had been trapped inside until my ancestor freed them. Centuries of stories being passed down—misconstrued and recreated—turned them into the winged, reptilian dragons. They are capable of disguising themselves as humans to walk among us.

"My ancestor realized the danger of these creatures and the ore in the wrong hands, so he got rid of the meteorite." Merlin seemed to almost forget she was there as he monologued. "To where and how, I do not know. There is no record."

"I've never heard of that. How could something like that go unnoticed?" Savannah asked.

"He thereafter filled the crater with water to create what is today, Loch Ness. The name originated from a peasant who witnessed the event, 'Tha loch 'nis ann, tha 'nis ann!' he had said, or 'There's a loch now, there's a loch now!'" Merlin seemed a little irritated by the interruption and continued on quickly before she could interrupt him again.

"Decades later, he would brand twelve brave, chivalrous knights and their honorable king with their new sigil, using a brand crafted from the meteorite. The combination of his own magic and that of olmerion gave those of the round table powerful abilities abiding by the elements. Lady Guinevere's, thine, is the control and conception of fire. You are the Ember Knight"

"I thought you said she was the queen?"

"Aye, she was, but King Arthur was not the most faithful of husbands and so she blackmailed him into taking the place of a fallen knight. And a great fighter she was as well," he added as if he had been there.

"The Merlin of old," he went on, his voice remained neutral but the air growing stale around them seemed to signal his annoyance. "unbeknownst to the thirteen, bonded the branded sigil to their souls as to be passed down through their first-borns and theirs after. 'Till death will they part."

Merlin held his hand up to stop Savannah from asking another question. "If a knight haveth no earthly children, their soul will take up residence within a zygote just conceived. That is why, m'lady, neither of thy parents have the mark.

"The others will wake shortly," he said as he stood up and put an end to the conversation. "Would thou like some tea whilst we wait?

"Coffee," she requested, glancing over at the fire. "With bourbon if you have it."

He was gone when she looked back as if he had never been there. *I'm not getting that bourbon, am I?*

# Chapter Nine

**A person dressed** in a *boshiya* strolled into a convenience store, eliciting a bell to sound. The cashier, an ugly kid with even uglier acne, jerked up at the noise a little too quickly and eyed the customer. There was a nasty bruise on his forehead.

"*Salaam*," the stranger said in a feminine voice.

Judging by the tone of her voice, the cashier could tell she was smiling. He returned the greeting but not the smile.

The newcomer nodded and went to the back wall where a wide variety of energy drinks lay behind frosted glass. After a brief deciding hesitation, she grabbed the blue Red Bull. Now she moved over to the hot dog roller and contemplated whether she should have one. Her days of tanning on beaches were over, but that didn't mean she wanted to get fat.

"How long have they been on there?" she asked the cashier.

"Just put them on," he answered.

The charred lines proved otherwise, but she had already made up her mind and placed one of the less-seared wieners into a bun, drizzling just a little mustard on top—her mother had always warned about the fattening effects of ketchup, so she avoided it.

She took up her selection to the ugly man-boy and waited as he rang her out.

"Can I ask you a question?"

He gave her an expression that said he couldn't do much to stop her.

"Who gave you that nasty bruise," she asked and not-so-lightly touched it.

He grimaced and acted as if to grab something around his neck that wasn't there. "Me and my friend were wrestling."

"And I'm sure that would be quite the sight, but really who? The person who did it may be a mutual enemy."

"He looked like every other Muslim in this hell hole," the cashier said.

"But there was another, yes?"

The boy nodded. "He was massive in both height and width. Like an even more jacked Arnold Schwarzenegger. Although, I guess he'd be more like the Rock with his skin color and baldness. He even had a tattoo."

"Of what?"

The kid stared at her blankly.

"Of the tattoo! What was the tattoo of? And where?"

"Chill. Sorry. It was a dragon that was on his left—" He actually made an "L" with his left hand. "No, right—forearm."

"You wouldn't know where they went, would you?"

"No."

"Thank you." She fiddled with the sleeve of her boshiya.

"So, what did they do?"

"Didn't your *umi* ever tell you to mind your own business?" She pulled out a slender knife from a hidden pocket in her sleeve and stabbed the cashier in his neck, piercing the carotid artery.

She stepped to the side before pulling the knife out and

avoided much of the spraying blood. The customer wiped off the blood on the dead kid's shirt and turned to the security camera pointing directly at her. She waved, knowing who was on the other side.

Back on the busy streets of Doha, she balanced the Red Bull and hot dog in one hand as she grabbed her phone with the other. While the phone rang, she pulled down part of her boshiya to take a very lady-like bite of the well-deserved wiener and chased it down with the energy drink.

A smooth voice answered the phone.

"Balthasar took Rajeev," she said, her mouth still full.

The phone was hung up just as quickly as it was answered.

# Chapter Ten

**They finished their** tea—Merlin never acknowledged the fact she wanted coffee—in a dining room as long as a football field at a table fit to sit fifty. A chandelier with hundreds of glittering crystals hung from a seventy, eighty-foot ceiling. Breakfast foods from stacks of chocolate chip pancakes to steaming bowls of oatmeal, from fluffy, full omelets to fresh, juicy fruits were piled on one end of the table. The smell of pot grew stronger as the others entered.

Merlin sat at the head of the table, Savannah to his right. On her right was a woman around her age. And judging by her blood-shot, slitted eyes she was the source of the marijuana odor. Attractive and with dark hair containing streaks of gold that fell short of her shoulders, she was introduced to her as Sir Tristan. Isabella Knowles—the name she called herself—was raised in Carlisle, England and could create any poison known or unknown to men, as well as other stuff she didn't go much into. Savannah made sure to keep her teacup away from the Brit's, not someone she'd want accidentally to drink after. The low-cut blouse she had donned left little to imagination, especially in relation to her mark—an arrowhead with something dripping off it.

Across from her was a black man with hair cut close to the head that crept up past his temple. He had white eyes that saw none, yet when being introduced as Sir Ector—the man never gave his real name, never talked at all really; maybe he was mute as well blind—he made eerie eye contact with Savannah. A perfectly trimmed goatee was further evidence he didn't need optics to see. 'The ability to travel between space,' Merlin had said his power was. Teleportation is what Savannah took that to mean. He was dressed in a suit, crisp and sharp as she figured he was.

And next to him, an Asian kid ate French toast drenched in syrup at a startling pace. His name was Masaru Kato from a small town north of Tokyo. Sir Kay, as Merlin dubbed him, was fifteen and had shaggy, black hair that stood up in areas. Along with an out-of-place pair of leather gloves, he only wore pajama pants and skin and bones protruded beneath pale skin. He didn't look like somebody who had the power of death.

"Nice outfit," Masaru said in perfect English but with the fast tilt of Japanese that didn't disguise his sarcasm.

"It's better than nothing," Savannah retorted.

"Is it?" he replied, smiling widely.

For thirty minutes they chattered over their food until her unwanted tea became cold. The talk was extremely dull as their past and family were strictly avoided, sticking to mainly icebreakers—there was only so much she could contribute to Japanese cinema. It seemed she wasn't the only one who had been burdened by her mark.

"I believe it is time we show Guinevere the pride of Camelot," Merlin announced, already standing, and pivoted out of the dining hall, the red robes spinning around him.

Savannah followed the group to a tetradecagonal room, a large round table—the Round Table, she realized—perfectly centered in the middle. Along the wall, suits of armor stood vigil from thirteen corners, each holding a shield with a sigil. One corner, however, only contained an empty stand. She found her burning heart being wielded by a knight with a fiery cloak the same color as hers. It was also the only one with breasts.

"The Round Table of old," Merlin stated the obvious. "Think of all the most important deliberations had here."

The knights took seats at the legendary table, while Merlin just stood to the side of it. Savannah hung back, feeling like a kid choosing where to sit in a high school cafeteria.

"Lady Guinevere, thy place is over there," he pointed at the area across from Isabella. "Nay, there, search for thy sigil."

She found her arms—still weird to think that it's hers—painted on the back of the chair below "Lady Guinevere," which was below another name, the gold letters crudely crossed out with a sharp object. All she could tell was that it started with a "G." They probably misspelled the queen's name—an easy thing to do—and rewrote it.

" 'Tis my dream to fill the rest of these chairs," Merlin said with almost sorrow in his usual indifferent voice.

"Where are the others?"

"Some we cannot find. Others do not want to joineth our table. And a few have unfortunately chosen a darker path."

He went quiet although his expression remained the same. Savannah thought about pursuing it but a quick glance around the room told her that would not be wise.

"Now that our hunger hast been quelled," Merlin began again as if he was reading from a script. "We may now seek out an adventure.

"Lady Guinevere, my ancestor did not just brand thee with powers, he crafted and enchanted weapons from the meteorite. These weapons are the only element that can smite a daegaryn as well as a fellow knight. I am sure thou knoweth of thy cellular regeneration. Borderline invincibility."

She regarded her finger, cringing at the memory of the bones mending, and nodded.

"The double-bladed staff thee saw me weld belonged to another, Sir Bedivere. 'Twas christened as *Radiance*." The self-named wizard didn't elaborate on how he came into possession of it. "Thy weapon is a longsword, *Ash*."

"Where is it?" Savannah asked, almost thinking he was going to pull the sword out of his asshole. *Now that would be some trick.*

"No," Merlin said curtly as if he could read her mind—*could he?* "It's in Turkmenistan. There thee will find the Darvaza Crater, known to many as the Door to Hell," he turned to Isabella. "Sir Tristan will accompany thee."

The British woman gave a slight nod but there was no other indication of how she felt.

"What? Is it just going to be sticking out of the ground?" Savannah asked.

"It would not be the first time that has happened," he answered with his usual annoyance at questions. "However, that will not be the case. The Darvaza Crater is indeed a door to Hell, though, I cannot be certain of the precise location. Only the ancestor of the Lady Guinevere may pass through."

*That makes absolutely zero sense, but okay.*

"Sir Ector and I have confidential business elsewhere," now looking at Masaru he said, "Sir Kay, thou hast charge of Camelot."

"Yes sir," The Japanese teen acknowledged with an exaggerated salute. "It's in good hands, Bossman."

Merlin stood up. "It is settled then, I will see ye three later."

"We're leaving now?" Savannah asked. She hadn't had time to breathe since the daegaryn. To mourn for James. Now she's off chasing a sword in some door to Hell with a British chick she just met.

He sighed but remained standing. "I know thou hast dealt with more in the last twenty-four hours than many will ever in a lifetime. But there are those like us that believeth they should rule the world. And I would be remiss not to mention the daegaryn are growing bolder by the day. We must be at our strongest as to stand against them and getting thy long-sword is essential to that mission."

"Why should I care?"

"Because thou hast done terrible things in the past, we all have." Savannah eyed the others, heads all pointed down. All but his, those icy, blue eyes stared through her soul. "This is thy chance for requital for thy grievous sins. And with *Ash* thou shall obtain a greater control of thy power."

She tried to think of a response, but the wizard was gone with Ector before she could get anything out.

# Chapter Eleven

**Rajeev had spent** all afternoon cooking dinner for his father. It was his birthday. How old was he? Rajeev was too afraid to ask. He had requested—although that may be too light of a word to use—machboo, a Qatari meal that consisted of rice, vegetables, and lamb.

The finished product was placed in the center of the dining table. It was perfect. The carrots, tomatoes, and onions were chopped into tiny bits and mixed evenly with the fried rice. Finely sliced pieces of lamb rested on top in the center. Parsley sprinkled over the dish was the final touch. He would love it, Rajeev knew with pride.

He heard a key turn in the lock and rushed to the fridge to grab a beer and put in the place where his father sits. The door opened and he entered. Rajeev didn't even have to smell his breath to know he had stopped at the bar after work at the dock. Mr. Patel was just as short as his son, but the similarities ended there. Decades of alcoholism led to a massive beer belly and a double chin that was hidden due to an unkempt beard.

"Happy birthday, baba," Rajeev said with practiced excitement.

"I told you not to call me that," he said in his usual sullen manner.

"I'm sorry, Omer," he didn't let any physical disappointment show on his face. "I made your machboo just the way you like it."

"I see," Omer scratched his rear and sat down before the food, taking a large swallow of the beer. "Did you get more Corona?"

"Yes, Omer." Rajeev joined his father at the table and waited for him to serve himself before filling his plate. "How was work?"

Omer just laughed and shook his head, taking a bite of the machboo.

"How is it?"

"Had better."

The usual silence followed Rajeev's feeble attempts at small talk, but it wasn't long until Omer finished his beer and waved the empty bottle at his son. Rajeev retrieved the drink from the fridge. As he walked over to his father, though, a foot stuck out, causing Rajeev to trip and spell the Corona all over the machboo.

"*Areyh Feek*," Omer screamed at his son, standing up surprisingly quick considering his drunken state. "You *shar-moo-ta*. Spilling my hard-earned beer all over my dinner on my birthday of all days. You know what that means."

"Baba—"

"Don't call me that!"

Omer took off his belt and whipped it at Rajeev, who was already bent over. He learned at a very young age to not fight it. The habit continued even when he first developed his powers. The creature behind him was not his father, not baba. No, it was force of evil possessing Omer.

"See, even with your magic I'm stronger than you." *Whip*.

"You're the reason your mother left." *Whip.* "She saw the devil in you, she told me herself." *Whip.* "And you dare to have that same birthmark as her." *Whip. Whip. Whip.*

Rajeev remained quiet throughout the beating, any pleading or grunts of pain only made it worse. He just had to wait for the evil to leave him.

Soon it did. He feared for the day it didn't. Omer left. Rajeev barely realized it, his attention on the steel lighting fixture over where his father sat for dinner.

Deep brown eyes opened to a high cave ceiling with stalactites pointed at him. He was in a bed, oddly comfortable for the environment he was in, with silk sheets and a feather mattress. The humming in his head had grown even louder.

*"Morning, Rajeev."*

He almost fell out of bed at the voice of his oppressor right next to him. She laid on her side and stared at him with reptilian eyes that had purple irises. They were both beautiful and frightening like most aspects of Catharsis.

*"Did you sleep well?"* She got out of bed and walked to a mirror over a dresser on the opposite side of the room, revealing a rounded butt not much more pale than the rest of her body.

Rajeev was suddenly aware of his own nakedness. He strained to remember what happened last night but couldn't remember anything past the kiss. "Did we . . ." He waited for her to answer before he finished the sentence, but she only smiled at him through the mirror. ". . . have sex."

*"Unfortunately, not, you were just oh, so tired. You had just fainted into my arms, and I carried you to my room. I believed it would be best if you woke up to a friendly face."* Catharsis turned her head back and gave him a flirtatious—*or was it cynical?*—smile. *"We are friends, aren't we, Rajeev."*

"Yes, of course," Rajeev said, nodding his head like an idiot, again functioning without any thought.

"*Good.*" Catharsis slipped on a pair of jeans sans any underwear to Rajeev's regrettable disappointment. But she still left her top half unclothed.

"You said you know what I am," Rajeev said, trying to focus on something else rather than her.

"*Ah, yes.*" She sat down next to him. *So close.* Rajeev felt something rise in him and quickly scrunched up his legs. He attempted to picture Yasmin but at that moment he couldn't remember what she looked like. "*Over fifteen hundred years ago, our planet, Farlorn, exploded when our galaxy, the Malatrox Gap collapsed on itself. Just like now, we lived subterranean and a horde of us were trapped in a meteorite broken off from Farlorn. We landed here on Earth, specifically in Scotland. A wizard, Merlin, found us and went to work harvesting the mystical ore of our planet. Olmerion is indestructible and holds a power barely even understood by us. Through living in constant contact with the element, we gained special abilities called* dji. *The wizard's great magic in addition to olmerion is what gave yours.*"

She pointed at the birthmark on his chest. It was shaped like a shield with a cross in the middle. "*That identifies you as Galahad the Iron Knight.*"

Merlin and Galahad. Those were characters from the King Arthur legend. Rajeev had never read any of the stories, but he did watch that *Monty Python* movie. It wasn't the names, however, that really got the gears moving.

"My mother had that same birthmark. Does that mean she was . . . like me?" Rajeev asked. He always hated his mother for leaving but maybe there was a reason.

"*Too much information given in a single conversation leads to much forgetting,*" Catharsis said and stood up. "*Now, come. Let me show you to your quarters; I don't fully enjoy having a roommate.*"

The covers were ripped off him and he hurriedly moved to cover himself.

*"Odd what the cold air does to men."* She threw a pair of jeans at him.

He got dressed, awkwardly turning his back to her while she stared at him with that same joyless smile, and then followed her out the "door"—just a red silk curtain. Catharsis led him down several winding passages, occasionally running into another daegaryn that just stared at him like he was prey. Rajeev attempted to keep track of the path taken but with there being no discernable landmarks or even knowing how deep he was in the cave, he doubted he would be able to find his way out.

They stopped before a doorway that seemed like every other he had passed except this one had bars running up and down in the opening. It was a jail cell, yet unguarded.

Or maybe not as a daegaryn suddenly materialized in front of him, this one white but not nearly as fair-skinned as Catharsis. And even more naked—no pants gave him the semi-decency of the daegaryns. A dragon tattoo over his shoulder, shook its head when he nodded to her.

*"Eyron can camouflage himself,"* Catharsis explained. *"Gives you a little more privacy."*

Eyron unlocked the cell and Catharsis gently prodded him inside. There was even less light than in the halls—only a single torch next to the entry—so it took a little while for his eyes to adjust.

"Rajeev!" a familiar, unwanted voice called from the shadows. "I cannot tell you how happy I am to see you."

Finally, Rajeev could fully pan over his new "room" and saw Dmitri Smirnov, bare belly hanging out, with an eyepatch sitting up on the lower bunk bed. But other than that, he seemed perfectly fine; his beard was even cleaner than usual. Though, Rajeev was surprised by the number of scars on the Russian. Some of them rather nasty.

*"I'm so glad to reacquaint you two and will allow you to catch back*

*up.*" And with that, she locked them in together.

"Oh, what a beauty she is, eh?" Dmitri said. "She was the first woman I screwed without stretch marks in decades. Did you do the devil's tango with our lovely host?"

Rajeev just narrowed his eyes at his former employer.

"No? Problems getting it up, oh? It's no worry, no worry. It happens to all of us. Well, not Dmitri Smirnov. No, no. Though, after the romping she gave me, my member may never work again, ha."

"I thought you were dead," Rajeev said. "And gay."

"No, no, I am what is known as bisexual, I just prefer the touch of another man. And, really, Rajeev, you think that Dmitri Smirnov—"

"Stop saying your fucking name, I know who you are," Rajeev exclaimed. The Russian wasn't what would get him out of there. His days of ass-kissing were over.

Dmitri wasn't fazed, however, and actually smiled. "I love the emotion, Rajeev. Our conversations can get so dull sometimes. It can be like talking to a wall.

"But no, *Dmitri Smirnov*, doesn't die that easily. They took me to find you."

"You lost an eye for me?" The Russian was full of surprises.

"Oh, no, no, no," The golden teeth flashed at him. "Rajeev, you misunderstand. They took my eye because they don't like me. I'll admit, I can be a bit loose with what comes out of my mouth. But I think it fits me, eh? Gives my handsome complexion just a little more character, ha."

*That makes more sense.*

"Why do they want me?" Rajeev asked.

"What everybody wants," Dmitri said, golden teeth flashing. "Power, my boy. Power."

# Chapter Twelve

**Cries arose throughout** Kroger as a portly man in a pink Hawaiian shirt ran behind a glass counter. He tripped over something and nearly slammed his head into the corner of a metal table. The man hurried to his feet, just glancing at the obstacle.

*Connie. Oh fuck, Connie.*

But there was no time and he ripped open the heavy cooler door, stacking boxes of cheese in front of it. The man looked around for a weapon, visible, icy wisps of air swirling in the frigid air each time he took a breath. He settled on a slab of salami and then prayed for the first time since sixth grade.

Two long minutes passed before the cooler handle was jiggled but the boxes held strong. The man waited, frozen in a position with the salami in two hands over his shoulder like he was about to hit a cheese ball.

Then suddenly the door is flying at him. Something popped in his shoulder, releasing a flaring of fiery pain. He laid immobile under the massive door, only his head visible. A shadow approached him slowly, a large hammer half the size of the figure held in—*its?*—hand. The murderer stopped in front of him, staring at the man from under its hood for a minute before removing the cowl. The fat man in the Hawaiian shirt let out a hideous, shrill scream before it was silenced with one swift blow of the hammer.


The shadow moved up the driveway—seemingly floating— blending in perfectly with the dark woods to the sides, the warhammer fitted into a sheath on its back. A small house—a cabin, no more—laid ahead.

The figure broke through the door with a quick jab of the heel of its palm that shattered it to pieces and then drifted to the kitchen smelling faintly of chili. It opened the microwave and then searched the room, pulling open drawers before shoving them closed. Not finding what it was searching for, the phantom slid its hand into the folds of the shadowy robes it was cloaked in, pulling out a handful of something. It shoved the item—no, items; there was clattering—into the microwave, closing it carefully and hitting the number eight.

It entered the next room and moved past the bed to the small table next to it. The shadow picked up the picture frame placed on it, staring at the woman's charred face as the air around it grew warmer and smoke filled her nose. Then threw the photograph behind it and exited by slamming the hammer through the wall.

# Chapter Thirteen

"**And there I** was in the courtyard of Petak Island." Dmitri stretched out his hands comically as he told the story. "I walked up to biggest *sukin syn* guarding that cold hell and asked of him, 'Do you know who I am? I am Dmitri Smirnov the greatest spy the Mother Land has ever known and you will let me out.' Then whacked him in his giant *hoc.* And you know what they did?"

"No, what?" Rajeev asked, staring up at the ceiling and focusing on every bit of metal in his range. Dmitri had no problem filling the silence of the prison and had told many wild stories. Whether they were true or not had yet to be determined.

"He punched me right above the eye and knocked me out cold." The Russian laughed as if he told the greatest joke ever. "But later on I made my escape. They thought me stupid. Oh, but Dmitri Smirnov proved them wrong, I did, I did. So, here it went, I dropped the soap—"

The door creaked open and Catharsis smiled at them with Eryon over her shoulder.

"Ah, there is my love, Catharsis," Dmitri rambled. "Such a beautiful name, did I ever tell you? We going back to your room, for a little romping? I know you liked it, Dmitri Smirn-ov could tell. Rajeev here could come and watch, take some notes, eh? He could use the help, hehe."

*"Dmitri,"* Catharsis started, that evil grin not wavering. *"One of these days I'm going to rip out that tongue and really enjoy eating it."*

"Oh, Catharsis you little flirt." Dmitri said but spoke no more.

*"Rajeev, now that you've had time to process your past, perhaps now we may discuss your future."*

"Like what happened to my mother?"

*"Poor Rajeev, your mother is the past. I speak of the future."*

"What *happened* to her?" Rajeev was way past frustration with these creatures, but he still realized he would never be able to fight even one them one-on-one, not to mention how many currently resided in this cave.

*"How about we make a deal, Rajeev. You help me get what I want, and I'll tell you what you want. An incentive in addition to the life of your beloved—Yasmin, that's her name, yes?"*

"Stay away from her," Rajeev demanded, his anger on full display, and realized at once from the daegaryn's expression that that was a mistake. "She has nothing to do with this?"

*"Oh, Rajeev. You love her so that means she has everything to do with this."*

He sighed and tried to reset himself. "What do you want from me?"

*"To simply find the Holy Grail."*

"Merlin, Galahad, and now the Holy Grail. What is this? Some children's fantasy."

*"You would be surprised by how many stories told to you in your youth are actually based in truth,"* Catharsis said. Rajeev found himself getting lost in her purple eyes and had to turn away. *"You have inherited the spirit of Sir Galahad the Chaste, a sacred member of King Arthur's legendary Round Table. The blood of a knight*

*flows through your veins mixed with the magic of Merlin. LOOK AT ME WHEN I TALK TO YOU!"*

Rajeev spun around and stared at a very angry and very dangerous woman.

*"You, Rajeev, as was your mother, are the only person alive who can locate the Holy Grail. It's an extremely powerful artifact.*

"How can I find something that I barely know what it is?"

*"Do you feel the humming in your head? I've heard it's hard to miss."*

And it indeed was present, louder than had ever been. He had been almost grateful for Dmitri's ramblings since they helped distract him from it.

"Yes," Rajeev said carefully. He had a feeling she already knew.

*"That humming is like a homing beacon,"* Catharsis said. *"It has a radius of twenty-five-hundred miles. Is it louder here or in Qatar?"*

Rajeev knew he should say it was quieter here and give them less to work with but when he spoke, he said the opposite. He was just glad he wasn't crazy.

Catharsis opened her mouth but then placed two fingers on her temple. She stayed that way for a minute, her beautiful, frightening eyes still fixed on Rajeev.

*"It's Azarox,"* she finally told Eryon. *"He just got back. I'll handle it but take them to be fed and prepared. We leave for the Grail first thing tomorrow."*

They followed the daegaryn through the halls of Halgarth, his bare ass not nearly as tantalizing as Catharsis's. Deeper and deeper they went and further and further were they from the exit. The dull, brown scenery, broken up by the occasional red curtain, continued as before. But without warning, the two-shoulder-length walkway opened up to a large cavern, where daegaryns of all ages milled around or sat at stone tables. Twenty of them, it looked like. There appeared to be a larger ratio of men to women. five-to-one or something like that.

*"This is the dining hall,"* Eryon said. *"Find yourself something to eat and meet me at that table in the corner there."*

It was a cafeteria for monsters, Rajeev now realized. He worried about what kind of food there was.

When Rajeev and Dmitri moved away from the daegaryn, the Russian whispered to him, "What's the plan, Magneto?"

*"Try to escape, and I will rip you apart, Russian,"* Eryon called after them.

"Ah, I was just joking, my friend. Come on, can we not just have some fun," Dmitri yelled back and then whispered to Rajeev. "I didn't know he had super hearing too."

*"I don't, you're just loud."*

As they approached the supposed beginning of the line, Rajeev avoided eye contact with the daegaryns while Dmitri smiled and even waved. The creatures, even the kids—the youngest being perhaps twelve or thirteen—stared back at them unabashedly. Some, mainly the older ones, had hate in their strange eyes but most were just curious.

"What's the odds you could protect us if they all decided to attack," Dmitri asked and for once they seemed to be on the same page.

"Using you as a distraction, I might be able to save myself," Rajeev said lightly. In fact, he worried even the smallest may be too much for him to handle. It's odd to fear something that he had never seen fight. There was an air about them. They knew about him, yet let him roam around free. Confidence is terrifying.

Dmitri had said something else, but Rajeev had been too preoccupied to hear it and only nodded.

The lunch line itself was just like the one he had in high school except no lunch lady, smelling like a mixture of ham and flowers, resided on the other end. It was self-serve and the selections were just as mysterious as what he was used to. He scooped some ground meat of unknown origin—*please, dear God, don't let it be human*—pita bread, corn, and something that looked like mashed potatoes. Dmitri got the same with larger portions and threw on some green mush as well. "I've been missing my Vitamin C gummies," he said.

They found Eryon at the table he told them to meet with four others. One was Balthasar, the others were a woman, a man—who was the first daegaryn Rajeev had seen without a visible tattoo—and a boy.

"*This is your team,*" Eryon said. "*All with unique* dji *that will help complete your quest. You've already met Balthasar. Nobody is quite as strong as him. Glanderos is intangible. Diomedes can fire laser beams from his eyes and see through walls. And young Kalynst had just lost both his father and uncle this morning. He will come with us to avenge them.*"

The kid didn't appear distraught as he should be and only nodded when the deaths were mentioned. He was white and no older than sixteen with a dragon tattoo around his abdomen. His pants were made of a different material, than the jeans of the others. Almost like leather.

"My team?" Rajeev asked.

"*Yes. You are the only one who can find the Holy Grail, so, they will follow you.*" Eryon leaned forward. "*You are not our enemy, Rajeev. We keep you captive here, only because we need you. Evil is out there and the Grail is essential to eliminate it. After you have retrieved it, you are free to go.*"

"What about me?" Dmitri asked. "Rajeev has his magnetic abilities. You daegaryns have your *dji*. But I'm just little ol' poor Dmitri Smirnov. Powerless and small versus you mighty people. And I'll admit, not in my best shape." He patted his bulging stomach, sending it jiggling. "You don't need me. So…shall I see myself out?"

"*There's no need to worry about travel,*" Eryon said. "*But we're not done with you yet. You will be staying here with me."*

Dmitri seemed satisfied enough with that answer to keep his mouth shut for once.

"You're not coming?" Rajeev asked.

*"No, my place is here. Catharsis will take my place once she returns from her urgent business."* Eryon stood up, giving Rajeev an unfortunate eyeful of his manhood. *"Eat up, then I will escort you back to your cell. Get plenty of sleep, Rajeev. You will need it."*

# Part 2

---

# The Binding of Fates

*"...for love cometh of the heart and not by constraint."*
*"That is true," said the king; "for love is free."*
-James Knowles
*The Legends of King Arthur and his Knights*

# Chapter Fourteen

**The pair of** young women stood on a sidewalk in the bustling city of London before some school with the famous tower far behind them in the distance. Their hair—one auburn, the other with golden streaks among the darkness—whipped around in the British wind.

"So, why couldn't Merlin teleport us the rest of the way there?" Savannah asked, shivering in her blue jeans and sweatshirt saying "Keep Calm and Mind the Gap"—whatever the hell that meant—that she got from a gift shop. "And what's his real name anyway."

Isabella flicked off a taxi driver that ignored her frantic waving. "First, he's never told me, and I never asked; somebody who calls himself Merlin and carries around that ghastly weapon is not to be messed with." The cool winds didn't seem to bother the British woman in her low-cut blouse and yoga pants. "Second, he wants us to *quest* for our weapons. I had to do the same thing for *Snakebite*." She kicked the ski bag at her feet with the six-foot spear in it.

A taxi finally squealed to a stop in front of them, spraying their legs a little with dirty gutter water. Isabella acted as if to say something but held her tongue with some very apparent difficulty. The women packed their bags—a concealed, ancient spear and duffel for Isabella and a mostly empty one for Savannah—into the back of the cab. Savannah sidled in next to her on the worn leather seat, wiggling her nose at the lingering smell of cigarette smoke.

"Where to," the obese, white man with a scraggly beard—not quite appearing like the British she had seen on TV—asked.

"The Port," Isabella answered.

The driver grunted and skirted out onto the busy road, blasting his horn. He also turned up the radio, playing some rapper. The Next, the screen read.

*Cocaine on my face like the Stranger*
*Oh, help me. I think I'm in danger!*

"If we can't use modern *devices* to get to Turkmenistan, then why are we in a taxi?" Savannah asked over the music that conjured the question.

"Let's just say people around here do not like me very much," Isabella answered almost proudly. "This keeps me off the streets from prying eyes."

*I should've guessed,* Savannah thought.

It would be a little bit of a drive, so Savannah took the time to check the scenery. It had been a childhood dream to travel Europe. She didn't really know what to expect. Maybe those Red Robin guys with the tall hats walking around town with their rifles. But there was really nothing extremely different from the states—except for driving on the opposite side of the road, of course. The buildings were more colorful and gothic—was that word she wanted? There were even restaurants from America like Starbucks and . . .

"There's a KFC," she said to herself in amazement.

Isabella didn't even glance out the window. "Yup. Your state does make some bloody good fried chicken."

The large office buildings and stores gave way to smaller cottages and bait shops as they neared the River Thames. A fishy smell penetrated the cab, forcing the girls to roll up the windows.

"How are we going to find this guy Merlin mentioned?" Savannah asked her forced partner.

"You'll know."

The bright red exhaust of a cruise ship was the first visual sign of the Port of London, appearing when they stopped at a security depot. Soon, other boats appeared. Massive cargo ships, horns blaring as they entered and left. Several white, shining yachts were docked in an area all to themselves. Graceful sailboats, sleek speedboats, and dingy fishing boats filled the rest of the Port.

"Which one . . ." Savannah's voice trailed off when she saw the giant galley at the far end of the dock. Three large masts waved sporadically in the wind that was even more wild by the River. *Merlin's Breath*, she read off the side when they got closer.

"Is the captain like us?" Savannah asked.

"No," Isabella answered. "He's just some Irish bloke who has an old ship that he named after the actual Merlin and needs the money."

The taxi slowed down in front of the large boat, where a short man with a clean-shaven face and curly, red hair stood grinning from ear to ear. The British woman handed the driver some cash and exited the cab.

Immediately after removing their luggage, the taxi sped off. Isabella murmured under her breath. Something that had to do with *pounds* and *toxins*.

"You must be the ones Marlin spoke of," the Irishman squeaked. "Odd, he never gave me his last name. Must be like one of those one-name American singers like Madonna and Adele."

"Adele is British," Savannah said hesitantly, thrown off a bit by the mispronunciation of Merlin's name.

"Oh, is that right?" The sailor paused in thought as if the world's greatest question had been answered. "Anyhow, my name is Cormac Murphy."

"I'm Isabella," the Brit said, ignoring the man's oddities and shaking the offered hand. "And the American there is Savannah."

"A long way from home," the man said but did not ask the reason. This was obviously not his first off-the-books voyage. "Well, we have the wind at our backs, so we best be off. Marlin paid me for thirty hours and I'd hate to have to throw you floozies overboard." He smiled heartily.

They followed Cormac onto the wooden deck that creaked with greeting. Fifteen minutes later, they were off sailing to Calais, France.

# Chapter Fifteen

**Six figures hunkered** down behind an SUV-sized rock as a large gust of wind swept sand and gravel at their covered faces. All still wore no shirts as per their ancient tradition but black, woolen scarves were wrapped around each head. Mecca was only thirty miles east but couldn't be seen in the storm. The weather was only getting worse and flying wouldn't make it any better.

"Couldn't we do this tomorrow?" Rajeev screamed through the roaring air. "I can't see anything out here."

"*That's why we have Diomedes,*" Catharsis said clearly without appearing to raise her voice. It almost seemed to come from inside his head. "*And your internal beacon.*"

"What's the rush?"

"*Recent circumstances have called for immediate action.*"

"Don't you have someone with a *dji*—or whatever you call it—to control the weather or wind or something?"

"*No, we don't choose our* dji. *Now be quiet. You wouldn't be the first to drown in a sandstorm.*"

This was insane but within minutes, Balthasar had him wrapped up and they were in the air. Small particles ripped through his skin that healed immediately. It was like he was being whipped.

The thought made him think of his father.

Balthasar and the rest of the daegaryns, on the other hand, didn't seem to be affected as the sand just bounced off their mostly bare skin. Rajeev strained his eyes through the tiny slip in the scarf and saw that Diomedes was in the lead with Rajeev and Balthasar diagonal to him. Catharsis was on the opposite side with Kalynst and Glanderos behind them. They were flying in v-formation like birds migrating south for the winter.

For thirty minutes they continued in the same direction—*north?*—without questioning Rajeev. They appeared confident as usual, but he wasn't sure if that was a pretense or not. For all he knew they could be heading for Qatar. Though—it could have been his imagination—he did think the humming was growing louder. And after another thirty, he was sure it was. Catharsis turned to him and tapped her hairless temple. He pointed a finger up—he no longer cared about the harm of helping them so long as he could go back to Yasmin when this was all over. She was satisfied with the gesture, so they continued on.

Hours passed by and the storm's wrath did not dissipate but the humming only grew louder and louder. Every thirty minutes, Catharsis touched her head and Rajeev responded the same. Every second was agony and he prayed for them to reach their destination.

Catharsis flew to him and whispered in his ear. He shivered at her closeness and hated how much he liked it. *"There are rumors that the Grail is in Jerusalem. Your beacon has supported that theory. If you hear the humming decrease at all let me know but the plan is to land there. We'll be there in eight hours. There'll be no stops, so I hope you don't need to relieve yourself."*

She returned to her spot.

*Eight hours.* The last—Rajeev tried to remember how

many times Catharsis asked him about the humming—three(?) hours had felt like an eternity. He didn't know how he could make another eight. Closing his eyes, he focused on the metal below him. There was a city. A small one, more like a village. Soon he was separating the large blob that glowed in his head into the specific. Iron was a light blue. Steel a dark blue. Copper blood-red. And so on. It was like a radar where he could only see the metals in a certain circumference. The change of concentration helped and soon the pain and irritation seemed a little further away.

The thirst came first. His throat felt dry enough for someone to be able to light a fire in there with one strike of a flint. Sand somehow found a way to get past the scarf and he really began to wonder if it was indeed possible to drown in it.

Rajeev waved at Catharsis to get her attention and then pointed at his mouth. She shrugged then held her right palm out and one finger on the other. *Six more hours.* He was kind of surprised two hours had passed. But he couldn't imagine another six of this. He found out a long time ago that he could heal from any type of injury, but what about dehydration? Catharsis seemed to believe he would survive this treacherous trip. At least he knew she needed him alive.

An hour maybe went by—his sense of time was completely off—and his concentration was wavering, his thirst punching through the colorful glows of the metals. But now, what he really worried about had arrived. His bladder was sending electrical signals up to his brain that it was full. He squeezed his legs and sent another prayer. After a short period of time, though, he knew would have to relieve himself.

Rajeev motioned for Catharsis to come over. She shook her head and held her hands out. He mouthed and swallowed sand for his efforts. His mouth was covered anyway. Completely embarrassed, Rajeev grabbed himself like a child. He could almost see her smiling as she gestured with one arm, in a "go ahead" movement.

He waited a few more moments and then tapped Balthasar's arm, giving him the same universal gesture. Behind him, Kalynst had already moved out of the way. It was best to get it over with, and he loosened the belt and unzipped the jeans. Rajeev pulled them down and waited but nothing came. He couldn't piss! Closing his eyes, he concentrated on the metals below him and eventually released to a sweet pleasure that overcame his embarrassment.

Time went by. If it was hours or minutes or seconds, Rajeev didn't know. It just went by. His mind soon became foggy and the metals below—just some random patches of iron ore—seemed further and further. Even Diomedes grew smaller in his fading vision.

How long he was out was a mystery, but when Rajeev woke up, the storm had abated for the most part. The reason became apparent with a quick glance around. He was lying next to a wall with four daegaryns scrutinizing him, their scarves discarded. Diomedes was the one missing.

"Huh?" was all Rajeev managed, his throat felt like sandpaper.

"*We're just inside the southern wall of Jerusalem,*" Catharsis said. "*How is the humming in your head?*"

"Screaming," Rajeev said. And it indeed was the worst headache he ever had. But he had more pressing concerns. "I need water."

"*Kalynst, find some,*" Catharsis ordered and the young daegaryn immediately sped off in a blur. Rajeev had an idea what his *dji* was.

Several minutes went by before somebody landed in their midst. But it was Diomedes, not the kid.

"*I found the Grail,*" he said. "*It's in a secret catacomb underneath the Church of the Holy Sepulchre.*"

"*Is it still closed down?*" Catharsis asked.

*"Yes, due to a recent fire."*

*"Good."*

Kalynst skidded to stop before them and handed Rajeev a bottle of water, who drank it greedily, the water slopping over the sides of his mouth.

*"Did you buy that?"* Catharsis asked.

He nodded.

She sighed. *"I'm sure a shirtless Caucasian boy with reptilian eyes wouldn't draw any attention."*

*"Sorry,"* he said but not a hint of apology touched his young face.

*"Let's take precautions,"* Catharsis told the group. *"Everybody change your skin tone to the light brown of a Middle Eastern. Use him,"* She pointed at Rajeev, holding the water bottle, now empty, in hand. *"as an example. And put your contacts in."*

All the daegaryns, except for Balthasar—already the needed color—changed their skin to match Rajeev's. He was too tired, though, to be very surprised at the transformation. They also reached into the pockets of their jeans to remove a contact lens case, which they opened and applied. Now they all had brown, human eyes.

*"Let's go,"* Catharsis said, and Rajeev was lifted up by Balthasar before he could voice an objection. The pace over the Israeli city was much quicker than before and no scarf protected his face. He squeezed his eyes and mouth tight as the airborne particles tore through him. But barely any minutes passed by the time they dropped in front of a building that could only be a church. The grand double doors were barred off with a large chain. A sign read: CLOSED FOR RECONSTRUCTION. At least on the outside, there didn't appear to be any fire damage.

The other female daegaryn—the only one to also have purple irises—grabbed his hand with a dragon-covered forearm and held Catharsis's with the other. He felt a wave of electricity rush through him and reflexively tried to rip away from the daegaryn, but her grip was a vise.

*"Glanderos is intangible"*, Catharsis explained. *"You will be able to move through the spaces between atoms. We are currently less dense than the stone beneath us, so there should be no fear of sinking."*

Glanderos took a step forward, and Rajeev copied her just a little more hesitantly. Six more steps and her right foot had disappeared through the door. After all he'd been through, walking through an obviously thick slab of wood, at that moment, seemed to be the craziest thing he had ever done. But three more big steps and he was inside. The passing-through was extremely trippy, with, perhaps, century-old oak all around him, including *in* him. It almost felt like he was drowning.

Not much could be seen inside, the sandstorm hid the normally bright, shining, Middle Eastern sun and since it was closed no bulbs were lit.

*"We had originally meant to bring another daegaryn instead of Kalynst, who could become a human light bulb, but something came up,"* Catharsis said.

But that wouldn't be an issue as Diomedes—phased in by Glanderos, along with Kalynst, while Rajeev got a grasp of his surroundings—found a light switch within seconds.

Directly in front of them, eight lamps with red crosses lit up over a large slab of stone to illuminate a mosaic filled with people—*disciples of Jesus*, Rajeev thought, realizing the prophet from his religions class in high school—placing their god into a tomb. A plaque next to the wall painting went into further detail about the scene.

Catharsis moved into a passageway—followed closely by the other daegaryns, except for Balthasar, who must've been standing guard outside—not bothering to look around at the ancient, religious artifacts. Rajeev hurried after them, hating the idea of being there alone. They walked past a flame waving in a vase, another mural—this one with Jesus being nailed on the cross—and an out-of-place bottle of sanitizer, placed sacrilegiously on a pillar, before stopping in another room.

A large shrine, brightened by electric lights rather than candles—though there were a multitude of them—sat in the center. A doorway was in the middle of it, below thirteen faces. *The disciples and Jesus or the Knights of the Round Table and King Arthur?* Impossible to tell in the gloom, and he would've believed either at this point. Twelve men following one they held up above all others. Not too different, really.

Inside the shrine, more extinguished candles lay in their golden homes with an emergency light being the only source of illumination in the shrine. Above a stone bench, a blue banner with the words ΧΡΙΣΤΟΣ ΑΝΕΣΤΗ was sewn on with yellow thread.

Diomedes pointed at the bench, *"That's where the Grail lies."*

*"As expected,"* Catharsis said and climbed it with Glanderos. She motioned for Rajeev impatiently.

Glanderos grabbed his hand immediately once he was up. The drowning feeling happened again as they sunk down into a secret chamber. The size was impossible to guess since no light extended past a few feet around them.

Catharsis pulled out a flashlight while Glanderos floated up like an angel to retrieve the others. They were in a mausoleum, made known by a stone tomb that had just been out of sight of the upstairs light. No writing was inscribed upon the top, nor were there any neighbors. Compared to above, this room was plain. And cold, but Rajeev didn't think the goosebumps that appeared on his mostly naked skin were just from the cool air.

Diomedes was down and moved to Catharsis, giving her a single nod. She slid part of the cover over without any explanation. Rajeev leaned forward and saw the expectant skeleton with a sword held in its hands. On top of it, a shield with a red cross over a white field—strikingly similar to the birthmark on his chest—and a chalice that could only be one thing.

"That's . . ." Rajeev forgot the knight's name for a second. "Galahad."

"*Indeed,*" Catharsis said. "*He went on a quest to obtain the Holy Grail with Percival and Bors. Only he returned. Some believe it was due to his chastity. Others think he used his fellow knights as a sacrifice to be able to obtain the ability to harness its powers.*" She put a large hand on his skinny shoulder, sending a shiver through his body. "*But all we do know is that only his descendants can touch the Grail. Anyone else will perish in a most painful way.*"

"*Just don't touch the shield,*" Diomedes said and Rajeev saw with the corner of his eye Catharsis give the daegaryn a narrow look.

"*Don't try anything,*" Catharsis told Rajeev and he knew he wouldn't. "*Now pick up the Grail.*" And he did as he was commanded.

But as his hand reached down, a shrill alarm screamed through his head and his fingers brushed the shield instead.

# Chapter Sixteen

**Rain attacked Savannah** while she hung over the railing. Her lunch of Reubens wrapped in cabbage was long washed from the side of the great ship where she had expelled it. But an abrupt lurch below her feet that had her stumbling made her believe not all had made the great exodus.

The squall had come upon them without warning. No gray cloud in the distance or drop in temperature. The rain didn't even begin in a drizzle, it just "dropped," like God decided to take a piss right on them and nowhere else.

Isabella was still in her cabin, the Brit's stomach made up of a little more steel than hers. Actually, everybody else was below deck, probably cracking jokes about her being a weak-tummied American. Cormac said it would take less than thirty hours to get to Calais; she didn't think she could wait that long.

She glanced up from the dark waters below her and jerked back on deck when she saw a massive wave that hid the already barely visible horizon.

"Oh shit!" *Can I die from drowning?*

A large hand suddenly grabbed her shoulder and pulled her down, holding her with one arm. She let out a scream that was muffled in the wind, before realizing the person was trying to help her. Savannah turned her head to try to get a glimpse of them but could only see the free hand holding onto a deck rope. Judging by the hair on the arm and the color of it—the same as the rest of the crew—he was an Irishman.

"Hang on, we'll ride her out." The voice was surprisingly calm for the circumstances.

Savannah didn't verbally respond but just nodded, her neck brushing up against a bristly beard.

The ship rose from under them and then tilted violently. She felt herself sliding on the wet deck, but the man tightened his grip on her and hooked his leg onto the rope tied along the bottom of the railing of the boat, securing them both. The galley was almost at a ninety-degree angle now and stayed that way for what seemed like forever. But eventually, it leveled out and the man released her.

Savannah staggered to her feet and emptied her stomach of whatever was left of that heinous sandwich. She turned back to her savior, wiping away the bile from the side of her mouth. The man was a giant—six-seven, at least—with broad shoulders and rippling muscles that popped through his worn crewneck and pants. A fiery beard hid most of his face, while his egg-shaped head was barren.

The Irishman stared off into the distance. "That should be the worst of it."

She didn't believe he was able to see anything in the black void in front of them, but she took his word for it anyway.

"They call me Killian, by the way," the man said.

"What do others call you?" Savannah asked, not able to help her tongue-in-cheek response even under the circumstances.

"Killian, I suppose." He chuckled and seemed a little bashful for such a big guy. "I have a question for you." The Irishman turned back to her and went on without waiting for a reply. "You're obviously a long way from home, traveling with a Brit, and travelling by galley when you could get to Calais by the Channel Tunnel much faster. Where are you going?"

Savannah stared at his feet, wondering what she should say.

"I'm sorry, my curiosity has always been my biggest weakness." He again seemed ashamed of himself.

"That's fine, I guess." She was suddenly ready to go inside. *Could there be dragon tattoos under that shirt?*

*They walk among us.*

Savannah shivered. "It's a business trip." She wasn't exactly lying.

Killian's face darkened just for a second before he nodded and smiled. "Ah, of course."

She backed up until she reached the door going below deck, making sure to keep an eye on the man—if he even was one. Once inside, she sprinted to Isabella's cabin—Merlin had made sure that they got separate accommodations—surprising a few sailors along the way. Isabella was somehow sleeping on her cot and was not very happy to be woken up.

"What in the bloody hell do you want?"

Savannah explained the situation with Killian.

"He probably just wants in your pants." She closed her eyes and laid back down. "And maybe you should let him, a little dogging might loosen you up a bit." The Brit opened one eye when Savannah didn't respond and sighed. "The last place one of those creatures would want to be is on a wooden boat in the middle of the ocean. Relax and go to sleep. We have a long day tomorrow."

Savannah left and sought out Cormac, keeping a wary eye out for the Irish giant. She located his quarters and knocked gently. He opened it almost immediately. There was no sign of sleep in his brown eyes and his red, curly hair was unruffled. She did not wake him.

"Can't sleep either, eh." He smiled up at her. "Like my dear old da used to say, dark skies lead to long nights."

"I would think you'd be used to this by now."

"Aye, but Marlin paid me a lot of money to get you and your friend across the Channel." The heartiness he had exhibited earlier seemed to have mostly left him. "Americans with deep pockets can make great mates. Or even worse enemies. I'd rather not get on his bad side." He spoke as if he had experience with something like that. "Why did you come to see me anyway, lass?"

"What can you tell me about one of your deckhands, Killian?"

"Killian." He pursed his lips. "Hmm, you must be mistaken, I don't employ anybody by that name."

# Chapter Seventeen

**Rajeev felt like** his body was being yanked through the shield itself, contorting itself in impossible angles. Just with a blink of a brown eye, the cold, dark tomb turned to a humid, well-lit brothel, the humming gone for the first time in probably years.

Women wearing only thin white shifts danced with each other to music only they must've heard. The source of their thraldom appeared to be the only man present. He was scrawny and average in height with long, blond hair split in a middle part that had long gone out of style. If there was still any mystery about who the man was, a brand on his chest identical to Rajeev's own, gave it away.

Sir Galahad the Chaste smiled at him while a woman with red hair sat on his bare lap.

"Rajeev," he said with a slightly nasally voice. "It is such a great pleasure to finally meet thee."

The knight gestured at the prostitutes around him. "Now please, choose thy own pleasure."

"Where am I?" Rajeev asked, forcing his eyes onto his ancestor—a much easier task than with Catharsis.

"Ah, a man of urgency. Have somewhere important to

be?" Galahad sighed and patted the ginger's back, who moved aside for him to stand up. He was more impressive from the waist down. "Alas, mortals always have important business to attend to. Especially those with blood as powerful as thine running through their veins."

He walked to Rajeev until they stood within a foot of each other. Not many people could stand tall and stare right into his eyes. Galahad was one of the few.

"Thou art in my personal heaven, given along with the gift of eternity by the beloved wizard Merlin the Wise and Powerful. It is a great life I live but I do, believe it or not, get bored. It is so delightful to have a guest even if it happens only once a generation or so. In fact, I believe it was your mother who visited me last. Such a lovely lady and a rarity for a knight's descendent to pass down their powers along with their own genes. She must've told great things of me."

"She left when I was young," Rajeev said. That night would always be fixated on his mind. His parents had fought for hours while he lay in bed, fifteen years old. He remembered thinking if he should go down and give Omer what he deserved. Instead, those thoughts remained a fantasy until his mother came up to his room. She was smiling but her eyes were red and sad. There was somewhere she had to be, and she would be gone for a while. He was told to be strong for his dad. Then she was gone.

"A pity," the knight said with no such emotion.

"Do you know where she is?" Rajeev asked

"Dead," Galahad said, poorly feigning a sympathetic look. "Four years ago. I am sure thy powers manifested around that time, yes?"

Rajeev felt sick to his stomach even though he had expected it for longer than that.

"Why am I here?" he asked quietly

"To obtain what is rightfully thine by birthright," Galahad said. "*Irontruth.*"

Right before his eyes, a sword grew from his hand beginning with a cheap, steel hilt and finishing with a dark gray—almost black—blade with runes inscribed onto it. He squinted and saw cracks running up and down the blade as if it had been shattered and then repaired. "*Irontruth*'s blade was welded with olmerion—the ore from the daegaryns planet, Farlorn—and enchanted by Merlin. It can be wielded by only thee. Thy mother shattered the blade, using the old wizard's smith." The pieces of the blade separated and flowed around the knight for a minute before again retaining their shape. "Each shard of *Irontruth* can be controlled telepathically by you, just like any other metal. Gives quite the advantage."

Galahad handed the sword over and immediately Rajeev felt a rush of pure power flow through his veins like none he's felt before. He slashed it back and forth in the air a couple of times. It was like swinging a toy, yet he knew that if he tested the edge with a finger, half of it would end up on the floor.

"*Irontruth* gives its wielder more control of their abilities. Thou hast amazing power hidden within that thee haven't even tapped into yet. This sword will allow thee to."

The knight nodded back at the whores. "Thou can test it out on one of those bimbos if thee would like." Rajeev didn't waste a reply. "No, all right. Well, you best get going; thy mistress won't last much longer without her medicine. Which has already run out, by the way. Should've put on the full chemo bag instead of waiting for the other one to run out."

Rajeev gripped the ugly steel hilt tightly. "Why have you been wasting my time then? How do I get out of here?"

"Thou sure thee doth not want to stay?" The knight said, curling a finger in the redhead's hair. "It gets real lonely here sometimes. Even with my girls."

"Galahad!"

"Fine, fine," he held a finger to Rajeev's forehead. "Just

make sure to give those daegaryns hell. Especially that lady one. The pretty ones are always the most dangerous."

"What about you?"

"Boy, I fight with a different sword these days."

The finger landed and Rajeev again felt himself being contorted in a disorienting but not painful way. And just as abruptly as before he was standing over the skeleton of the man he just talked to.

"Ra—" He didn't let Catharsis finish and whipped around *Irontruth* in a full one-eighty to take off her shoulder at the elbow, the forward momentum also causing the blade to sink deep into her side.

Flipping around just in time, he blocked twin laser beams from Diomedes's eyes with the sword and reflected them back to cut him in half diagonally.

He was covered in blood by the time he turned on Glanderos. *Irontruth* only passed through her each time Rajeev swung it. The daegaryn didn't even care about stopping him, going to Catharsis instead. She grabbed her intact arm, the other gushing blood with each pulse of her non-human heart.

Changing tactics, Rajeev released the shards from their magical binding and sprayed them at the pair. But then a strong force punched him across the face, sending him rolling. He glimpsed up from where he fell and just saw two pairs of feet before they disappeared through the ceiling.

The attacker was, of course, the remaining daegaryn, Kalynst. The kid stood over him, his face containing no triumphant smirk, just a blank expression.

"*Catharsis will want you alive,*" he said.

"How would you do that?" Rajeev retorted.

A single shard shredded through the back of Kalynst's left leg, shearing the hamstring. The daegaryn crumpled with a short cry.

Rajeev stood over him and reformed the sword. Raising

it up in preparation to kill, thoughts surged through his head. The kid's dead father and uncle. The senator's daughter. And most powerfully, Yasmin. He let *Irontruth* drop to his side.

"Stay out of my way, kid," Rajeev said. "Because next time I will kill you."

He stepped over him and to where they had dropped down into the tomb. The shards tore through the rock like butter, going back and forth as dust and small rocks fell on him. One large chuck hit him in the shoulder dislocating his shoulder, but he popped it in without any thought. Soon, there was a large enough gap for him. Several golden lamps hung above him and he used them to pull himself up, then swing himself to the floor of the shrine.

The remainder of the church flew by in a blur as he propelled himself forward with his internal magnet, knocking down priceless artifacts in his rush. It took minutes before he was again on the streets of Jerusalem. There were no signs of daegaryns but with how much the storm had progressed, they could be right in front of him.

Rajeev closed his eyes and concentrated on the metal around him. Cars, pipes, and appliances all lit up in his mind's eye. He used *Irontruth* as a valve to regulate his raw power and soon smaller dots, almost microscopic, appeared. These were the metals found in all humans—and considering their food source, daegaryns too. No one was near him. The monsters must've escaped.

And for Yasmin's sake, he had to go too.

After a quick mental search, he located a nearby Ford Explorer and cut off the driver's door with his sword. Just like he had done many times before, he stepped on it to use it like a magic carpet. Though on those occasions, he wasn't in a sandstorm. Taking some upholstery from the car, he wrapped it around his eyes and mouth, leaving his nose exposed. He would have some terrible sand boogers, but the upholstery would make it impossible to breathe. He didn't have time for added protection.

The door and its passenger left the paved, stone ground and soared up in the air then in the direction to where he believed Qatar and his wife would be. They had gone north of Mecca, and when he woke up from his faint, Catharsis said they were in the south wall of Jerusalem. Right? Then they went north, maybe northwest. Considering Balthasar had taken him mainly west of Doha, he needed to aim southeast. Rajeev wished he had a better sense of direction and paid more attention in geography class, but it didn't matter now. He just had to get back to his wife.

Further on into the unknown Rajeev went, his skin being ripped apart at almost as fast of a rate as it was being healed. His nose soon became clogged, so he had to remove the upholstery from around his mouth. With the speed he was flying, however, the whole thing ended up coming off and his entire face became exposed. He closed his eyes and only took breaths when he needed, each time swallowing a fistful of sand.

Consciousness soon left him.

# Chapter Eighteen

**Even though Savannah** tried to stay awake all night, she must've fallen asleep at some point as there was a note on her bedside table.

She leaped off her bed, sparks flying from her in her fear. Her cabin was empty. It was small but cozy, with a cot screwed flat to the ground and a cramped closet that she left open last night. Only naked hangers and a life jacket occupied the space.

Savannah let herself cool down—a problem the rain had helped with last night—before picking up the slip of paper. An address was scrawled upon the paper.

*109 Sárkány sikátor, Budapest.*

*But why?*

There was a knock at the door, and she quickly tucked it into the back of her only other pair of jeans.

"Let's go, *Lady Guinevere*," Isabella demanded. She was wearing a low-cut crew neck along with her yoga pants. "I'd like to get this bloody quest over with as soon as possible."

"Yeah, I'm coming."

Savannah grabbed her duffel from atop the coffee table and opened the door.

"Any visits from your boyfriend last night?" Isabella asked as they walked down the corridor. Her voice was filled with mostly humor. But just mostly. Underneath there is something else. Concern maybe?

"Cormac said he never heard of the guy."

"Shite!" Definitely concern. "Why didn't you wake me up?"

"I thought you were going to stab me with your spear if I woke you up again."

"Did he have reptilian eyes? Dragon tattoos?" She had dropped her volume when some sailors had begun staring at them as they walked.

"No," Savannah's heart accelerated with her companion's unnatural worry. "But he could've been wearing contacts and he was also clothed from head to toe."

The British woman suddenly dropped her luggage and unzipped the ski bag, pulling out the deadly weapon. Seeing it for the first time up close, Savannah saw it was almost as tall as her—a five-foot-eleven power forward for all of middle school and some of high school before her broken finger magically repaired itself—probably pushing seven feet. The blade was unnatural, broad almost as it was long—the size of her fist—and it was the color of charcoal, yet it gleamed to illuminate some type of runes on the side of it. The shaft, on the other hand, was the boring dull gray of steel.

"Merlin said they might be able to track that inferno in your belly." She gathered up her bags again. "I just don't understand why it didn't kill you if it truly was a daegaryn."

"It saved me actually."

"Yeah, there's most definitely a long-term game with you." They entered the open deck, mist rising during France's dawn. "We have to get out of here quickly."

Cormac was standing next to the left—starboard?—side staring off into the Port of Calais, surprisingly busy considering the early hour. He turned at the sound of their feet on the old-fashioned, splintering, wooden flooring. The bags under his eyes were dark and puffy and they widened at the sight of *Snakebite.*

"Any problems last night?" he asked but the joy was back in his voice now seeing they were almost off his ship. "Liam and Sean never reported back to me."

Savannah almost forgot he sent guards for her, yet she didn't remember seeing anybody when she left her cabin. She raised an eyebrow at Isabella.

"Oh, those wankers, I sent them off just a minute ago," She stamped the butt of her spear onto the deck. "I'm the only protection she needs." The British woman flipped her golden-streaked hair in the ocean breeze as she turned to the nearby ramp. "And by the way everything's fine. My friend here imagined the man, Killian, in her fright." Isabella handed him a wad of cash she had removed from her cleavage, while Savannah watched this exchange in amazement. "Cheerio, bruv. Thanks for the ride."

Savannah followed her apparent friend out onto the bustling dock and saw the reason for the busyness. A cruise ship loomed over them in the next dock over. In their hurry, they never noticed the giant boat. Shuttles were receiving luggage and delivering it to the supposed terminal, a large building at the edge of the port.

"*Salut!*" A skinny, Black man with a smooth flattop called to them from a golf cart. "*Bienvenue en France.*"

Isabella pointed *Snakebite* at him and scowled.

"Woah," He raised his hands but smiled kindly and spoke in English with a beautiful French accent. "Mr. Cormac called on me to take you to the car rentals. My name is Luis."

Savannah turned to the Brit, mouthing *daegaryn.*

She shook her head and said a little too loudly, "I've seen skeletons with more meat on their bones."

The drive was short yet made longer by the tensity between the Europeans. Each question Luis politely asked as small talk was shut down by a harsh cough from Isabella. Considering the terrifying woman beside him, the Frenchman was surprisingly calm and upbeat. Not to mention that same woman had a badass spear sitting across her lap with the razor-sharp edge pointed at him.

Luis dropped them off with an *au revoir* at the rentals and hurried back to the docks. The line was short—strange with a cruise ship docked in the harbor—and soon they were greeted by an elderly woman with red hair. *"Bonjour, comment puis-je vous aider?"*

*"Anglais?"* Isabella asked.

The lady shook her head.

Isabella already had her phone out and was rapidly typing something down.

It wasn't until then that Savannah realized her own iPhone had been destroyed in her own fire. She never could leave home without it and relied on it for everything. Like for comfort and reassurance from James.

Now, what was the point of having one?

While lost in her own thoughts, Isabella had secured a ride and was marching off to it. Savannah hurried after her. The British woman stopped in front of a sleek, silver sports car, low to the ground and built for speed.

"2020 Alfa Romeo 4C Spider. Two hundred and forty-seven horsepower. Goes zero to sixty in just 4.1 seconds. And it's an absolute beauty," she said, appearing at her happiest since Savannah first met her.

"I didn't know you were a car person," Savannah said peering inside at the velvet seats, appearing brand new as if nobody ever sat in them.

"You met me two days ago; how would you know anything about me?" When Savannah didn't respond she said, "I inherited it from my dad. I just wish we could get an earlier model, but we have thousands of kilometers to go and need at least a little reliability." She regarded the other luxurious rentals in the garage with envy for a moment before opening the driver's side door. "Let's go. We need to put as much distance between those dragon bastards as we can."

# Chapter Nineteen

**The European phallus** stood erect as the man walked—with grace for one his age—down the steep stairs of the Gulfstream V. His beige trench coat bristled in wind just strong enough for him to feel the need to keep a hand on the matching fedora. It was a cool day—twelve degrees Celsius if his damned meteorological app was correct—but the locals would've disagreed. He could never get used to this weather.

A freshly shaven man dressed in a navy blue sports coat greeted him at the bottom of the steps. A white, tinted-out limousine idled behind him. *Bulletproof too, I'm sure*, the visitor mused.

*"Monsieur Santos, Bienvenue à nouveau."* They exchanged lipless smiles as he continued in French. "We were expecting you."

*"Oui, oui."* He spoke French as well but with an Argentinian accent. "He's home, I suppose?"

With his luck, Biron would be on vacation at one of those nude beaches Santos so endeared.

The Republican Guard nodded and opened the door to the limo. Inside, Santos was delighted to find a bottle of Amargo Obrero. Sitting on the plush leather seats, he added a finger of the stuff to a frosted glass. Opening the cooler, he took out a plastic container of grapefruit juice. It was generic and with a large score of added sugars, but it would have to do. He added it to the bitter, mixed, and took a sip. *Ecantador.*

He removed his fedora that had covered white, recently trimmed hair to show more of his face, lighter than that of most of his country's neighbors. An inch-long scar through the corner of his beardless mouth had long ago become his excuse to not smile.

Santos laid back and let Mercedes Sosa and the cocktail bring him into a doze.

Light penetrated his eyelids but he kept them closed; a ghost danced naked in a hotel in Costa Rica.

"Monsieur, we are here."

With a sigh, Santos stood up and let his eyes adjust to the sun's glare. They stood in front of an official-looking building in the typical fashion of Europe: the wings running perpendicular to the main section, hugging the courtyard. It was made of faded bricks the color of his coat with a cacophony of windows occupying the rest of the external structure. Élysée Palace. Named for the final resting place for the heroes of Greek mythology, it seemed misused for the residency for French government nobles.

Biron's man led him inside. Gold and art dominated the interior architecture of the Palace, stinking of power and riches. Chandeliers with thousands of crystals glittered above them as Santos was guided past portraits of French royalty. Napoleon Bonaparte appearing as a baby in a man's body. A woman he didn't recognize. *Louis XIV*, the golden plate underneath read. *European art was so drab.*

They stopped at a pair of French doors—*French doors in the capital building of France, how about it*—where the Guard gently rapped before pulling them open.

President Jean Biron waited for them behind a—*how astonishing*—golden desk covered with what was surely important documents, and in front of a large portrait of himself. The president was young for a man of his profession—couldn't have been much older than forty-five. He was clean-shaven but the heavy bags under his hazel eyes illustrated his current worry and restlessness.

"Fernando. Thank you for coming," he said, putting on a tired smile as he spoke Santos's first language.

"You learned Spanish, I see?"

*Kiss ass much.*

"Just a little, my friend," He answered. His face firmed up but still pleasant as he got down to business, never one for small talk. One thing they had in common. "We were expecting you."

*Do these damn Frenchies have anything else to do but expect? Not much to do here, I guess, except peruse hideous art.* "I've been busy."

"Of course," Biron's tone didn't agree with his sentiment.

Santos finally took a seat in a velvet chair across from the president when it was not offered. The Guard had left and closed the doors on his way out.

"We are on the brink of war," the president said.

"Yes," Santos said in his usual calm manner. "It is a difficult situation."

"*A difficult situation.*" The president's nicely gelled hair quivered as he spoke. "We were nuked, Goddammit!"

Santos bristled at the blasphemy. "As I said, a difficult situation.

Biron raised his voice to be just one octave under yelling. "Strasbourg is gone because of your people."

The ghost appeared in his head briefly before he blocked her out.

"First, just because I was born with similar abilities does not mean I'm like them." Santos straightened his suit. "And second, how do you know it was caused by someone like me?"

He frowned, not wanting to tell Santos how he knew a knight did the most sinister of deeds. "Intel showed that a young girl was taken to a high-security prison in the Western United States." Biron stared at Santos for a moment, preparing his next words. "Were we correct?"

Santos told Biron. "American, Nathan Stromberg, is the most powerful human being on the Earth. He was responsible for the destruction of Strasbourg. But he didn't do it personally. He somehow got into the ear of Prime Minister Malory of the United Kingdom. A threat perhaps? Maybe all the money he could ever desire? It could even be to see a lost loved one again." Santos paused just briefly after he said that. "What mattered is that it happened."

"What do we do?" he asked, his already chalky complexion growing paler and paler by the minute.

"Prepare for war but wait for me," he told the president in French. "I will try to win over the Brits."

Santos stood up to bid the Frenchman ado, but the Biron had one more thing to say.

"Can't you turn back time?"

"The past can't be changed, not truly. Time is unforgiving. If I stopped the nuclear reaction in Strasbourg, there may be a bigger one in Paris."

Santos had found that out the hard way.

# Chapter Twenty

**The Alfa Romeo** sped off Autoroute 31 onto A4, cutting past an SUV full of kids. The father flicked it off and was quickly reprimanded by his wife.

Inside the convertible, Savannah hung onto the side for dear life, while her auburn hair whipped around in the wind and endless trees and cars flew by them in a blur. Hours ago, she had learned the reasoning behind "white-knuckling it."

She glanced at the speedometer and cried out, "Why are you going 160?"

Isabella seemed unfazed and just glanced, annoyed. "It's 160 *kilometers* per hour, not miles per hour. I almost forgot you Americans use that system. I'm only going about a hundred miles per hour." "Calm down. We need to put as much distance between us and your boyfriend."

*A hundred is still a lot.* But she did have a point. It's not like they could die anyway.

The Brit took a short drag from a joint to Savannah's chagrin. Apparently, a lot of the knights smoked to calm down since anger and stress can cause one to lose control of their powers. It explained the slight weed odor at Camelot. Isabella had offered her some after showing her a massive plastic bag of the stuff. Savannah turned it down but did accept a pack of cigarettes at the gas station. However, she was too afraid to attempt to smoke it at this speed especially since Isabella is making her use her hands to light it. What she really wanted was a vape, but the Brit firmly denied the request without giving a reason. She felt like a toddler.

Red lights appeared in the distance. Isabella cursed and hit the brakes a little too hard. Traffic. When they had slowed to a manageable thirty-five kilometers per hour, Savannah let out a sigh of relief, careful not to let her companion see. Without the thundering of the engine and roar of the wind, she could discern somebody rapping in French over the radio.

The quietness gave her a chance to figure out what the hell was going on now that Killian was—hopefully—far off.

"How long 'till we get to Turgekistan?" She sat back and relaxed, allowing the sun to warm her on this cool day.

"Turkmenistan," There was no hateful laugh at her ignorance; she was too busy staring holes into the back of the white Camry in front of them. "Eighty-five hours from Calais."

*Eighty-five! So, it's not in Europe then.* She was never great at geography. "Where is it?"

"The Middle East. Part of Old Russia."

She tried to place it on a map inside her head to no avail. Now she was starting to miss her phone. "Remind me again why we aren't flying there?"

"I already told you, Merlin's orders." She honked her horn at a familiar SUV. "These frog wankers don't know how to drive." They drove in silence for a moment before Isabella continued. "It's because he wants us to quote 'experience the countryside of thy travels.' " She was again cut off, leading to the horn and the most unholy finger. "Sometimes I wish I had Immanuel's powers."

"Immanuel?"

"The Congolese man."

Savannah was still confused.

"The black guy."

"Oh, him." Savannah nodded. "He never gave his real name, but he could teleport, right?"

"At its simplest, yes." The traffic was starting to ease up, and the Brit got on the tail of the SUV, daring them to go faster. *She has a serious anger issue.* "He tried to explain it to me once, but it went over my head. Quantum mechanics and all that shite."

"I didn't know he could talk."

"Yeah, he prefers the quiet. Says it helps him see—with his ears, that is."

"What's his story, how'd he get blind?" Damn, she was turning into one of her deli coworkers. Always gossiping about the girl in dairy who had just gotten knocked up by her boyfriend or the stocker whose dad had just died. Strangely, she actually missed those old birds.

Isabella paused, even letting up on the gas a little. "I asked him when I was too foolish to know better. He stared directly into my eyes—*directly*—and stayed that way until I left. Since then, I've been too scared to talk to him alone." She shook the memories and sped up. The British woman then dangerously looked over at her. "I'd advise you to do the same."

They drove a while longer, back to the dizzying speed.

"What about you?" Savannah eventually asked. "What's happened for you to join Merlin?"

Isabella slammed the brakes and Savannah's head bounced against the dashboard. She wiped the blood from her healing forehead and took the hint to remain quiet.


Traffic let up soon after they had stopped to get something to eat. Actually, that was an understatement as there was not a single car on the road currently. The reason became clear when yellow signs with a familiar symbol came into view. Radiation.

Savannah turned to her driver, but Isabella didn't seem to notice. Or care. She was still moving at extraordinary speeds.

"Where are we going?" Savannah spoke for the first time in hours.

"Turkmenistan."

*Smartass.*

"Where are we *now*?"

"Just outside of Strasbourg."

"Didn't China just nuke them?" She remembered that day clearly. James had invited her over for dinner—the thought of him made her choke up a bit. Both their phones had gone off at the same time. **NUCLEAR EXPLOSION IN STRASBOURG, FRANCE.** He quickly turned on the TV, his glasses slipping down his nose in his hurry. A Fox reporter broke down the disaster, stating China was involved. They flipped the channel to CNN who said it was North Korea's doing. The other news outlets weren't any clearer. Fingers were pointed everywhere. It was the second Cold War. There was a fear of retaliation leading to World War Three. But in the coming months, local news shifted to the roaring Cincinnati Bengals, behind the incredible Joe Burrow. It was another world's problem. But now here they were.

"It wasn't China or any of the other countries, it was one of us."

"How . . ." But Savannah's question trailed off when flashing blue lights danced through the sounds of trees up to their left. Isabella slowed around a bend, where two police cars blocked off a makeshift gate. Police, not government, that might be good. Officers—four of them—were already standing outside, hands out as if that would do anything against a speeding Alfa Romeo. But the Brit stopped anyway and cut the engine.

"Don't say anything," she warned. "Hold your breath after my signal."

"Wha—"

But she was already out of the car, tugging her shirt down to reveal more cleavage.

"Hey officers!" the British woman said with the naïve cheer of Reese Witherspoon in *Legally Blonde*.

The police noticeably relaxed. Just a lost British tourist. "Mademoiselle, this a restricted area, one of the officers said in crisp English. *The captain*, maybe, Savannah thought. *I can't even differentiate between American police badges, so theirs definitely don't help.*

"Unfortunately, me and my partner," Savannah perked up and smiled politely when they turned their attention onto her. "Have business here. We come as representatives of the United Kingdom, sent personally by Prime Minister Malory. We're SIS." Isabella showed the assumed captain the inner flap of her wallet. *Does she have a fake secret intelligence badge? Or is she actually an agent there?* Savannah would've believed either of them at this point. Anyhow, a floozy spy was an interesting cover.

The captain and the other officers inspected the badge, gathering close.

"I'm sorry, we were not made aware of that." The policeman looked at his partners, worried. "Let me make a call to the captain."

*So not the captain. The lieutenant maybe?*

He stepped into his cruiser and spoke through a walkie. Behind her back, Isabella stuck up a middle finger. *The sign.* Then, *What a bitch.* Nonetheless, Savannah held her breath.

The lieutenant stepped out of the car, with a wide smile. "Good news . . ." He went into a coughing fit that caused him to bend over. The others joined, eventually falling to their knees and then to the ground where they stayed, unmoving.

Savannah was too scared to take a breath and questioned what just happened. *Poison, her power is poison. She killed them with poison!*

Isabella physically checked each one of them before turning back to Savannah. Her eyes were a vibrant pink, and she was grinning, proud of her work.

"Calm down," she said. "I gave them a dose of domoic acid, commonly known as amnesic shellfish poisoning. It will give them some memory loss. They'll forget the last few hours, probably not much more. It can take some time for those symptoms to appear, so I added propofol—a common hospital anesthetic—to the mix. That's what knocked them."

Savannah didn't respond, still holding her breath.

"Breathe, dammit. The poison is gone, and it probably wouldn't have hurt you, anyway. Having you hold your breath was just a precaution."

She released her air and took a hesitant breath. No coughing, at least not yet. She felt fine. "How?" Savannah asked, still a little pissed.

"What? You should be proud of me. ASP is only transferred through consumption. I could have snogged each of them, but I think I would've been tased before I was finished. So instead, I created microscopic, artificial spores in my right lung—which contained the concoction. I breathed them out and they breathed them in. Although they were a little more fuzzy than I intended, hence, the coughing."

"So, they're not going to die?"

"No," the British woman seemed offended at the question. "I never mess up my doses.

She scrutinized her victims. "Now, help me move these obnoxiously nice bastards."

Isabella removed some rubber gloves from her duffel— *not her first time doing this?*—and they started dragging the officers to the side of the road.

"Shite!" Isabella exclaimed and sprinted to the Romeo. Savannah glanced around her, not knowing what to do. The Brit grabbed *Snakebite* and threw it at a tree. The sharp sound of metal against metal was followed by the crash of the spear with something else in the woods. Isabella whipped her head frantically around, sharp eyes taking in everything before going to retrieve her weapon.

"A security camera, frack," she said, emerging with her weapon and a small object just bigger than her hand. "We have to move."

"What are we going to do?" Savannah exclaimed, wide-eyed.

"Secrecy is a knight's best friend. Secret levels of governments all around the world have been trying to find us. We need to find that tape and destroy it before someone connects the dots of four officers being knocked unconscious without being touched."

A sudden thought made this tough girl shiver. "Or Merlin finds it first."

# Chapter Twenty‑One

**A dark apparition** floated across the cold, stone tomb of a knight not as great as legend would tell. Two halves of a body lay gruesomely in a pile of congealing blood. An arm without a host was directly at the base of the stone coffin.

It peered into the final resting place of Galahad. A sword rested in his bony hands and a legendary, but simplistic, shield was placed over it. The stranger slowly reached down to it, a short index finger drawn and ready. Their body tensed in anticipation inches from it. The finger and shield connected.

Nothing.

"Damn," a feminine voice resounded. "Oh well."

The important item here was that the Grail was missing. Not much she could do about it except include it in her report.

She clasped her hands and looked at the grisly scene. It was cleanup time. Most of the damage could be blamed on Israeli delinquents but the daegaryn would be a different matter.

Gloves were slipped on and a garbage bag opened.

"What's a girl gotta do for a vacation," she asked the dead knight and went to work.

# Chapter TwentyTwo

**They hurriedly finished** clearing the road and Isabella broke the lock of the gate with *Snakebite*. It was ten minutes before they were in the lost city of Strasbourg.

It was worse than she had expected. She had of course seen pictures on the news. It was all over Facebook and Instagram too, but she was never one for social media even when...

There was a shadow of a small child against the remnants of a gray—God, everything was gray here—building. *A little kid died here. Not with family, a friend, or even a kind stranger. They died alone. Alone with no one to hold their hand. No one to lie to them that everything was going to be okay.*

"There were no survivors," Isabella said in a sad but strangely monotone voice, like that of a documentary narrator. "The largest single-day genocide in history—nearly half a million died—yet nobody knows who did it. Or at least that's what most of the world thinks."

Isabella paused as if waiting for her passenger to ask a question, but Savannah was barely paying attention to her, instead, a destroyed house, burnt to a crisp, grabbed it. *I wonder if a family was in there? A father and a beautiful daughter? A wife that loved them? Did they die together in each other's arms? Or separately like the little kid?*

"It was a knight—maybe two—who did this," Isabella continued. "The ones Merlin mentioned who had gone down a darker path."

"Why?" Savannah asked faintly.

"The specifics are for Merlin to tell, but the motive was to kill another knight."

"Why?".

"Again, that's Merlin's story to tell."

They continued down the dark, dusty road, trying not to think about the horrors that happened around them.

"He told me to bring you here to show what we're up against, and also what we're capable of."

Savannah finally glanced at her partner and saw something raw there. This was her first time here too.

She shakily pulled out a Marlboro before remembering Isabella didn't allow her to buy a lighter.

A Bic landed in her lap. She eyed the Brit.

"You'll light it yourself next time," was all she said.

The poisonous smoke felt reassuring as it swirled around in her lungs, then releasing out into the gray solitude. Gray on gray, everything was gray, like Death had sucked all the color away. The nicotine cleared her head but perhaps for the worse. *Did they all die quickly? Or did the radiation slowly destroy some of them from the inside out?*

*Radiation. Shit.*

"Does radiation do anything to us?" She blurted out.

Isabella's eyes widened slightly at first but quickly reduced to the usual annoyed squint. "Merlin wouldn't send us anywhere we could be harmed."

*That's reassuring.*

Fifteen minutes later they had reached the perimeter of the city and got onto an autoroute. A short while later, familiar flashing blue lights appeared in the distance.

"Just follow my lead," Isabella ordered.

"What are we going to do?" Savannah asked, not as concerned as she probably should be.

"Get captured. They'll take us to the closest security depot. Hopefully, that is where the camera was being transmitted."

"What if it's being transmitted to multiple places."

"We'll be screwed because I don't know how to tell, I was a dentist before I came here, not some kind of tech nerd."

*A dentist. Interesting.* Savannah looked at *Snakebite* in the Brit's free hand, angled for the butt to sit next to her feet. *I don't think I'd want her prying around in my mouth.*

Déjà vu hit as they slowed to a stop before the barricade with the officers—six of them this time—waiting for them with guns drawn.

"Mesdemoiselles," an officer said curtly. *Was this the captain?* "Please step out of your vehicle."

"*Pas de français,*" Isabella responded mildly but put her hands up.

"Please get out of the car."

They both slowly exited the convertible.

"Put down the spear." All politeness was out of the captain's voice.

The British woman still held the ancient weapon and didn't release it at his command. She eyed the police in front of her. Four men and two women, all pointing handguns at her. Then, without warning, she reeled *Snakebite* back and threw it. Gunshots went off. The spear flew well over their heads. Blood spurted from Isabella. She was on the ground motionless. Yelling. So much yelling.

The event played for Savannah in snapshots as she tried to process what had just happened. An officer, a woman, appeared in her face. Screaming and pulling at her. Savannah looked back at her friend and went with the cop. She was taken past the captain who appeared shell shocked as he should be, muttering "I'm sorry, I thought she . . ." to her.

Handcuffed and in the back of the cop car, the fog cleared. She knew all too well they couldn't die from gunshots; the wounds healed almost immediately.

*You tricky bitch.*

# Chapter TwentyThree

**Both anatomical and** wind-driven sand glued Rajeev's eyes closed. Not that he really wanted to see. The quietness and scorching heat let him know he was alone in the desert, somewhere in the Arabian Peninsula. Though, that was if he was lucky. He could've been in Africa or gone north instead of east and ended up in Syria.

The only thing that allowed him to pry open his eyes was the thought of Yasmin. Blurry sand and rocks, accentuated by waves of heat, stretched in every direction, broken up by the rare desert bush. The dry surroundings were nothing compared to the arid environment of his mouth. This was somehow even worse than the flight to Jerusalem. He coughed and only dirt exited.

The limits of his body were still a mystery to him. He never tested it with internal destructive elements like bleach or tried to cut off an arm to see if it would grow back, but for all Rajeev knew, he couldn't die. Did that mean his body could magically produce water to rehydrate his cells? Rajeev had a feeling that if he didn't find water soon, he would discover his limit.

The door of the Ford Explorer had to be nearby. He could use that to find the nearest town and hydrate, then find out where he was. Rajeev closed his eyes and found the door some twenty feet in front of him.

His stomach growled as he climbed to his feet, reminding him he hadn't eaten in almost two days—Catharsis didn't want Rajeev to eat yesterday morning, so as not to expel it as soon as they took off. His legs felt heavy, a sure result of a lack of water, electrolytes, and food.

He stumbled in the direction of the door and weakly held his hands out. Rajeev magnetized to it and was pulled forward back onto his face. Physics played a lot of part in his powers. If something was heavier than him, it would pull him and vice versa. That meant the door must've been buried deep in the sand. Or he really had lost much of his strength. It was probably a combination of the two.

Another idea popped into his head. He jumped up and then pulled. A brilliant idea if there was any sense to it. A rock, five feet away, hidden in the sand knocked some into him.

His weakened state made him think of the power he had yesterday, given to him by *Irontruth*. Rajeev searched for the ancient weapon and found it about thirty feet in the opposite direction. He gently tugged on it with his mind. It barely moved, stuck as well. Using the door as a sort of anchor he pulled with full strength on the sword, praying that he didn't rip himself apart. The tendons in his shoulders felt like they were going to snap, but *Irontruth* found its way into its master's hands, sending a volley of sand into his face. Power immediately flew through him. Colors flew into his vision as all the microscopic metals mixed in the sand appeared. Only one mattered though, the dark blue of steel that made up the majority of a certain Ford Explorer's door.

*Irontruth* didn't change the rules of physics, but it did give him the strength needed to lumber to the spot in front of the door. It was definitely buried deep in the sand to the point where he could only see with his metal-vision. The enhanced sight also gave him depth perception, letting him know that the door was somewhere between five and ten feet under. Not wanting to face plant again, he started digging.

With his hands free to dig, he felt some of the strength that *Irontruth* gave him drain. Now was not the time to worry about becoming dependent on it.

Sweat dripped down on his brown arms and sand, turning it a similar color. A good sign that there was some water in him. And eventually one of those moist hands brushed a hard surface.

He rolled back onto his feet quickly, gladly retrieving his sword, and pulled the door the rest of the way out. Not wasting any time, Rajeev scrambled on it and zoomed away. *Irontruth* took away his fatigue, but it wouldn't hydrate him. He needed water and Yasmin needed him.

Staying around twenty feet in the air, Rajeev surveyed the desert, not with his eyes but with his magnet. Ten. Twenty. Thirty minutes go by and still no sign of civilization. He was physically and emotionally drained but *Irontruth* and his wife were his batteries. A source of water and a helpful guide would come along soon; it was only a matter of time.

His hidden fear evaporated and green—the color of trees in a rainforest—appeared on the edge of his metal-vision. Tin. A metal not to be expected found in the middle of a desert in the Arabian Peninsula.

Rajeev opened his eyes and indeed saw something glint in the Middle Eastern sun not so far away. He increased the speed of the door and soon realized it was a house. A small one made of bricks and a tin roof, but a house usually had an owner, even one this far out in the desert. Rajeev refused to believe it was abandoned.

The door took him to the foot of the house as the sun moved past its highest point. He stepped off and climbed up the wooden porch. The butt of a cigarette discarded next to a rocking chair gave him hope of occupation. Rajeev knocked on the front door with more fervor than he intended. Seconds felt like minutes while he anxiously waited for a savior. It opened up just a bit with a loud creak and an older man with a kind face peaked in through the crack. He smiled widely, causing bushy, white eyebrows to move up his wrinkled forehead.

"*Salaam*," the man greeted Rajeev in Arabic. "You appear to be lost," he said as if they weren't in the middle of the desert.

"*Naeam sayidi*," Rajeev said and then, forgetting his manners, blurted out, "Can I have some water, *min fadlik*?"

"Of course, what am I thinking? Being out in this heat, you must be very thirsty. Those phony weathermen had said we were going through a heat wave. Hmmph. I could've told them that. I can't even smoke a cigarette without sweating my ass off."

Rajeev followed the man through the door without comment. The inside of the house seemed very similar. Almost like his growing up, come to think of it. He half expected to see a twenty-four pack of Coronas in the fridge.

The old man was still going on about the quality of weathermen these days while he poured Rajeev a glass of water from the tap. His mouth felt even drier at the sight.

". . . I worked an honest job at the quarry before I retired out of here, yet those posers make more money than I ever did."

He walked over to Rajeev with the water. "What's your name, anyway?"

"Rajeev, where are we, *sayidi*? What country?"

"Isn't that obvious, boy?" Rajeev reached for the water but the man just pulled back. "You're home."

Rajeev turned to a frame on the wall, holding the photo of a family within. *His* family. With his mother and father standing over him, one hand on each of their shoulders. The memory of his father's smile was almost faded as that of his mother's face.

"You never asked my name, boy." Rajeev faced the old man again, but he was not the old man anymore. "A rude thing to do when asked of yours."

Omer scowled down at him and poured the water on the dusty floorboards. "That's what you get for spilling my beer, boy."

His dead father unfastened his belt and removed it from around him. "And this is what you get for scaring your mother away."

The belt took him in the ear, and Rajeev was bent over before the next hit came. Precious water leaked from his eyes to mix with that spilled by Omer.

Whip. Whip. Whip.

# Chapter Twenty-Four

**Being shot hurts** like a bloody bitch, but the wounds healed almost immediately—an uncomfortable feeling similar to a fly crawling under one's skin. The blood, however, continued to soak through her crewneck, sending alarm through the froggies. The chaotic commands in quick French made her almost crack an eye, but she had to keep them closed to play the part of the barely conscious victim.

It took longer than expected before somebody came to check on her vitals and then attempt to stop the bleeding that never really started. She groaned at the pressure, hoping they didn't rip her shirt or else they'd be in for a surprise.

An ambulance siren could be heard in the distance and soon she was positioned onto a stretcher.

"You will be okay." a paramedic said to her in poor English.

There was whispering between the man and the officer in charge. *Haguenau.* A city. It was close; they had passed an exit for it like forty minutes before reaching the first barricade. That must be where the camera was transmitting to. And if not, so help her God.

She was lifted into the ambulance, feigning a grunt at the

sharp movement. An oxygen mask was immediately placed over her mouth as they pulled out. Murmuring in French, the medic stabbed two IVs into the pit of each elbow. There was a cold tickle of metal against her skin then the shirt was being cut. She expected this would happen sooner or later. The man released a gasp when he reached the spot where the wound should've been.

"Surprise." Isabella ripped out the IVs and pulled off the mask, rolling off the stretcher almost simultaneously. The paramedic—in his thirties but already balding—turned to the policeman next to him. They made the mistake of not hand-cuffing her. She lunged at the officer as he reached for his handgun, punching him below the sternum at the solar plexus and then ramming her knee into his forehead as he bent over.

While the froggie lay cold, she kneeled down and kissed him on the lips, delivering the concoction she created earlier. It was much easier to contain that way; she didn't want to knock out the driver. The window was closed and the poison was designed with a short half-life, but Isabella didn't want to take any chances.

The paramedic sat in the corner of the bench, holding his legs in a fetal position.

"What? Never been snogged?"

She calmed him.

The window to the driver was hopefully soundproof; she didn't need any calls for backup. Isabella pulled it open now. An older woman drove, listening to soft French music and oblivious of everything that happened.

"*Bonjour,*" Isabella greeted.

The woman jumped in her seat and then reflexively reached for the walkie.

"I wouldn't do that if I were you." Isabella touched the police officer's gun to the back of her neck.

The driver sat back, stiff like an ironing board as she

should be. "What do you want?" Her English was just a little better than the paramedic's.

"Take me to Haguenau."

In the rearview mirror, she could see the French woman's eyebrows knit. "That's where I was told to go. The Centre Hospitalier de Haguenau."

"Take me to the security depot there."

"The police station?"

*Police station, duh. What the bloody hell is a security depot?*

"Oui."

It was twenty-five minutes before they arrived in Haguenau. It was built like the majority of European cities where the buildings are all attached, all different from one another unlike the uniformity common in America. The windows of every third building, though, were shattered. Graffiti was scrawled everywhere. She couldn't really understand French, but she knew what skulls and bloody bodies meant. The perpetrators of the morbid art couldn't be known since the streets were empty, probably all hunkering down for nuclear war.

The ambulance came to a stop in front of a faded red building. *POLICE NATIONALE HAGUENAU* was written over a castle—with four towers placed over a wall to appear as a crown—a five-petaled flower, and an "F" placed through the hole of an "R." The intricacies of the coat of arms were difficult to decipher since a slur was painted over it satin red. Other than that, there weren't any other signs of vandalism.

"Thank you for your help," She sucked a finger then reached over and harshly shoved it in the driver's mouth. Too far to kiss her.

Before she got out, Isabella wrapped some gauze around her face, only leaving her mouth and nose uncovered. She wasn't going to make the same mistake that caused her to be here.

Outside on the sidewalk, she summoned *Snakebite*, activating the ball of power within her to create a beacon. After just a moment, her spear flew at her at stunning speeds. Isabella turned her body at the last minute and grabbed the staff that warmed at her touch. This weapon was the reason she made it here in an ambulance instead of a police cruiser. *Snakebite* is not meant for anybody but her.

Isabella spied a camera and spit a yellow-orange acid with the vigor of a reptile. The mixture of hydrochloric and nitric acid known as aqua regia, dissolved the device in less than a minute. It was a trick she had just recently learned to use. The ingredients of the acids are already being produced naturally in her, so she just needed to create the chemical reaction. But for stronger metals, she had stored some inorganic chemicals in an indestructible pocket in her stomach.

Now, she calmly pulled the door open giving the young male secretary a small smile as if her face wasn't wrapped in bandages and she wasn't holding a spear. *"Bonjour."*

He stood up quickly and reached for his piece with one hand while picking up the phone with the other. *Snakebite* took the latter one. The officer got one shot off before he passed out from the domoic acid—a dose less than the more common deadly one—and propofol mix that Isabella released into the air. The bullet went wide and shattered a photo of a *surely* decorated frog.

Other froggies heard the shot and rushed in one at a time through a door in the back. The air was so contaminated that they passed out almost immediately, leaving a pile-up. She disposed of two cameras before moving the officers out of the way. *This is taking way too long,* she realized, thinking about potential calls for backup. The last thing she needed was a national emergency and the government to get involved. Eventually, she created a gap to move into the next room, searching for a cowardly policeman. *It'd just be my luck if I knocked them all out.*

But there was one. He was sheltering inside a locked gun closet, yet he was unarmed. And he was old, had to be to be close to retirement, not the type she would've expected to be hiding.

"*Anglais?*" she asked.

"A little," he answered, his voice trembling.

"Security tapes. Where?"

He pointed a shaky finger behind her at the rows of desks, overfilling with paperwork.

She jabbed the spearhead at him, "Sorry, you're going to need to be more specific than that."

"Across." He pointed in the same spot. "That door."

There were three doors on the other side of the bullpen.

"Get your pathetic arse up and show me."

He slowly got up and moved at a snail's pace to the door he pointed at. The man looked back at her as if asking "what next."

Isabella impatiently motioned him to open it.

A cool draft of air blew at them as he did as she said. Inside were four computer monitors filled with different camera views. Behind it, were two tall, mechanized structures with flashing lights. *The hard drives,* or at least that's what she thought it was.

"Strasbourg gate cameras. Pull them up," she ordered the bobby.

He nodded, a little more confident that she wasn't going to kill him, and fell into one of the office chairs. With a few clicks of a mouse, the screen was filled with a different set of camera views, one of them blacked out. She told him to run that one back two hours. Through a curtain of green branches, she saw the two police cars with their trunks against the gate to Strasbourg. The officers were still in them then. Fast forwarding twenty minutes, he slowed it down when the rented Alfa Romeo stopped on the edge of the panoramic. They watched until Isabella threw *Snakebite* directly at the hidden camera. Acid spit would've been more efficient, but she didn't want any of her other powers to get caught on video.

"Delete everything," Isabella ordered the older man, who was rightfully shocked at the display.

A few more clicks and the screen went blank.

"Did this tape go anywhere else?" she asked.

The froggy just shrugged.

She figured he'd know as much. "Where do you keep stolen cars and stuff like that?"

"A compound, two blocks."

"Thank you, now get out of here."

When he left, Isabella turned to the supposed hard drives. *It wouldn't hurt.* She gripped her spear with both hands and slashed and stabbed at the machines with speed and precision until everything was completely obliterated.

Now that the evidence was cleared, Isabella waited by the doors of the station, keeping a wary eye on the unconscious policemen while also waiting for Savannah to arrive.

*They should've brought her here by now.*

Images of police cars smashed and burning flashed in her head. A daegaryn, maybe two or three of them standing over Savannah's broken body.

Sirens finally could be heard in the distance and soon two cruisers appeared. Something is wrong. There were *three*.

Six officers exited from the two cars, the last one with a hand on her archetypal mentee—allowing Isabella a sigh of relief. Oddly Savannah seemed embarrassed rather than anything else. Isabella waited for them all to enter, before quickly dismantling them with the staff of *Snakebite*.

"What the bloody hell happened?" Isabella asked, staring pointedly down at the American.

"I tried to melt my handcuffs and cause a little distraction to buy you some time."

"Wait, I thought you were scared of fire?" She kept checking out the front windows for anybody, police or concerned citizen.

"Fire's all I have now." Savannah worked her jaw. "It's been with me longer than anybody else."

Isabella was never the consoling type and moved on. "What happened to the cruiser?"

"I accidentally caught some of the seat on fire." Her downtrodden countenance soon changed to one of embarrassment.

"Your bum is hanging out isn't it?"

She nodded, her jaw at work again.

*She's on a quest to obtain a magical sword in a crater of fire as she's being chased by creatures that could rip her in half, yet she's about to cry about some public indecency.*

"Go to the lockers and find yourself a pair of pants." Isabella was barely able to keep a straight face. "But hurry up, we have to go."

The American slunk off and she got a good look at her rear.

"Nice arse, by the way."

# Chapter Twenty-Five

**Thirty-five thousand** feet in the air, a phone rang.

"Santos."

The voice on the other end was both frantic and alarming.

"I'll handle it," he said calmly and hung up.

He pressed the intercom. "Return to Paris, please."

Back in Élysée Palace, he again sat in front of the desk of President Jean Biron. Next to him stood the Minister of the Armed Forces, Jules Bernard. Standing, she was just as tall as the sitting president. And while Biron had more of a timid nature, hers was less fluid. She was not fond of Santos or the involvement of an Argentinian in the French government.

"When did it happen?" Santos asked.

"Three hours ago," Bernard answered, glowering, her dark braid almost trembling with her anger.

"Show me."

The Minister pushed a phone in front of him, tapping the middle of the touchscreen. He watched without comment, his face never changing from the pleasant mask he put on at the private airport.

Once the spear had brought the video to an end, Bernard ripped it away and scowled at him as if it was his fault for the incapacitation of her police. "There was also a tape on the other side of Strasbourg of her being shot but there were no reports of her admittance to the nearby hospital in Haguenau. Instead, the police were attacked with some kind of chemical weapon. Unfortunately, the cameras there were not backed up to a server. I'm interested to see what the officers have to say once they wake."

"I assume you have deleted it from all the servers," Santos said.

A curt reply came from both the French leaders.

"And the police will be sworn to secrecy?"

Unhappy nods from both.

"Good, then it is settled." He stood up to leave.

"Not so fast," Bernard stopped him.

"*Oui?*" Santos turned around, the small smile still on his face. He was pleased to at least see Biron was alarmed at his subordinate.

"You're not going to do anything about your *freaks?*"

"I'll deal with them," he answered in French and slowly approached the Minister. "But if I find out that you went after them . . ." he walked around the desk, towering over her, and put one finger to her temple. His eyes glowed a blinding gold while hers rolled into the back of her head. "I'll bring about this future." It was not something he could control but she didn't know that. There were a thousand potential futures and this was just a rather unfortunate one. And it worked as tears ran across her wrinkly cheeks.

The president made himself busy with some papers on his desk.

"*Je comprends.*"

Santos attempted to leave again.

"Are they the bad ones?" Biron asked, finally speaking, in

his soft French.
    "We'll have to see."

# Chapter Twenty-Six

**Again, Rajeev found** himself dying in the desert of some Arabian Peninsula country. At least this time, he had passed out on his back. The lack of light shining through his sand-glued eyelids and the cooler air, let him know it was night. He reluctantly rubbed his eyes and pulled them open. And quickly sat up.

Someone was standing over him.

Rajeev stumbled backwards, crab walking away from the stranger before taking to his feet. It was too dark to see who the person was. He pulled *Irontruth*— mercifully on top of the sand not far from him—to his hand, sighing from the gained strength.

The stranger didn't seem worried about the weapon and stepped closer to Rajeev, who strained his eyes. It was Kalynst and he was holding the Holy Grail with a blackened, necrotic hand—a sign of its power—but it was what was in the other, that drew Rajeev's attention. He raised his sword but didn't strike.

"Why are you here?" Rajeev asked.

*Why didn't you kill me?*

"*You let me live,*" Kalynst said. He was standing up straight with no apparent pain as if the sliced hamstring had no effect. There were no vehicles in the area, either, meaning he walked here. Curious. "*And for that, I owe you. It's the way of the daegaryn. To be in debt to another is an embarrassment.*"

Lowering Irontruth, Rajeev stood tall and commanding. "First, you will hand over that water." He greedily ripped the bottle from the daegaryn and drank half of it in a couple of swallows. He didn't believe he ever felt a greater relief. "Then, you will take me to Doha, Qatar. To my wife. Once I'm there, you will be free of your debt."

"*Then let's not waste time,*" the kid said and held out his free hand.

"Your *dji* is superspeed, correct?" Rajeev asked.

Kalynst gave a single nod.

"How were you able to run here after I slashed your hamstring in two?"

"*Weapons forged from olmerion will cut through the nearly impenetrable skin of daegaryns and prevent the natural process of healing; that is true. But the Grail will reverse those effects.*"

The daegaryn turned around and pulled back his torn pants, revealing that, indeed, there was no visible injury or even a scar.

Rajeev didn't bother with a reply and finished the water, tossing it to the side, before grabbing Kalynst's now waiting hand. The kid threw him over the shoulder—almost causing Rajeev to drop the ancient sword—with no warning and as casually as a camper's knapsack. Then again without admonition, they were speeding off into the desert.

The journey was cumbersome being held in a fireman's carry on uneven terrain. The desert floor—changing to rock on occasion—went by so fast it became disorienting and Rajeev had to close his eyes for the rest of the trip. He felt every bump and sand kicked up into his face, filling his orifices, but it wasn't nearly as bad as the flights had been. Kalynst's body blocked most of the spray, anyway. But worse than the flight was the damage super speed did to his body. The wind ripped through him, tearing his skin worse than the sand ever did. His brain banged around his skull, giving him the worst headache imaginable. Worst of all was the feeling of his internal organs bouncing against his ribs and spine, rupturing and rehealing before their contents contaminated his insides.

But he couldn't ask for a break; his wife needed him.

Kalynst was extremely fast, but it still took two—maybe—three hours until they were on the outskirts of his hometown. They took a quick break for Rajeev to tell him where he lived and soon they stood within several heartbeats of Yasmin.

Rajeev fell to his knees and vomited up the lining of his stomach. He had to wait an eternity until the world had stopped spinning before he could stand to face the daegaryn.

*"My debt to you has been repaid,"* Kalynst said.

"Where are you going to go now?" Rajeev asked. The expression on the kid's face did not say he was going back to Halgarth and just handing over the Grail.

*"Revenge against the man who killed my father and uncle."*

Rajeev nodded then walked up the stairs to his duplex. He paused at the top and turned his neck to look back at the daegaryn. "Thank you."

*"It is my duty."*

"Can ask one more favor of you?"

*"You can ask."*

"My wife has cancer." His voice trembled as he realized what his next few words could mean. "Can you use the Grail to heal her?"

He seemed to give it great thought, while Rajeev's heart pounded within his chest before finally nodding.

Inside they went.

"Yasmin," he called, keeping his voice casual as if he hadn't been missing for three—almost four days—only to return in the middle of the night.

There was no answer, but that didn't worry Rajeev much. There were days when she would sleep for the entirety of it. Then there were other more memorable ones where the pain kept her up all night. He laid *Irontruth* by the umbrella he kept near the door and hurried upstairs, not even bothering to flick on the lights.

At the top, he crossed creaky floorboards to their bedroom and threw open the door.

Immediately he knew something was wrong.

Both the pain medicine and chemotherapy bag were empty. Rajeev rushed to her side and felt her cold neck. Nothing. He laid his head over her chest. Nothing. Placed a hand over her slightly open and blue-tinged mouth. Nothing. Nothing. Nothing. Nothing.

"Yasmin!" Rajeev cried out. "Come back to me! Come back to me, my *ləv*. I love you. I love you, so, so much. Come back!"

He squeezed her limp hand and felt the ruffle of paper. It was a note addressed to him, written in the shaky handwritten she had adopted a few months after the diagnosis.

*Dear Rajeev, my heart,*

*I have decided to take my life. It had been a miracle to live this long. But the pain has become unbearable. Though, worst of all is the guilt I retain for the burden I have put on you. What you do at night gives me nightmares. Do not act like I don't see the news. I know you do it for me—and for that, I'll always be grateful—but I can't let you keep hurting others just to keep me alive for a little longer.*

*Please do not mourn me and go and live your life. Meet someone else and be happy. That is my dying wish: for you to be happy.*

*I will always love you, Rajeev. Now you must let me go.*

*With all my love,*

*Your heart.*

A flood of grief flew through him, cramping up his stomach then rising through his narrowing throat, up to his twitching face, and broke the gate at his eyes.

He laid over his wife of not even a year, convulsing as the tears soaked into her Beatles tee. Memories of them together rapidly flew through his brain almost too fast for him to process. Dinner at that expensive steakhouse by the sea for her birthday that he saved up for months to afford. Evening walks on the beach—almost a daily thing before the tumor. Her laugh at his terrible pickup line after a long, twisting buildup.

*I'll never hear her laugh again.*

Rajeev had to turn to the side as his empty stomach heaved and bile exited out of his dry mouth.

Crawling into bed next to her, he held his heart for one last time, never realizing that Kalynst was long gone.

# Chapter TwentySeven

**With a quick stop** at the police compound just outside Haguenau to steal back the Alfa Romeo, the girls entered Germany around five o'clock.

Savannah, sporting a stolen pair of navy-blue slacks and her British gift shop hoodie, let out a yawn.

"We'll find a place to sleep in Salzburg." Isabella had donned a salmon sweatshirt she had dug out of lockers but kept on her bloody yoga pants, reasoning that "a proper person shall not question the stains on the britches of a lady." Savannah just assumed she didn't want to wear the police pants; they weren't exactly comfortable. "I'm shagged too," she continued. "I can get us there in four hours if we don't hit traffic."

They got there in just over three.

The Austrian city rested before the silhouette of the Alps. The center, set upon a hill, juxtaposed the flat area surrounding it. Numerous teal cathedral-like towers dominated the landscape, looming over the rest of the town.

They crossed a bridge over a river that glistened in the setting sun. It was a beautiful, calming city, so much different than Strasbourg.

"I went here as a kid," Isabella said. "It was like entering a fairytale." They turned onto a narrow street, paved with cobble. "It still is."

Savannah turned to the British woman. She still faced forward but her face seemed softer and eyes elsewhere. This was the first time Isabella had ever mentioned her past, but Savannah decided to not say anything for once and just enjoy the serenity.

They pulled under an alcove of what looked like a hotel. Well-dressed men opened the doors for them, and Isabella dropped her keys and some money into one of their waiting hands. The inside of the hotel was as breathtaking as the city it resided in. A golden chandelier with thousands of crystals sparkled from the domed ceiling of the same color. Even the tile beneath their feet seemed to glitter.

A young, fair-skinned concierge greeted them behind a platter of fluffy pastries covered in powdered sugar. Her eyes never once trailed off to the blood on Isabella's pants. *She was right*, Savannah thought as if the assertion was ever in doubt.

"*Willkommen*," the concierge greeted them, smiling brightly.

Isabella worked with the translator on her phone, while Savannah tried one of the Austrian delicacies. Two crepe-like slices sandwiched a vanilla custard. It was delicious and reminded her of how she hadn't eaten all day outside some gas station food that morning.

"Come. There's a sit-down just a couple blocks away," Isabella said, reading her mind, stuffing a pair of keys into her soiled yoga pants.

They left the hotel just as quickly as they entered, nodding at the valets standing at attention as they passed. The streets—narrower than those Savannah was used to—contained a scattering of Austrians, nothing like the bustling roads of London. And most seemed to have the directiveness of locals rather than the wandering of tourists. She asked Isabella about that.

"After Strasbourg, tourism in Europe has decreased significantly. Everybody's waiting for retaliation."

"But they don't know who did it."

"It doesn't matter." She led them to a building. *Königsschwert*, the dangling sign read. "Nukes don't come out of nowhere."

A couple drinking a hot beverage on the patio smiled and murmured a foreign word of greeting as Savannah and Isabella passed them to enter. Inside the maître d' brought them to a table in the back corner near a pianist playing soft music. The restaurant was mostly empty, not unexpected for the hour of nine. The interior was reminiscent of an Italian restaurant her parents had taken her for special occasions as kids: Philomena's. *I guess that goes to show how cultured I am,* Savannah thought.

The maître d' laid down some menus, giving a curt bow and a couple of words through a clean-shaven smile before leaving them. Savannah pored over the menu but only recognized a few words. She looked over at her companion who seemed to be having an equally hard time. *Merlin should've given us a translator. How are we supposed to cross Europe and the Middle East without understanding the language spoken around us?*

"I'll order for us," the Brit said.

Five minutes later a different man returned with the same countenance as the maître d'. "*Was für dich?*"

"*Wir werden das Wiener Schnitzel und die Frankfurter Würstl haben,*" Isabella ordered in jumbled German.

The waiter bowed slightly and hurried off.

"What did you order," Savannah asked.

"Schnitzel and Vienna sausage," the British woman answered, pulling out her phone to do God knows what.

"My parents would always pack me Vienna sausage for lunch as a kid," Savannah said. "The other kids made fun of me, but I loved it. I'd never thought I'd have it in Austria."

Isabella just gave a thumbs up without looking up from her phone.

Savannah scowled at her forced partner. "What are you doing, anyway?"

"Wordscapes."

"A word game?"

"Obviously."

"'Blate' is not a word, is it?" the Brit mumbled to herself.

"How long have you known Merlin?" Savannah asked abruptly. "Been a part of this . . . group?"

"You just do not like the quiet, do you?"

"Nope."

"Your parents must've gone mental with you."

"They're both dead."

"Figured." Isabella finally sat the phone down. "Four. Maybe five; time works differently in Camelot. But Merlin didn't join until I had been there a couple of years."

"Then who found you?"

"A man named Everton, knighted as Percival. He was from Jamaica and had the ability to control the wind. He was one of the best I've ever known."

"What happened to him?"

"Daegaryns."

Before an awkward silence shrouded the table, the food arrived. The Vienna sausage looked much different than the kind she ate from a can. They were a good deal darker and had some kind of red sauce drizzled on them. The other dish contained a fried surprise—what she could only assume to be the Schnitzel—on top of some mashed potatoes.

"What is Schnitzel?" Savannah asked her companion once their waiter left.

"Pork. Perhaps veal." She shrugged. "All that matters is that it tastes good."

And it was good. So was the Vienna sausage, but it lacked the nostalgia of the can.

Once finished, Isabella paid the check and they returned to the hotel, falling asleep in their separate, spacious rooms almost as soon as their heads hit the feather pillows.

# Chapter TwentyEight

**A shadow walked** across the deck of a ship, the slapping of waves against the hull the only sound in the night. Red-headed bodies leaking liquid even more red, littered the deck.

"Why?"

The cry came from one of the bodies. He was a short man, clean-shaven with curly hair. A shard of bone jutted out of his left arm above the elbow. And when the phantom crossed over to him, he saw one of the man's eyes bulging out of its socket.

"*Orders*," came the ghostly whisper.

The wraith lifted its hammer—the dark blade glistening in the moonlight—and brought it down with force, rupturing the Irishman's skull as easy as a watermelon. A pale hand wiped bits of brain and skull from its cloak.

Sirens could be heard far off in the distance as the apparition glided down the ramp and moved to a sleek cigar boat, just as black as the demon. Minutes later the boat roared out of the River Thames.

The devil walked through the door. Or at least that's what the intruder looked like to Lieutenant Boucher. He and the other Command Corps had been stationed here soon after the events of Strasbourg, replacing the police forces. President Biron had wanted the locals not to be worried, so they dressed as police. Now, Boucher had to man the desk tonight in Haguenau after he drew the shortest straw. It had been quiet—even with the measures to ensure calm, the civilians still lived in fear of another attack—but he remained vigilant. They had been assaulted earlier today by terrorists with chemical weapons. Only one was reported but there had to be more; one person couldn't do that much damage. And now he had to deal with this guy.

"*Bonsoir.*" Boucher greeted the stranger. *Or rather,* bonjour, he thought as he glanced at his watch. How can I help you?"

No answer came from the ghostly figure, but it still continued to walk—no, glide—toward him. Boucher unclasped his sidearm and flicked off the safety, keeping a steady hand on it, all while his welcoming smile never wavered. It was then that he noticed the large warhammer hanging to the side of the phantom.

Boucher pulled out his MAC 50 and pointed it at the possible enemy. "*Congelez!*"

It never even flinched and continued toward him. Once it was within five feet of the desk, Boucher fired one shot to the head—a rash decision but after this morning, he wasn't taking any risks. The creature's neck snapped back but only the hood fell.

His heart stopped as he stared at a melted face. There were holes where its nose and mouth used to be and a single eye that seemed to droop inside its socket. But most frightening of all was the gaping hole on the top of its head that slowly closed as he watched.

"What are you?" he asked in French, trying not to allow the fear to show in his voice. It did.

The monster dropped a handful of bloody insignias on the desk in front of him. "*Death.*"

And it came mercifully quick for Boucher.

# Chapter Twenty-Nine

**Oh, what great** *of a loss it is to lose a bride at so short of a sacrament. It may be only comparable to that of losing a parent. But the loss of all three is truly a terrible thing. Perhaps, it is payment for the lives of strangers taken without mercy or any thought. All truth be told, it will be a dreadfully long life for an individual as such.*

It was the smell that woke him up. Rajeev sat up in his bed and slowly and solemnly looked down at his decomposing wife. He had almost hoped it had been a nightmare or Yasmin had just gone into some deep, cancer-driven, coma. But the odor wafting from her said differently.

With barely any will, Rajeev stumbled over to the shower. Not giving himself the luxury of warm water, he turned the temperature lever all the way to the icon of a snowflake and washed all the sand and two days of filth off of him. Even the freezing cold water felt good after being without it for so long. He took deep mouthfuls of it, hating himself for even the smallest bits of joy that his wife would never be able to experience again.

Afterward, he lumbered down the creaky stairs and to the

kitchen. There wasn't much there. But he found some stale bread and soaked it in a can of Campbell's chicken noodle soup. He later found some old celery sticks in the back of the fridge to chomp on. They were both fairly bland which was exactly what he was looking for. Their only purpose was to fill his stomach up a little and give him some strength back.

The daegaryns had taken the one thing he truly cared about. And now he didn't have anything except for the black hole of revenge. Those monsters don't realize what they did, creating a being with god-like powers and nothing to hold him back. A being without fear. He was coming and wouldn't stop until they were dead.

The thought of Kalynst saving him in the desert came to mind, but he shook it out of his head. The kid was just repaying a debt. Rajeev had a feeling he wouldn't be so kind next time.

Taking his time, Rajeev packed the essentials—food, water, and a picture of Yasmin and him at the steakhouse—into his metal pack, then left his and his wife's duplex for the last time. He stood outside for an inconsequential amount of time. It was such a big deal for him to be able to move out of Yasmin's parent's tiny house and move into this even smaller place. They even lucked out and the other half would be unoccupied for the short length of their marriage. It was a place he had dreamed for him in his new family to grow up in. Rajeev should've known there was no chance for happiness in his life. He was a cursed child.

Rajeev raised his arms up slowly in dramatic fashion until they were held over his head and then slammed them towards the ground with the full force of a god—ripping apart pipes, wiring, and ductwork—bringing the duplex down and burying his Yasmin in the rubble.

As dust bellowed around him, Rajeev hit a button on the pack, triggering a pair of wings to retract from each side. He dropped it to the ground and flew away from the sirens in the distance. From his hometown. His past. His heart. And to a future he knew that would only end in blood.

Doha blew up below him and then slowly shrunk to an eventual blip as he distanced himself from his hometown. Rajeev had a good idea of how to get to Halgarth from here, but he put Mecca in his wife's phone—his was God knows where—just in case. It was an almost fifteen-hour drive to Mecca and probably had taken half that when Balthasar flew him there.

The weather was great and the sky clear. Rajeev sat down on the transformed pack, letting his legs dangle as he enjoyed the flight and scenery below. He hated every ounce of his joy.

The phone had died an hour ago—Rajeev had neglected to charge it fully before he left—forcing him to fly straight with a little bit of blind faith. He considered chucking it into the rocky terrain of Saudi Arabia but thought better of it, stuffing it into the back of his jeans instead. It was one of the last pieces of Yasmin he had left. Instead, he read her letter over and over again. He knew he should've left in the rubble of their duplex but somehow it ended up in his pocket. It was the "why" of this path he had put himself on, and a reminder of past failures he could not let happen again.

Not another hour had passed before the skyline of Mecca appeared on the horizon. The hoverboard dipped down while Rajeev searched for the hidden passageway into the daegaryn lair. But in his concentration, he didn't see the object shooting at him from behind. It impacted him, causing him to break his magnetic attraction on the board and sending him sailing to the ground. Rajeev turned at the last second and pulled *Irontruth* to him where it was held snug in the straps of his pack. His spine cracked and legs went numb when he landed awkwardly on a jutting rock, sending waves of pain through the parts of his body that could still feel anything. He had to wait a minute for the broken pieces of his vertebrae to mend and regain neural connectivity in his legs. The daegaryn took advantage of this and charged down at him, using the sun as cover. Rajeev shaded his eyes and realized at the last second that it had launched a projectile at him. He rolled to his left and turned to see the spot in the rocks where it was sizzling from some type of acid.

Then he landed on Rajeev, pinning him to the ground. The monster stared down at him, as he struggled for a breath. The daegaryn looked like every other one except this one didn't have any visible tattoos just like Diomedes. That mystery was solved a second later when his tattooed tongue shot out and wrapped around his neck, taking away the rest of his air.

Rajeev fruitlessly tried to pull at it before summoning his sword—abandoned a few feet away—to him and slicing the sticky member clean off.

The monster backed off with hardly a grunt and Rajeev hurriedly took to his feet now that his spine was finally healed. The daegaryn attempted an acid spit, which he anticipated and sidestepped easily. Rajeev advanced but he took off into the air.

*Al-ama.* He was probably going to warn his brethren. Rajeev fractured *Irontruth* and sent the shard after the daegaryn like hell missiles. The daegaryn was just a shadow now but Rajeev could tell when the shards struck and the blob fell to the earth.

One down, who knows how many left to go.

Back on his homemade glider—retrieved some twenty meters away—Rajeev combed the rocky terrain and soon found the entrance to Halgarth without any more difficulties. He could understand how humans never once stumbled upon it. From above, it just looked like the shadow of a valley. The transformed backpack and its passenger hovered over the opening for a couple of minutes, waiting to see if anything would come to challenge him. He'd rather fight a daegaryn out in the open than in the darkness of the cave. But nothing arose and so Rajeev descended.

It was deeper than he remembered. And so much darker. His glider eventually hit the ground and he stepped off, taking a dueling stance—knees bent, sword out in front, and head on a constant swivel. He stayed that way until his eyes adjusted to the dim and rare light of the sparse torches. There was no one in the cavern where he had first met Catharsis. Rajeev sensed a trap but continued on into the widest offshoot with the most light.

The hallway was recognizable but then again there was not much to differentiate them from one another. Rajeev looked ahead with his metal-vision and a rainbow of color popped into his head. The mass explosion of light in his head caused him to cry out and drop to one knee, cradling his temple with his free hand. One of the daegaryns was somehow messing with his metal-vision. He would be going in blind.

On and on he went until a barred door with the person he had dreaded to see smiling at him appeared to his right.

"Rajeev," Dmitri said, teeth glinting in the firelight. "How happy I am to see you. I knew you would come back to save your favorite Russian."

"Dmitri, where are the daegaryns?"

"*Behind you.*"

An arm wrapped around Rajeev's throat, and he got choked for the second time that day. *Irontruth* fell to the stone floor as he grabbed at the invisible arm of Eryon with both hands. He tried to stomp at the camouflaged feet to no effect. Reaching for the bars with his magnet, he pulled, sending them both at him. Rajeev used the surprise and momentum to turn the daegaryn so that Eryon's head hit one of the bars with a great thud, simultaneously smashing the fingers of

Dmitri's left hand, releasing a series of Russian swear words. The collision caused the daegaryn to release his hold just a bit for Rajeev to duck out and point his sword at where he guessed Eryon's neck to be.

Eryon released his camouflage and stared back at Rajeev without letting any emotion touch his face. The tip of his blade was in the daegaryn's neck.

"Where are the others? Where's Catharsis? Balthasar?" Rajeev screamed at the daegaryn.

"*Waiting for you*," Eryon said and nodded into the dim corridor ending in darkness.

"Then they'll join you." Rajeev brought *Irontruth* back for the kill stroke.

"Wait!" Dmitri yelled.

"What the fuck do you want?" Rajeev asked, irritated but didn't bring the sword down.

"Well, first, screw you for slamming that creature's thick skull into my fingers. I think you broke them. Yes, I think you did."

Rajeev stared daggers into the Russian.

"Right, right," Dmitri sighed in exasperation. "If you kill him and try to kill his friends, you will die. Now, hear me out. You'll have your chance to kill them but now is not the time. You are one against hundreds. There are others like you who could help, plus there's the Holy Grail that looks to have just slipped between your little fingers. It could even the odds some."

Dmitri had a point, though Rajeev would never admit it. He couldn't get revenge if he was dead. "Then what am I supposed to do now?"

"That's up to you, my boy. But Eryon, here, has a piece of the daegaryn hivemind in that damaging, cruel head of his. You could use it to find daegaryns out in the wild. Find them and you could very well find others like you. Then you can get the revenge you so desire. Your wife died, didn't she?"

Rajeev didn't need to answer for the Russian to see it on his face.

"Yes, I have seen love leave the eyes of many people throughout my long life. Many have sought revenge; none have been truly satisfied." Dmitri's rare, serious face changed to that of one keeping a secret. A hilarious one at that. "But seeing the aftermath is a great joy, so go crazy."

"Don't act like you're not part of the reason she's dead," Rajeev said, releasing one of the shards of *Irontruth* and shoving it in front of Dmitri's face with a flick of his wrist. "If you had given me more medicine at less of a cost. She'd still be alive."

"Oh, so it had nothing to do with your extended absence." The bastard had the audacity to smile. "A lonely heart can be deadly."

"I'm leaving," Rajeev always hated how he felt like he was always storming away from the Russian. "Move," he told Eryon.

The daegaryn led the way out of the tunnel with *Irontruth* right at his back.

"What about me?" Dmitri moped.

"What about you?" Rajeev taunted without turning his back.

"You wouldn't leave old, poor Dmitri Smirnov."

"And why wouldn't I? You are less to me than shit on the bottom of my shoe. At least that smells better. Not to mention you told them where to find me."

"Well, first Rajeev, I didn't tell them anything about you; they actually never asked. I assume you think this because of the loss of my eye. They removed it because, one, it was easier to show you my eye than have to fight you. And, two, they just don't like me very much."

Rajeev just glared at the Russian.

"All right, all right. You want a reason to save me? It's because, Rajeev Patel, you think of yourself as a good guy. If I really was trying to brown my nose I might even say a hero. You will break me out of here because that's the right thing to do."

*Dammit.*

Rajeev stomped back and cut the top and the bottom of the bars—*Irontruth* slicing through them like butter—keeping a careful eye on Eryon as he did. He hurried the daegaryn on without waiting for the Russian. Every now and then, he would look back and nearly smile at the sight of Dmitri trying to catch up, all sweating and gasping and body fat jiggling.

Back in the entry chamber, Rajeev balanced him and Eryon on the hoverboard and brought them out to the very welcoming sunlight. After they were on solid ground, he let the pack back down for Dmitri. Surprisingly, he got on without complaining and exited the same way.

"*And who first do you want me to find?*" Eryon asked in a way that he knew he was not going to be a prisoner.

"First, we must steal a car from Mecca, since traveling on this thing." Rajeev pointed at the manufactured glider. "Will be very difficult, not to mention uncomfortable, with two people."

"Two people?" Dmitri interrupted. "What about me?"

"You can find your own way from Mecca."

"Why? We could have a great adventure. Not to mention I know much about your kind. I even have one of their numbers. An old friend, ha."

"Why did you never mention this before?" Rajeev asked, irritated but not surprised.

"I cannot play all my cards at once, my boy. It makes me less valuable."

"Fine you'll come. And then once we have the car, I'm taking the Grail from Kalynst."

# Chapter Thirty

"**Merlin told me** to train you," Isabella said as they stood in a pasture of some random farmer just outside Salzburg. She held *Snakebite* and seemed fully ready to use it. "And considering your little predicament in Haguenau . . ."

Savannah blushed at the all too recent memory.

". . . it's better to do it sooner rather than later."

Earlier they had purchased some clothing from a store near their hotel. Isabella found a new pair of jeans with a dull pink blouse that of course showed cleavage. It was a wonder she wasn't shivering in the cool autumn air. Savannah, on the other hand, bought a heavy gray sweater and jeans. The Brit made her take the flammable sweater off leaving only a sports bra of the same color. Isabella preferred her to be completely ly naked—"it would probably get burned off, anyway"—but Savannah wouldn't go any further.

"Our power comes from right here." Isabella patted the dripping spearhead mark on her left breast. "You've felt this?"

Savannah nodded. Every time she was even around fire it seemed to warm.

"Have you ever tried to use it as an anchor when you

control fire?"

Savannah shook her head. "What do you mean?"

"Some abilities are harder to control. Mines are easier than others. I create most of my poisons and acids, either with elements I produce naturally or those I have to consume," she paused for a second and gazed over at the skyline of Salzburg. "But accidents do happen." She spun her spear. "Yours, on the other hand, is one of the hardest to control; Fire is unpredictable. So now, are you sure you don't want to strip down? The only person who is going to see you is me." She grinned naughtily. "I'll join if that'll make you feel more comfortable."

Savannah just scowled at her.

"All right, then take out those ciggies."

She removed the pack of Marlboros Isabella had bought her in France sans a lighter and brought out one.

"Good, now light it."

Focusing on the furnace inside her, Savannah tried to direct it to the cigarette. But as it began to spread beneath her skin like a parasite, she quickly quenched it. She was still scared of it.

"When I direct poison to a specific body part," Isabella said. I treat it as a spigot with multiple hoses coming out of it. You have to block off the hoses you don't use, leaving just one. Try it."

Savannah closed her eyes, trying to imagine the source of her power just as Isabella described it. She slowly let loose some of the flames up and into her left arm, using her mark—her furnace—as both the anchor and the source. It burned as it traveled through her arteries and even among her fears it felt amazing. It always did. The fire reached her hand and then fingers, finally enveloping the Marlboro that burst into flames, causing her to reflexively drop it and extinguish the fire with the heel of her shoe.

"Once the element of your power leaves your body," Isabella taught. "It becomes much harder to control since you no longer have your anchor. Instead of being physiological it is psychological." She kicked at the cigarette still smoldering in the grass. "But good work for your first real attempt. Now do it again."

Savannah tried again only to achieve the same result.

"Fire inside you is connected here." She tapped her mark. "Fire outside you is connected here," she tapped her head. "Again."

Once the flame had reached the tip of her finger, she focused her mind on it and then slowly released it into the cigarette. Immediately, she grasped control of it with her mind, reigning the fire in and only allowing it to light the tip before releasing it. Savannah waited for it to explode in her hands, but it burned only at its usual slow pace, smoke curling from the end. She took a hesitant hit, but nothing strange happened.

"Brilliant," Isabella said, her supportive face now replaced with the annoyed one Savannah was used to. "You managed to light a ciggie. So much that will do against daegaryns."

Savannah glared at her trainer from where she was bent over, hands on knees and almost dripping sweat. All that to light a damn cigarette.

"Those monsters," the British woman continued. "have claws and teeth that can permanently damage us. Merlin believes they are as much of the meteorite that brought them here as these blades." She gestured with *Snakebite*. "And now we really train."

"But I've just started," Savannah said, ashamed of the slight whining in her voice.

"And you hadn't even started when the daegaryns first attacked you."

"Can I at least get some water first?" Even though she

was trying to stall, Savannah was indeed thirsty. Extremely thirsty.

"Here," Isabella tossed her a water bottle from a small duffel bag she had purchased along with her clothes. "Heating up your body that much can result in dehydration."

Savannah gluttony gulped down the water, finishing within moments. She looked to the Brit who gave her another. Half was gone before she was finally satisfied.

"Now we begin," Isabella twirled her spear and advanced on her trainee.

"What if you cut me?" Savannah spurted. "I wouldn't be able to heal."

"Oh, I'm too good for that," the British woman said before she attacked, swiping *Snakebite* diagonally from right to left.

Savanna's furnace reacted faster than she did consciously, heating up to a dangerous intensity. She thrust her hands forward reflexively launching a beam of fire right into Isabella's chest. The Brit flew back—managing somehow to hang onto her spear—and landed on her back over thirty feet away.

But there was no quit from her trainer and with skin seared off, she jumped up and launched *Snakebite* at Savannah, who twisted at the last minute. Then, suddenly a sharp pain came through her right arm. The spear had returned to Isabella's hand, which the Brit sat down to rip off her blouse that was still aflame. There was nothing under except for raw skin that was quickly healing.

"What the hell!" Savannah exclaimed, gripping her bleeding arm. "I thought you weren't going to cut me."

"I didn't think you were going to ruin my bloody new shirt," the Brit yelled back. "Anyway, it's better you know what it feels like now rather than be surprised when a daegaryn inevitably mars you."

And as Isabella approached, she did see a long wound

along her abdomen covered with something. The Brit's eyes glowed a brief pink before she hawked something up into her hand. She moved to place it on her trainee's wound, but Savannah jerked away.

"Relax," Isabella said. "It's a compound we used in the Royal Navy that's like superglue. Since the wound can't heal, you need something to cover it to prevent bleeding out."

"I didn't know you were in the military," Savannah said. The way she dressed certainly didn't give any indications.

"There's a lot about me you don't know." She slapped it on harder than it needed to be without asking for permission.

Savannah knew better to pursue but there was one thing nagging at her. "I dodged that spear without thinking. I'm no athlete. Not at this age at least."

"We didn't just inherit these elemental powers from our ancestors," Isabella said. "We also got their physical attributes like increased reflexes and their fighting ability."

The Brit worked at a zit just below her collarbone, reminding Savannah of her nakedness.

"Can you please put a shirt on?"

"You're the one that took it off." She grinned and stuck her prominent chest out just a bit. "And it was the only one I brought, too." The Brit rolled her shoulders back. "Now get ready." Isabella attacked.

# Chapter ThirtyOne

**Unlike the other** residences of political powers, the executive office of the United Kingdom Prime Minister was rather shabby. It appeared as any other office building, although maybe smaller with its three floors. And only an unimpressive gate with a few officers—as well as the customary blast-proof windows and front door—acted as protection from attackers.

10 Downing Street. A terrorist's dream if any gave a damn.

Santos now stood in front of that gate, while a policeman spoke softly into his walkie. While he waited, he took note of the guards, wondering if any worked for neighboring governments. Europe, after the destruction of Strasbourg, couldn't have been more tense.

Now approved to enter, the officer guided Santos across the famous street, past the blue front door—appearing as oak, but he knew better—and into the house of Prime Minister Alice Malory. The inside was much more reminiscent of other governing residencies. Pictures of old, white men decorated the walls. And the furniture gave an air of a more traditional era, vestiges of when kings had ruled. A simpler time, where a man with great powers would be praised and never questioned. He sighed. It was all for the best, however. The Lord knows what some would do with that type of control.

And he hoped he would never have to find out.

The English leader greeted him in her office behind a mahogany desk plastered with a horde of documents. Santos couldn't help thinking that if Churchill had been a woman this is what he would've looked like. Malory was a fat woman with bright red drooping cheeks that sagged almost past her double chin, wearing a black suit that stretched along her stomach. He feared a button would pop off and take out one of his eyes. She even peered down at him through spectacles resting on the tip of her nose. At least she didn't have a cigar stuck between those fat lips. Santos abhorred the odor of tobacco smoke. It was a putrid scent, indeed.

"Mr. Santos," she said, surprised as if he had not called that morning. "Can I get you some tea? Coffee, perhaps?"

If it was any factor, she did have a soft voice for such monstrous lungs.

"Tea would be superb," he removed his fedora and took the unoffered seat.

"Earl Grey, Green, English—"

Santos cut her off with a wave of his hand. "Whichever you prefer, my dear."

"Earl Grey it is." She smiled and nodded at the well-dressed man behind him.

Once he left, the wrinkles in her pudgy face subsided as she adopted a more serious expression. "Why are you here, Fernando?"

"M'lady," Santos said solemnly. "I fear war."

"War? How so?" She took a deep breath and grabbed her breast dramatically, causing Santos a momentary worry that she might go into cardiac arrest. "Does this have to do with Strasbourg?"

He nodded, letting her come to her own conclusions before he tweaked them.

"Who did it?" Her breath leveled as she unconsciously became morbidly interested in the matter.

"Well, I am not quite sure, yet." He leaned back and crossed his legs. "I have been running an investigation."

"There would have to be some reason for it." Her eyebrows slammed together beneath dark bangs that hid her large forehead. "A strategic one."

Santos inclined his head as the door was opened behind him and the tea sat down. They stared at each other in silence, waiting for the door to close before resuming their discussion.

"It's Germany, isn't it?" Malory asked. "Strasbourg is right on the border. Two miles, if I remember correctly."

Santos took a sip from his tea to hide a hint of a smile. Malory was always quick to point fingers.

"Remind me of the radius of the bomb."

"The majority of casualties were found within a fifteen-kilometer radius," Santos recited from memory. "Evidence supports a one megaton warhead. Eighty times more powerful than the one dropped on Hiroshima."

"So, they took damage themselves?"

"Nearly a third of the casualties were German."

"It doesn't make much sense, does it?" The Prime Minister began to dig through the mess on her desk. After a few minutes, she found what she was looking for. "Germany does not manufacture their own nuclear weapons, do they?"

"No, ma'am," Santos said. "They have twenty B61 gravity bombs from the US, shared with them as part of a NATO agreement."

"B61." She skimmed through her notes again. "Those have a blast yield of no more than 340 kilotons."

"Indeed."

"Did they build any in secret?"

"They have the mechanical prowess."

"It seems unlikely, though," Malory leaned back in her chair, the back struggling under her immense weight.

He made no physical or verbal reply.

"Us, the US, France, Russia, and China all have bombs of that size. We also know India, North Korea, Pakistan, and Israel possess nuclear weapons as well, but we do not know their specifications. We can rule out us and France, of course."

She again smashed her eyebrows together. "There were not any reports of military aircraft of any nationality, right?"

Santos tilted his head.

"Is there any likelihood the bomb went off on the surface?"

"Considering the damage inflicted," he said. "Yes, there is indeed a likelihood."

"No concentrated levels of radiation leaving one of those countries?"

Now this is where Santos would step in. "Actually, mum, I never thought of that. Let me make a call."

He stepped outside and moved past the two members of Malory's security detail. Out of earshot, Santos created a pretense of making a call, complete with minor gestures. After a moment he returned to where an anxious Prime Minister waited with those enormous eyebrows raised.

"It appears my satellite detected radiation leaving India," Santos said with a grave expression. "The levels matched that of a one megaton nuclear warhead."

He had no such satellite and even if he did it wouldn't be able to pick such a minor measure of radiation. But Malory didn't know that nor would she question it. The air around Santos was otherworldly; nobody would second-guess him.

"Oh my God," she gasped. "It's them, then. What should we do?"

"I'll need more information before we can be a hundred

percent sure, so keep this between us. And then maybe I can try to reason with President Arole." He gave her a hard look with a little reluctance mixed in. "But it may be preeminent to peek into the future and prepare for war."

In the queen's limo, on the way back to the airport, Santos's phone rang. He pulled out his iPhone but saw only the default lock screen of a waterfall. The ringing continued and he slowly removed a flip phone from inside his beige coat, an unknown number on the screen.

*Fóllame.*

He answered it.

# Chapter ThirtyTwo

**Instead of going** into Mecca and having to act casual with a naked prisoner and shirtless Russian—not to mention they'd probably have to sneak in since Rajeev was the only actual Muslim there—he and Eryon waited on the side of the road while Dmitri lay on a backroad to the city. It had taken much haggling to get the Russian to agree to the plan.

It wasn't long before an old, black BMW cruised smoothly across the blacktop with the top down. As it got closer, Rajeev could see that it was three teenagers listening to music probably frowned upon by Islamic elders. They noticed Dmitri a little late and skidded to a stop just a few feet away from them. Rajeev maybe could've helped him out a little by squeezing the brakes with his mind, but what's the fun in that? He enjoyed the look of pure fright on the Russian's pudgy, bearded face.

Now Rajeev moved from his spot behind a rock and prodded Eryon to the convertible. Two of the kids had jumped and were trying to help Dmitri, while the driver clung to the wheel with equal fear to the man he almost killed.

"*Salaam*," Rajeev greeted them. "What a beautiful day to

drive that beautiful car. Unfortunately, we're going to have to take it off your hands."

Dmitri jumped up with the spryness of the old, fat fuck he was. "Got you *ublyudki*, ha. You're right, Rajeev, this was fun. Reminds me of my childhood in the great nation of Russia."

Realizing he had been duped, the driver broke out of his frozen state and reached into his glove compartment for supposedly a gun. Rajeev waited patiently for him to fumble with loading bullets into the cylinder of the revolver and flick back the hammer before walking towards the kid.

"Put it down before you get killed," Rajeev said. "I don't want to hurt you." But he did. He wanted to hurt Eryon and Dmitri and the other two teens who cowered down inside the car. He wanted to hurt everybody and let them feel the pain he felt. Rajeev wasn't sure how long he could hold back.

Either the short guy with the sword was the reason the kid didn't worry about the threat, or it was the short guy with the sword that was what led him to pull the trigger. Rajeev caught the bullet as it exited the barrel and waved it in front of the wide eyes of the teen. That became enough motivation for him to get out and run away toward Mecca with his friends.

"You know they'll tell others about a brown, pocket-sized Orlando Bloom, stopping bullets with a thought," Dmitri said, opening the passenger door and sweeping something off the seat.

"And what, the alternative is to kill them instead?" Rajeev asked, knowing that's exactly what the Russian wanted.

"Eh, it doesn't matter," he sat with an exaggerated sigh. "They most likely won't even make it a mile outside of town."

"What is that supposed to mean?"

"C'mon, Rajeev. You're a smart kid. Knights and daegaryns have existed here for centuries. You'd think it'd be difficult to keep a secret for that long. And you'd be correct. There is an, uh . . . *system* to keep your kind unknown."

"How did you find me?" Rajeev asked. The thought had come to him a few times before, but he never brought it up. He was a wanted man with a dying wife; there wasn't much of a chance.

"Once upon a time, there were four of us who made a pact to make sure knights never became a threat to the world." Dmitri was digging around in the back while he talked. "I was a spy, yes, but only in my early years. Once I saw what was going on in India, I made a career change."

"And what was going on in India?"

"A story for another day, my boy." Dmitri found an open bag of chips and loudly crunched on a handful. "But your mother was involved. I found you through her."

"What'd you do to her?" Rajeev jumped and attached to the car, pulling himself to stand on the hood and directing *Irontruth* to be within foot from the Russian second chin.

Using the distraction, Eryon disappeared. Rajeev noticed this from the corner of his eye and fractured the sword, sending the shards in the sparse area where the daegaryn had been. Eryon's camouflage broke just a few feet from where he had stood. Two shards stuck in chest just below the dragon tattoo, a third in his thigh.

Rajeev hopped off the car as *Irontruth* reformed to the hilt he still held and rushed to the side of the daegaryn as he fell. "Where is Kalynst?" he asked frantically but Eryon was already fading and he got no answer. A moment later his head lolled to the side, eyes forever glued to the Arabian sun.

There went his best chance for revenge, but he still had to deal with Dmitri.

Back on the hood with *Irontruth* in place, he glimpsed pure fear break Dmitri's normally jovial countenance before returning back to normal. "What a brutal display of power, killing your best shot to bring the daegaryns to their rightful extinction. But I didn't do anything to your mother."

Only narrowed eyes were received from him.

"Rajeev, Rajeev. I'm hurt that you would think I'd ever harm another person. I don't know how she died. We tried to convince her to join our little group, but she wouldn't have it. My boy, have I ever lied to you?"

And he never had, to Rajeev's frustration. He just never tells the whole truth. His sincerity didn't matter now, anyway. With Eryon dead, Rajeev needed another way to track down Kalynst. There was the possibility of a return to Halgarth to kidnap another daegaryn, but the scrambling of his metal-vision gave him the idea that a return trip wouldn't go as well.

Though, Dmitri did say he knew others like him. Maybe they could help. Rajeev asked him about this.

"Well, um," the Russian stuttered. "We had made a deal not to ever contact each other unless it's of dire importance."

"Does a magic sword made of metal from another planet point at your neck not qualify as 'dire importance?'" Rajeev retorted.

"Uh, well maybe it's time we caught up," he reached into his pocket and it came out empty. "Blasted. I forgot that beautiful she-devil had taken my phone and most likely destroyed it. Oh well."

Rajeev almost did the same thing before remembering his was lost too and his wife's dead in his pack. "We'll go into the next town—not Mecca—and find a payphone. Please tell me you remember the number."

"Of course, my dear Rajeev. Back in my day, we didn't have your little phones to remember our contacts; we had to memorize the numbers ourselves."

"Okay." Rajeev lowered the sword. "But get in the back because you really do stink."

"Hey, Fernando," Dmitri greeted inside a booth with the phone squeezed between his ear and shoulder. He gave two thumbs up to Rajeev. "It's your old friend Dmitri Smirnov. Ah, yes, yes. Well, you remember Aisha Patel. I found her son. Rajeev, a nice enough kid." He gave Rajeev a wink. "Ah, of course you know about him. Your shadow stretches far, it does, hehe."

They were in the Ta'if, about an hour's drive from Mecca. An hour of Dmitri telling stories, some that really made Rajeev rethink whether the Russian really did always tell the truth, none that were of any help. It didn't help that they had to go through some narrow, windy mountain roads, dimly lit in the twilight, causing Rajeev to get nauseated. He would've vomited what little was in his stomach if he knew that would shut up Dmitri, but he figured the Russian would just use the incident as fuel.

"So, he's trying to connect with his fellow knights." Another wink. "I know you're busy, but I was hoping you can point me in the direction of others. Anybody occupying Camelot these days? Ah, very interesting. A quest you said. Very fun, very fun.

"And one last thing, Fernando." Dmitri turned away from Rajeev and lowered his voice, but by straining his ears Rajeev could hear. "How is . . . Okay. Good, good. It's been a long time, Fernando. It was good to hear your voice."

He hung up and smiled his golden smile. "Success. There are five knights currently in Belgrade, Serbia and at least two of them will be crossing into Turkey from Bulgaria sometime Tuesday.

"Turkey is a long way from Halgarth," Rajeev noted.

"Well, you should've thought about that when you killed our daegaryn GPS."

Rajeev sighed. "What day is it now?" He racked his brain

to remember when Balthasar had taken him but couldn't come up with an answer.

"Sunday."

"And how far is it to Turkey?"

"Well, for Istanbul in particular. . . I have no fucking clue." Dmitri exited the phone booth to stand in front of Rajeev. "What do I look like, the map from *Dora the Explorer*?"

Rajeev ignored the satire. "We'll need to find an iPhone charger. I think the BMW has a cigarette port with a USB connector, so I can charge it on the way."

"*Charge it on the way?* Rajeev, we have almost two full days to catch up with them. Let's find a hotel to rest up. Actually, before that we need to eat; I'm famished. I saw a food truck selling falafel and I swear on my dear mother's ashes that somebody walked away from it with what I think were jalapeño poppers. I would kill a man for some jalapeño poppers."

"I want to get to Turkey as soon as possible," Rajeev said, "so we can hopefully catch them at the border."

A boy carrying a steaming tray of some fried food walked by and Dmitri practically drooled at the sight then said, "You won't be able to get there if you run that German excuse for a car into a ditch in the middle of the desert after you fall asleep. And that's if it doesn't break down before you leave the city."

"Fine," Rajeev conceded. "But we leave first thing in the morning."

"That's my boy!" Dmitri clasped his hands together. "Now where was that food truck?"

# Chapter ThirtyThree

"**Do you think** we could stop in Budapest?" Savannah asked hesitantly. "It's kind of on the way, right?"

They were in the Romeo driving through rural Hungary. That afternoon, after an awkward stroll through the streets of Salzburg, clothes badly singed and torn but still keeping them decent, the pair showered and then checked out.

They had fought for hours, not quitting until Isabella felt that Savannah might not die in a two-on-one fight with a daegaryn. Savannah had slept for the last couple of hours and still felt tired, yet the Brit barely seemed affected by the training.

Now, so close to Budapest, this might be Savannah's only chance to figure out why Killian had left that address. It might be a daegaryn lair, but Killian seemed . . . sincere. Her gut told her to go and that was enough to at least ask—*always asking, where did my freedom go?*

"It's like an hour and a half *out* of the way," Isabella said. There was no suspicion on her face but why should there be? "Why?"

"No reason, really. I've just always wanted to go."

Savannah had considered telling the Brit about the piece of paper, but something told her to keep it a secret for now. Again, she was trusting her gut like she was back in high school. *It's easier than rationalizing how I have superpowers due to being the descendent of a fantastical queen—well not really descendent but inheriting her soul through some abstract means I will probably never understand.*

"You can go sometime else," Isabella said, resolute. "We're on a mission, not a tour."

Well, that was it. It seemed fate had a different plan and Savannah wasn't really complaining; she could just imagine Isabella chasing her in the dark with her spear. She had to stop herself from rubbing her shoulder at the thought. It was weird to have a cut that didn't heal. But maybe even more odd, she liked it.

*There's a way out.*

Two hours later, long after all light had left the sky, farmlands gave way for the Alfa Romeo and its passengers to the small city Szekszárd—a town, no more. It was flat, vastly different from Salzburg wrapped by the Alps. And trees towered over many of the buildings. Only a single tower—from a chapel, perhaps—illustrated the dominance of humanity. To some, it may seem peaceful. To others, imprisonment from the world. To Savannah and Isabella, it was just the next stop on their journey.

They pulled into the parking lot beside a small inn with a single floor. In the dark, it gave Savannah bad vibes like something out of a horror movie. The rooms weren't much better with stained sheets and moldy corners and the musky smell of mildew. She had a feeling the bed bugs were going to bite tonight. But even with those worries, it didn't take long for her to fall asleep.

In the morning, they drove to a nearby café. There, a square-jawed man with tree-trunk arms and a bulging chest greeted them and brought coffee without asking. Savannah took a sip and grimaced. It was a strong mocha and compared to other black coffee, it was pretty good. But she needed cream and sugar for it to be palatable. Isabella, on the other hand, took long sips while scrolling through her phone.

The waiter came back and asked them something in quick Hungarian.

Savannah turned to Isabella for a translation who just shrugged. "English?" she finally tried.

The man's eyebrows scrunched together under his shaved head.

"Creeaam and suuugaar," Savannah said slowly as if that would help while making a pouring motion over her cup.

He nodded and returned with exactly what she wanted. He said something, sounding out each word just like she had. Savannah gave a horizontal cutting motion, pointed at the coffee, and then gave a thumbs up. *Maybe there's a McDonald's here.* She thought as her stomach grumbled. *Or a KFC.* The waiter smiled almost shyly and moved off.

"Thanks for the help," Savannah said to her companion.

"What?" She again shrugged. "The translation app doesn't have Hungarian."

Savannah scowled and then poured in two dollops of cream and just a dash of sugar from their metal containers and then mixed with the little spoon provided. She took a sip and was much more pleased with the taste.

"What happened?" Isabella asked suddenly, her eyes still glued to her phone.

"What?" Savannah glanced behind her to see if there was something going on.

"I don't know." She finally faced her. "With your life."

Savannah just narrowed her eyes in confusion.

"Well, you obviously want to talk. And now that your therapist boyfriend is dead—" Savannah shot her a dirty, hurt look. "What? Everybody around us dies. Get used to it. So, talk if you want, don't if you don't."

Savannah twirled her spoon in her coffee, eyes glazing as she recalled memories that haunted her every night.

"I was a junior in high school in Alabama." The words came easy for her, they always did. "There was a party the night after the homecoming game. It was at one of the football player's houses. The star receiver. Bryce Woeste. My best friend is the one who invited me. I had never been to a party before—at least none like the one I knew it was going to be—but I was a self-conscious girl who just wanted to be liked, so how could I say no?

"That night, I came with Lauren—my best friend—but I lost her soon after. There were a ton of people inside, making it impossible to walk anywhere without bumping into someone. Which happened as I drank a Jack and Coke. It was Bryce. He apologized to the point where I was the one embarrassed and brought me another drink. We talked for a while—just about school and, you know, the usual small talk—and soon I was feeling the effects of the alcohol. I didn't have a high tolerance back then—that would change.

"Anyways, he asked if I wanted to go upstairs with him. I said yes. And no, he didn't roofie my drink; I watched him as he poured it. One thing led to the other and we had sex. He asked me multiple times if I was sure I wanted to do it. Maybe he took advantage of me in my drunken state, but it didn't feel that way. It was my first time . . . and I didn't have any birth control and he didn't have any protection.

"Two weeks later, I missed my period." Savannah finally brought her tear-filled eyes up to Isabella's dry ones. "Tests confirmed it: I was pregnant at sixteen years old. I was scared, so scared. Another week went by before I got up the nerve to tell my parents. They were . . . were furious with me. They told me to abort it. Abort my baby. All to save me from shame.

I told them no. They screamed and screamed at me. I cried and cried.

"And then I exploded. I don't know how it just happened." Tears erupted from her dull, blue eyes. "I killed them both." She shook her head and snapped her fingers. This was the first time she ever told anybody about that. Who else would be able to understand? "Just like that."

Savannah wiped her eyes with a napkin. "I left after, of course, driving until I made it to Georgia. Why there? Why not? I had nowhere else to go.

"I lived in a Planned Parenthood until I gave birth," She clenched her fist and looked away from Isabella, focusing on her furnace; it was starting to heat up. It eventually cooled but her tears sizzled as they hit her coffee. "It was burnt to nothing. Her. She was a girl. All shriveled up and blackened and smoking. She was fine until the contractions started. I killed my unborn daughter. If I aborted her, I would still have my parents and my sanity.

"I moved again. To Tennessee this time. There I got a job at UPS and eventually things got better. I met a guy at a bar—I went there almost every night. Caleb was his name. He bought me a drink and the next thing I knew I was in his bed. It became a regular thing. And a year later we got married. The wedding was just us two and a minister we found on a website; we didn't have anybody else.

"He wanted to have a child, but I took birth control in secret. There's no way I'm having a repeat of what happened. After two years of 'trying' we adopted a beautiful little girl, Paige. She was three when we got her.

"For years, we were as happy as we could be. Just us three; we didn't need anybody else. Then Caleb found my birth control pills. We got into an argument." Savannah waved her arms as fresh tears fell down her cheeks. "and history repeated itself.

"After that, I started trying to find ways to kill myself. I drank bleach and immediately vomited it back up. I shot myself in the head and immediately healed. I tied a bag over my head and woke up with it off. Nothing worked.

"I moved to Kentucky and history repeated itself yet again."

Throughout the whole thing, Isabella did not have any verbal or visual reactions but never took her eyes off her companion. And even when Savannah was done, she remained silent.

"Is that it?" Savannah said to the Brit, irritated. "I dump my life story onto you, and you just sit and say nothing?"

"What do you want me to say?" Isabella finally spoke up. "That I'm sorry? That's not going to bring anyone back. That's not going to erase the past."

"I just wanted you to say it wasn't my fault," Savannah said quietly.

Isabella stared back at her. "It's your fault they're dead. It's my fault the people I lost are dead. We're monsters and monsters kill."

# Chapter Thirty‑Four

**An old, beat‑up** station wagon of some unknown manufacturer kicked up dust as the brakes squeaked with joint pain to slow down beside a group of three teenagers. They were innocent kids and eyed the car with relief even though they knew not who drove it. Ted Bundy had taken advantage of that exact same unwariness created by the modern world's facade of safety.

The stranger would follow in his footsteps.

"*Salaam*," she greeted after she had rolled her window down, smiling through her boshiya. "Do you need a ride? It is such a hot day to be hiking to the Holy City."

"No, thanks." One of the boys with just a hint of a moustache on his face said curtly.

The other two barely looked at her as they followed their leader down the dusty road.

She frowned but was not deterred and drove up again alongside them. "What happened for you three to be walking to Mecca with no adult in sight? It surely can't be safe."

"Allah told us to," the same one answered and hurried along, obviously worried about the stranger.

Now aggravated, she sped up and slammed the brakes, kicking up dirt into their faces. "Was there a man with a sword that could control metal?"

That did it, and the boys turned to the other with wide eyes. "Our car was stolen," the leader answered. "One of the thieves had a sword and looked like an Arabic Orlando Bloom. I tried to shoot him with my father's gun, but he stopped the bullet." He raised his hands, palms out. "But I only used it in self-defense, *sayyidi*." The boy dropped his eyes to the ground. "We ran away as fast as we could."

"The devil's work," the woman nodded her veiled head. "Satan knows he cannot enter the sacred lands of Mecca and walk the same grounds from whence Allah gave Earth Mohammad to preach His holy truth. So, instead he uses unbelievers as his weapon against God's people."

The three boys looked at each other, mouths slightly agape at being in the presence of the supposed devil—because who else could it have been?—and living to tell the tale.

"But it shames God to have His children run at the personification of sin. For the Quran says, 'And it is to be heard that all believers of the holy truth, shall not hideth among the shadows against the face of evil, but stand tall and let the spirit allow them strength and protection against sin's soldiers.'"

The shortest of the bunch raised his hand hesitantly. "*Sayyidi*, you must be mistaken. That is not in the Quran."

"You're a smart little shit aren't you?" All kindness had left her voice. "You always have to let everybody know you're right. I knew kids like you and killed them all. You just can't let something go."

A knife found a home in his left eye.

His two friends stood in horror as they watched him fall on his back with barely a gasp.

"Now what I was saying before I was rudely interrupted," she said from her seat. There was no sign where the weapon had come from. "Is that you two are a couple of pussies."

Two more knives from hidden compartments in her boshiya took the teens in the throats, eliminating their rising protests.

The stranger exited the station wagon and ripped up the clothes of the kids and spread their quickly flowing blood wherever she desired. Any passerby would assume they had been attacked by a wild animal. Perhaps even one possessed by the devil himself.

# Chapter Thirty Five

𝕶ragujevac was the closest city in Europe to the ones Savannah had recognized back in America, yet even still the tallest buildings couldn't scrape the sky. Did the reminder from her home make her feel any better? No. There was nothing there for her anymore. There was nothing here either. In Turkmenistan a magical sword awaited her and maybe she could potentially do something good with it.

More likely she'd just screw it up.

So, why did she continue this fantastical quest? To right her wrongs? To fulfill a sense of purpose? Boredom? Her mind became clouded at those thoughts. She was scared of her indecision but maybe most of all, she feared the answer.

For now, all she could do was put one foot in front of the other and hope they didn't get tangled with someone else's.

The drive through Hungary and into Serbia was quiet and filled with tension, so thin it could have been cut by one of the Brit's hateful stares. No apology, no light conversation, only silence. Maybe Savannah should've been glad at Isabella's sincerity. James would always act as if a previous argument never happened. It was one of the few things Savannah ever hated about him. Laughing past the hurt.

Currently, she lay in the bed of a Serbian hotel, the softness of the feather bed not assisting in her transition from the realm of evil reality to that of hopeful dreams. Sleep was always difficult for her with the worry of the nightmares that weren't really nightmares, but rather memories. It didn't help that the room service food—a sandwich with only one slice of bread (can that even be considered a sandwich?) covered in cheese, mystery greens, and salami—left her with some indigestion. It's what she got for eating right before going to bed, but Isabella dropped her off at her room and never offered to take her out to dinner and Savannah wasn't going out into Kragujevac by herself.

She still couldn't understand why Isabella had reacted the way she did. The Brit was the one who suggested Savannah get everything off her plate. It just didn't make any sense. *I guess everybody can't be like James.* She thought of something and smiled at her foolishness. *It's because he is a therapist, of course. Listening, diagnosing, and advising is what he got a Ph.D. in. What he gets paid for.*

Thinking about James, reminded her of something he had said in regard to a question she had about one of her coworkers, "*You can never tell what's going on beneath the surface. I've studied psychology for eight years and still can't weed out everything about somebody. Even with you, I can see there's something you don't want to tell me when we talk about your past, which is fine, of course. But everybody is different. Don't be quick to judge.*"

Perhaps Isabella had a past even worse than Savannah's. Most likely not but still. She just had to be more understanding like James.

And, anyway, Isabella wasn't wrong. It was her fault. All she had done; it was her fault.

A tap at the window caused Savannah to jerk to a seated

position. A rational person would've assumed it to be a tree branch or perhaps a large insect and ignored it. She was not a rational person and was out of bed before the second tap came.

The pale face of a little girl with a face the color of coffee smiled at her as if knocking on someone's window in the middle of the night was the most normal thing. Not to mention she was on the second floor. There was one more thing off, though. Her eyes glowed a forest green.

She was a knight.

*And a few have unfortunately chosen a darker path.*

But this kid couldn't be one of them, right?

Every neuron in her brain told her to back off and call for Isabella. But her heart saw the girl's innocence—a shadow of her daughter—and opened the window.

"Hi! I'm Elise Laurent," the girl said in a flowery French accent. "Heir of Sir Gareth the Life Knight."

Savannah couldn't help but smile at Elise's bubbliness.

"I'm Savannah Hamlin. Heir of Lady Guinevere. The Ember Knight, I guess." She reached over and flicked on a lamp next to the window to get a better look at the girl. She had dark hair tied into a braid and on her back there appeared to be a quiver—but no bow—slung there. A young Katniss Everdeen. "Why are you here?"

"You missed us in Budapest."

"You're with Killian? He's like us?"

Elise nodded. "His actual name is Eoin."

Savannah was relieved to know the giant wasn't a daegaryn but instead like her. But that didn't necessarily mean he was on her side.

"I asked Isabella—she's my chaperone, I guess; I can't remember who her ancestor is, but she's like the Poison Knight or something—and she decided against it. There was not much else I could do."

"I know Isabella Knowles. She's the heir of Sir Tristan," the French girl said. "It doesn't matter, we're here now."

"We?"

"Friends," Elise glanced over her shoulder. "But we have to leave now."

"Where?"

"A safe place."

"What about Isabella?"

The girl's face hardened in a way someone her age shouldn't. "Isabella is not the person you think she is. She killed her whole unit in the Royal Navy as well as everyone in the Polish town they were staying in. She's a war criminal. I'm sorry but I only tell you this for your own good."

Savannah believed it—Isabella obviously had a bloody past—but she didn't think that the Brit meant to do it. She knew full well the difficulty of controlling their powers.

"Do you know what I've done?" Savannah asked.

"You killed your parents, unborn baby, husband, and adopted daughter," Elise said matter-of-factly. "A relatively low kill count for those like us."

The French girl's nonchalance to her murders surprised Savannah. She feared for what had happened in Elise's past to result in that reaction.

"How do you know this?"

"Part of my power lets me read minds," Elise said. "Let's go before your 'chaperone' awakes," Elise said.

"How long will we be gone?"

"Not long."

That ambiguity again. But Savannah had been curious about Killian—er, Eoin—and the address he left. And now here was this girl. Both seemed nicer and more normal than the knights she met so far. She felt bad about leaving Isabella—though not as bad after this morning—but she had to at least hear them out. And it's not like she feared death anymore.

"I'll go."

"Fantastic!" Elise moved away from the window, appearing as if she was floating. "Oliver will bring you down in a second."

"Oliver?" Savannah asked but Elise was already gone.

She peered out of the window and jumped back immediately at the sight of a bear. It balanced on its back legs and had its front paws held up.

"Don't worry," Elise called from below. "I control him. Just lower yourself out of the window and he'll grab you and let you down."

Savannah leaned out of the window and yelled, "I'm good. I'll just take the stairs like a sane person."

Behind the hotel, Savannah made sure to keep her distance from the bear named Oliver as she approached the French girl. She wore a cute pair of overalls that ended mid-thigh with a bright pink shirt underneath.

"Please tell me we're not going to meet your friends on that thing," Savannah said.

"Oh no, they are in Belgrade, two hours away," Elise answered. "Oliver has three cubs and a grumpy mate. We'll drive."

"You're not driving, are you?"

"If I can control a giant brown bear with barely a thought, why shouldn't I be able to drive?"

*Fair enough.*

Savannah followed the strange girl to the hotel parking lot. Elise pressed a button on the key fob she pulled out of her overalls and the headlights of a red, not exactly inconspicuous, Fiat blinked in response. Once they got in, Elise strapped a wooden block to the bottom of her right foot, filling Savannah with fear. She went from having Vin Diesel to Short Round as her driver. Why couldn't anybody trust her to drive?

Elise pulled out surprisingly smooth and continued down the road in that manner. Savannah felt herself dozing off and figured sleep might not be a great idea in this situation, so she began to talk to the French girl.

"How did you become . . . join . . . uh . . ."

"Change from a little girl born in the outskirts of Paris to a badass bitch that has power over all aspects of life?" Elise asked while thankfully not taking her eyes off the road.

"Yeah, I guess."

"It was two years ago—when I turned twelve—when I first started to hear what people around me thought. Later, I found out I could control them as well." Elise switched lanes without looking and zoomed past a sleek sports car, causing Savannah to grip her seat. *Why can I never get a sane driver?* "So, anyway, one thing led to another, and I had my English teacher—a real muscular guy—kill this girl who bullied me. Followed her into the bathroom and bashed her head into the toilet. It even made the national news."

Elise's eyes showed no remorse whatsoever. Savannah kept that in mind; she wasn't dealing with an innocent little girl.

"I wasn't a very well-liked person; everybody thought I was a bit of an oddball—which I am but still—and I was bullied often. They did mean things. The worst was where they would stuff things in places they didn't belong. So, using other adults, I killed them all."

Savannah reflexively reached for her phone, still not used to being without it. This girl was really starting to freak her out. Elise didn't see the movement or pretended not to.

"It wasn't exactly the smartest thing to do, drawing that much attention to the school I went to. But I didn't care. I was getting revenge and was loving every bit of it. Eventually, the inevitable happened and the daegaryns showed up. It was scary to find something I couldn't control." Her face finally began to show emotion: fear. "They came while I was in the cafeteria for lunch. I knew almost immediately they were there for me. So, I ran. But just before, I possessed the minds of every normal person there—something I didn't know I could do—and had them swarm the daegaryns. I escaped all the way to Dijon and tried to stay hidden, rarely using my powers.

"But apparently those efforts weren't enough, because I was found," She smiled to herself. "Not by an enemy but a friend. His name is Pierre Castillon. Heir of Sir Gawain the Earth Knight. He and Eoin are who we are meeting."

And so, they continued down the highway in silence as Savannah contemplated the psyche of the girl and if she was in danger. And if she even cared.

# Chapter Thirty-Six

**Santos stood next** to the pitcher's mound of a pris-on, fuming in a way only he could. With slightly reddened cheeks and speaking in a tone that was somehow both calm and tense.

"They killed her?" he asked the Secretary of Defense, Noah Riggs. He had, of course, known this not long after it happened, but he liked to keep his wide-ranging knowledge a secret. "This is the most secure prison on the planet."

Knowing full well the person that stood before him, Riggs managed to stand his ground and maintain a stern composure, made easy by his sharp suit that was surely stifling in the heat. "Sir, we weren't prepared for that kind of power."

And it was a brilliant display of power, a prison cell completely ripped away from its neighbor and sat on the baseball field around enormous chunks of earth. But Santos had seen worse.

"What? Like a nuclear bomb?" Santos asked.

If Riggs was insulted at the quip, he didn't show it. "It was the specificity of it. Not brute strength but strategic maneuvers. The creation of a rainstorm and the control of elks as a distraction. And then that." He stuck a thumb back at the cell behind him.

"I told you to be prepared for anything."

"How can we prepare for something that can't be killed?" Anger and frustration could finally be heard in his voice. "I saw the footage, a security guard shot one of them with one of your rifles. And he still got up like nothing happened."

"I saw the footage, as well. *Your* guy shot him in the corner of the head. A chip shot. It has to be shot in the center of the body, preferably in a region where the bullet won't exit out the other side."

"Why does it matter, anyway." Riggs mopped at some sweat on his balding scalp with a handkerchief. It was midday in the Colorado desert sun. He wished Santos had waited until later for them to have this conversation. "The girl destroyed a whole city that may start World War Three."

"Because one, she's a little girl." His scar stretched as his mouth tightened. "And two, her death may cause something worse than war between men. You have no idea the Pandora's box you just opened with your lack of defense."

"Does he have to come, too?" Riggs asked of the creature that was behind Santos. It was cloaked all in black with a hood that left its face in shadow and hovered over both of them like some agent of death. But instead of a scythe, a large warhammer was held at its side.

"Indeed," Santos said without any explanation.

This guy was really pissing him off. Like it was his problem. Riggs had been in and out of meetings with the president the past few months, trying to figure out how to deal with the situation in Europe. He didn't have time for this.

Santos had asked for a tour of their "special facilities." The prison for these freaks with abilities they got from God knows where. The Argentinian would never tell him anything except to shoot them with those weapons and hope it incapacitated them. And now he wanted to bring this guy to a top-secret area, without even giving his name, not to mention some proper forms of I.D. It probably was one of the freaks like Santos. Riggs still didn't understand why the president trusted him.

Inside ADX Florence, Riggs nodded at a guard as he passed by in the hallway. After the man had turned the corner, he placed the palm of his hand flat against a seemingly random spot on the metal wall. An elevator opened up in an area with no apparent perforations. The group moved inside and then Riggs typed in his code in the area where normally there would be floor numbers, making sure his "guests" didn't look over his shoulder. Above the passcode, he stuck in his key, triggering a hidden panel to open up with a scanner for his retina. With all the security checks completed, the elevator moved down. Far down, below the basement and sub-basement, the doors opened.

They stepped out into an area out of an alien movie. Everything was white. White walls, white floors, white noise. There was nobody here—no reason for there to be anybody with no prisoners to watch—and the only sound was the whirring of the air conditioning. Which was working overtime at his command. Riggs felt goosebumps creep up his arms and he almost regretted his decision.

"How many people know about this?" Santos asked.

"At ADX, the warden and a handful of guards she trusts," Riggs answered. "And then only the President, Vice President, and me."

"I want everyone here to have a background check," the Argentinian said.

"They already have."

"Do it again and make it thorough." Santos narrowed

his eyes. "Notify Barth immediately of anything that appears off."

"The President is too important for these kinds of things."

"And so am I, but here I am," Santos waved him on, ending the conversation.

Riggs guided them past the security guard's house and moved into the west wing where the girl had been held. The hallway looked just like the entrance except for the reinforced glass windows that were placed on each door and a passcode. At the end of the hallway, sunlight blossomed through where the terrorist had ripped out the cell.

The Argentinian peered into the closest cell. It was modest in size, a 10x10 cube with a toilet, sink, and bed. No need to waste taxpayers' money on these people.

"How do you feed them?" Santos asked, not moving away from the window.

Riggs punched in a code on the passcode. A panel slid to the side revealing a secret compartment. He punched in another code and the inside wall of the compartment opened up.

"You got somebody you want to lock up?" Riggs asked.

Santos ignored the question. "Would there be any reason for this door to open with a prisoner inside?"

"Never."

The man nodded at his shadowy companion. The thing picked up a heavy hammer as easily as a toy one and heaved it into the side of the cell, leaving a massive dent and setting off an alarm.

"What the hell are you doing?" Riggs shouted, but he was long forgotten.

The freak hit it again and again and again. The reinforced door that itself cost nearly a million dollars became only twisted metal laying in the cell.

"It seems you have an infrastructure issue," the Argentinian mused.

"An infrastructure issue?" Riggs couldn't believe it. "You blew that thing to pieces."

"I was testing it," Santos said in a calm manner. "It failed."

"Why should I care, anyway." His walkie suddenly went off and he quickly reassured the guard that everything was all right. *But was it really?* "This is your problem, not mine."

"Maybe not today, but tomorrow?" Santos turned back the way they came as the alarm turned off, followed by the creature. "Who knows? The world is on a ticking time bomb."

"What's going to happen?"

He ignored the question. "Get this fixed up," the Argentinian said instead.

"I don't work for you."

Santos looked over his shoulder and smiled. "Everybody works for me. Whether they know it or not."

# Chapter Thirty-Seven

**The blood-red** Fiat carrying passengers with a past of the same color parked in front of an empty bar on the fringe of Belgrade. Above the door, a wooden sign dangled in the nightly breeze: *Kyña Xepoja*.

"Why choose this place?" Savannah asked. She was feeling worse and worse about her decision to go with Elise.

"The isolation," the French girl answered, then hopped out of the car.

Besides being in the middle of nowhere the bar was in pretty good shape. The windows were all intact and the red paint was barely faded, only peeling in some places.

Elise opened the door, eliciting a bell to ring and signal their entrance. But it didn't matter as two figures sat across from each other at a table in the shadows, turning their heads to the intruders as they entered.

"Savannah," the smaller one said in a French accent as he stood up. "It's very nice to finally meet you."

Even squinting through the darkness, Savannah struggled to make out the face of the man talking. The bar was only lit with a handful of lanterns like they were in the medieval era.

"I'm sorry for the dismal setting," the Frenchman apologized, walking to her with a slight limp. "It's the only place we could meet in secret and the electricity has long been cut off. Though, I have a feeling a mutual *friend* would be at home in an area like this."

The man had reached her, smelling faintly of weed, and held up a lantern between them. A thin beard accentuated a sharp jaw that shifted up as he smiled at her with perfect, white teeth. His hair was messy but like that of a model. And turquoise eyes glittered at her like the Montego Bay.

"Merlin?" Savannah asked. "You know him?"

"I met him just briefly. An interesting character."

"Let me formally introduce myself, Savannah," a familiar voice came from behind the man. "My name is Eoin. Eoin McGowan."

The Irish giant Savannah had known as Killian reached a large hand out and shook hers.

"And I am Pierre." The Frenchman shook her hand too.

"Why did you bring me here?" Savannah asked.

Eoin let out one of his voluminous laughs. "I told you, Pierre, she's not one for bullshit."

Pierre sighed and motioned her to a table. They sat and he began. "Because Merlin—I'll call him Nathan, his real name—is not who you think he is."

"I was around him for less than twenty-four hours; I've barely formulated an opinion on him," Savannah said. It was a lie of course. Merlin was a very easy person to judge.

Eoin spoke now. "Almost four months ago, our mentor Everton—he was killed not long ago."

"Right, by daegaryns," Savannah said. "Isabella mentioned it."

The mention of the Brit's name made her feel guilty about leaving her, but their earlier argument helped push those feelings back.

"That's what Nathan told us," Eoin said, eyes tilted downwards. "Anyway, Everton caught wind of a young girl in Munich who possessed powers of radiation. Her name was Sabine Hochleutner.

"Everton brought me and Nathan along for assistance. As you know, people like us are very dangerous, especially when we can't control our powers.

"When we got there, I saw Nathan's immediate infatuation with the girl. He is twenty and she was eighteen and very pretty, so it shouldn't have been that weird. But the look in his eyes made it so.

"Sabine lived with her aunt and uncle—her parents had died two and three years earlier from different types of cancer. We believed radiation leaking from her may have caused their deaths. But the girl had no idea she even had powers. She was innocent. Nathan had to do some type of mind thing to convince her of what was inside of her. I swear the smile he gave her when he touched her shoulder." Eoin grimaced at the memory.

"C'mon, guys," Elise spoke up. Savannah had almost forgotten she was there. "This talk is getting really dark. And we really don't want to scare away our guest."

Elise turned to Savannah, smiling. In fact, she was the only one present who was smiling. "What is your favorite color?"

"Orange," Savannah answered, peering into the flickering flames within the lantern in front of her.

"Oh, like fire. That makes sense," she sipped noisily from a McDonald's soda they had picked up on the way to Belgrade. "What about animal?"

"Turkey."

"Hmm, interesting. And what about number?"

"Number?" Savannah looked at Eoin and Pierre for help. Both sat amused. She was not the first victim of Elise's question barrage.

"Yeah."

"I was number forty-three in high school basketball, so I guess that."

"Okay, cool," Elise said and then pulled out her phone.

Before Savannah could question the motive for the inquiries, Pierre had picked up the conversation. "Me and Eoin had been in contact for several months."

"I ran into him during my own quest," Eoin added. "I wasn't sure what I was a part of and didn't want to be responsible for getting Pierre stuck in it."

"He called me one night," Pierre continued. "told me his problem and we discussed a plan. I posted something on Instagram of me using my powers and then immediately deleted it. Eoin screen-recorded it and then showed it to Everton. A gusty move, for sure, but one that needed to be done. I was in Strasbourg, just four hours from Munich."

"Strasbourg," Savannah started, empathy in her voice.

"No, I'm from Bordeaux that's just where I happened to be when he called. For a very long time, I just traveled aimlessly around France, which is how I met Elise. I was too scared to leave the country yet too wound up to stay in one place.

"Everton agreed to check Pierre out," Eoin picked up the story. "And two days later we left. Nathan was quiet about the situation, but you could see disagreement in his demeanor. And when we 'found' Pierre watching television, I would constantly catch Nathan staring at him. Not with anger or anything like that, but just staring.

"That night the daegaryns came."

"We think Nathan may somehow control them," Pierre added. "How? We're not sure. For all we know it could just be conjecture. But there have been too many coincidences."

Savannah recalled those human-dragon things coming

for her and killing James. She also remembered how Merlin arrived just in time to save her but not her friend. Savannah tried to not let those memories cause any physical change but by the expressions in the strangers, she could tell they saw something.

"Too many coincidences," Pierre repeated.

"Anyhow, we fought them," Eoin continued. "But the extreme elements of the battle caused Sabine to . . . *explode*. Everton created some type of pressurized wind vortex—he controls the air—that kept us from being blown apart. Me and Pierre left with Elise before Nathan could get his wits together. After that, we have no idea but we don't think Sabine survived her bomb. And with Everton," the Irishman shook his shaved head. I fear he may have been killed by Nathan."

They sat there for a minute and Savannah tried to process what she just heard. It seemed very possible, but they could've easily just lied as well.

"What has Nathan said about this?" Pierre asked.

"He answered my questions about the daegaryns and who I am," Savannah said. "but didn't say much else other than that. It seemed that he doesn't like to talk much."

"No," Eoin agreed. "He listens and observes."

Elise jerked her head up from where she was sitting. Her eyes had been glued to the phone for the whole conversation, but Savannah could now tell they were glowing green. "She's on her way."

"Really sorry about this, Savannah," Eoin said, standing up to his full, towering height.

"And it was really nice to meet you," Pierre added.

"Same!" Elise agreed.

"Wha—" Savannah started but the right hook from the Irish giant came before she could finish.

# Chapter ThirtyEight

**Before the Middle** Eastern sun had even risen over the Ta-if mountains, Rajeev had woken and banged on the door connecting their two-room. A groan followed by the squeaking of floorboards resounded on the other side before it was opened by Dmitri.

"Jesus!" Rajeev exclaimed at the sight of the naked Russian.

"I thought you didn't believe in that guy," he said, scratching at his bare butt and yawning. Rajeev almost vomited at the horrid scent. He never should've let Dmitri eat that falafel with the Lebanese garlic sauce.

"Why are you naked?"

"What? That's the only way I can sleep. You never complained about that daegaryn. Although, I guess you did kill him," he eyed Rajeev carefully as his scratching hand moved to the front. "Do I make you feel immaterial? Do not worry, most men can't size up to ol' Dmitri Smirnov.

"Get dressed," Rajeev ordered and turned away in disgust. "We leave in fifteen minutes."

"Okay, I guess I can sleep in the car. But remember how

I sleep, Rajeev. Hehe!" He let out a tremendous fart before he closed the door, forcing Rajeev to make a charge at the windows.

It was over thirty minutes before they had left the two-star hotel paid with some emergency cash Rajeev had stashed in his old duplex and were in the BMW, roof up—being stranded in the open desert was too fresh for him.

After they had eaten from the food truck last night, the pair had found a clothing store to obtain some fresh wear that wasn't sticky with sweat or itchy from sand. Rajeev had gone in alone, while Dmitri shoveled Arabic food down. He returned with a black shirt—to prevent the visibility of food stains—for the Russian and a gray tank top for himself, complementing both with simple, monochromatic running shorts.

Dmitri plopped down on the black leather passenger seat. Rajeev was tempted to push him to the back again but wasn't up to dicker. It didn't take long for the grizzly bear snores to attack Rajeev's ears.

Hours passed and mountains flattened to a very unwelcoming desert with nothing to occupy his attention except for some music from artists he never cared to learn the names of and his own orchestra of melancholy thoughts. The frequent checks of the GPS on Yasmin's phone—charged to its fullest last night, though the lock screen of them on their wedding night brought him near to tears—did nothing to help the drive go by faster. Rajeev wished he could take his hoverboard and leave the Russian behind. Unfortunately, he needed Dmitri's contact.

"Dmitri," Rajeev knocked him on the arm with the back of his hand in a not-so-friendly manner. "Wake up." Dmitri might as well make himself useful.

Dmitri just let out a snort as a reply.

Rajeev attached to one of his golden teeth with his mind and wiggled just to the point of discomfort. That apparently was enough because he slapped his mouth, grumbling a few, surely colorful, words in Russian.

"What do you want?" he asked in a much less jovial tone than Rajeev was used to. Maybe Dmitri was really like a grizzly bear and waking him up from his hibernation could've been a mistake.

"Tell me everything." Rajeev turned down the radio. "No more dancing around the truth. We have . . ." a glance at the phone. "Thirty-three hours left. Plenty of time with not much else to do."

"Ah, Rajeev," Dmitri sighed and rubbed his eyes, forgetting for a second that one of them wasn't there. "I guess it can't hurt, but I was really enjoying my sleep. Where should I begin?"

"Start from when you were in India. You said you saw something there so significant that you went AWOL."

"Hmm, yes, yes. But Rajeev, what I say you may not want to know. Things that involve your mother. Do you still want me to continue?"

Rajeev glanced over and gave one, stiff nod.

"Do you promise not to kill me?"

"Don't ask of things you know the answer to."

"Hmm. Well, it was, oh God, I don't even know. Thirty years. Maybe more, maybe less, once you get to my age and live the life equivalent of three men, things get twisted. But, anyway, it was around the time when the hammer and sickle of the Soviet Union was lowered for the last time. I was a soldier, a really good one. And sneaky. So, sneaky that I was put on a special ops team, consisting of just a handful of men, unknown besides just a few more. We were known as the White Serpents—a team that was created even before I was born. Our mission failure rate was zero percent, which included the assassination of the abominable Adolf Hitler—"

"Hitler killed himself," Rajeev interrupted. "There was a

witness."

"Ah, my dear, innocent boy," Dmitri let out his laugh that was both childish, yet deep. "The Kremlin has long fingers. I just wish I was alive to be a part of it." No more explanation was given as he jumped right back into the story. "When the USSR was disbanded, the White Serpents stayed. Our leader—a great man, long dead with a name not worth mentioning—believed that there were still threats from certain countries following the end of the Cold War. I didn't disagree and wouldn't have due to the promise of death for disobedience. I was sent to India to follow-up on suspicions of the construction of a weapon never before seen.

"It took me probably close to a year to find it, meanwhile I attended cricket games, city council meetings, whore houses—though that was more for my enjoyment, hehe—not asking questions that could probably get me killed, but listening. It's amazing what you can hear when people perceive you as a tourist, traveling the post-Cold War world, rather than the threat you are.

"There were rumors of some military activity going out to the Lakshadweep archipelago, just off the southwest coast. I kept up my disguise as a tourist and rented a small fishing boat. The man I purchased it from warned me away from the islands, so I knew there was some substance to the rumors. I headed to the capital, Kavaratti, taking my time stopping every now and then to cast my line. I even caught a mahi mahi—or at least that's what the guide that came with the boat said. It was as tall as you. Taller!" he stretched his arms in emphasis. "Can you believe that? Not too bad for a little Russian who never fished in his life."

Rajeev just let Dmitri ramble, he was in no rush to get to the point.

"Ah, but that fish only helped to bolster my disguise when the islands came into view. But when I came within so many nautical miles—never really understood that unit of measurement—a speedboat intercepted me. It was military grade, not that I was supposed to know enough to distinguish it from a normal one. The driver was dressed in plain clothes with no visible weapon in sight. But I know what the bulge of a handgun tucked into the waistband looks like. He told me there had been an oil spill off the coast of an island I couldn't pronounce and sent me back to the mainland on my merry way.

"So, for the next week, I wondered about the markets of the coastal city, Kozhikode. I found that many soldiers favored one of the local markets and one day I followed one to the back of a building where he took a whiz. Little did he know that would be his last. I had a lot less meat on my bones back then—believe it or not, Rajeev, hehe—and the uniform fit, only a little snug. And then after that, well I won't go into too many details. Just know that it involved a few more dead men plus a self-inflicted gunshot in the shoulder. But my plan worked and I had touched ground on the island of Kavaratti.

"And oh, yes. A white man, one even with a really good Indian accent, would raise doubt, so I applied a hefty amount of makeup—just like Robert Downey Jr. in *Tropic Thunder.* The ploy wouldn't last long, but the blood of myself and my "comrades" should've distracted them enough.

"So, now in my many years in the Russian secret ops, I'd seen many military compounds and this looked no different; they weren't even trying to hide their presence, supporting my theory that this was a government operation. The plan for my first day there—after I was debriefed on the wee incident that happened in Kozhikode and sent off to the medic—was to explore the island and see if anything out of the ordinary stood out. It turned out to be much smaller than I predicted, taking me less than an hour. It'd seemed bigger with all the tents and buildings—plus an aquarium that seemed out of place, but I guess the smell reminded the Indians of their wives—ha. Oh, and the Trap House as they called it—I don't need to explain that one, do I? Fortunately, I managed to avoid it.

"But the day hadn't ended before I found a tunnel that connected each of the thirty-six islands—although they were more like atolls—of Lakshadweep. The goal for the mission was to get in and get out within twenty-four hours then report back. Any longer and the odds of my survival would not be great. That would've been impossible to do with the atolls being hundreds of miles apart, but thankfully they had a transport vehicle that could get up to a hundred-fifty miles per hour.

"Most of the atolls housed random bits of military machinery, equipment, standard weapons, or barracks. But one entrance was locked with a sign, reading *Classified Personnel Only* in Hindi. Naturally, that seemed to be the place I wanted to go, but the soldier I had killed wasn't 'classified personnel' and his I.D. card wouldn't open it.

"If I had more time, I would've bided my time and attempted to blend in, learning who had access and then steal a card when the opportunity opened for me. But since I was in a hurry, I knocked. Moments later, a man opened it and asked me what the hell I wanted. I bashfully showed him my shoulder, bleeding through the patch I had applied to it at the HQ. I told him I'd shot myself at the range and was too embarrassed to go the medic. He called me a pussy, and I jabbed two fingers into a pressure point in his neck, giving me enough time to jump through the doorway and choke him unconscious. I stuffed him in a broom closet, snatching his badge, and climbed the ladder to the surface.

"This was the smallest island of them all and an ugly metal building with no markings was the only sign of the military. With confidence, I walked in with a swipe of the new I.D., one hand on my own Vektor pistol, but it was empty of life. There was a long table and chairs with probably an 8x6 board with a bunch of pictures in notes bulleted to it. I got closer and saw pictures of people of all nationalities. They each had a name and power. I didn't know then, but they were knights. The Indian government had been studying your kind, Rajeev. And it appeared like they were coming up with a way to kill you.

"I didn't get much of a look, though as a rag was thrown over my mouth from behind, and I smelled the all too familiar odor of chloroform.

"I woke up in a dark room with a shirtless grunt staring down at me. I laughed and he punched me. Short-story-short, I was tortured and questioned about what I was doing here—you've seen my scars. I didn't tell them shit; my training would never allow it."

Rajeev glanced over and almost expressed pity for Dmitri before remembering all the things he had made him do. Forgiveness was never his best characteristic.

"I don't know how much time passed but one day a woman had replaced the soldier. Immediately, I knew she wasn't with Indians. For one, she was Middle Eastern. And two, she didn't carry herself in the all-too-serious-for-one's-own-good demeanor that we soldiers tend to have. Aisha was her name—your mother, Rajeev—and she saved me. I went back to Russia as soon as I got to the mainland, reporting my findings and retiring."

"So, no Rajeev, I didn't kill your mother, but I may have been instrumental in her demise and for that I'm sorry. Aisha was working with the Indian government, believing there needed to be a way to kill the gods that you are. She knew your kind were too powerful for their own good and that kind of power in the wrong hands could be devastating. But knowing the consequences, she still rescued a Russian spy she didn't know from Adam. I've been keeping an eye on you for a while now to honor her and only used you for my own selfish gain, I'm afraid."

Rajeev felt a tear tug at the corner of his eye and wiped it away angrily. "She was killed, so that means they were successful in creating a weapon."

Dmitri nodded.

"I assume it could be effective on daegaryns as well as knights."

"Most likely, yes."

Rajeev's head bobbed up and down in a nod that wouldn't stop.

Thirty-two hours left.

# Chapter Thirty-Nine

**As Isabella skidded** to a stop next to a Fiat in a bar gravel parking lot, she swallowed a small vial of mercury, mixing it with carbon, nitrogen, and oxygen in her stomach. She vaulted out of the Alfa Romeo and spit out the compound known as mercury fulminate via a crystal vessel formed of special salts. The door of the aging bar blew to a million pieces as well as much of the walls around it.

Before the dust could settle, several arrows flew at her, which she easily deflected by spinning *Snakebite* with supernatural reflexes.

A little mixed girl in overalls over a neon pink shirt—thirteen or fourteen years old—now stood just outside the blown door. Her eyes glowed green in the dark as the arrows returned to her open hand and a falcon landed on her shoulder.

While Isabella tried to process the threat in front of her, the ground beneath her collapsed. She fell fifteen feet before abruptly and awkwardly landing on her arse. Dirt and gravel rained down on her as she quickly leaped to her feet, her spear still held firmly in hand. Taking a second to assess her situation, Isabella hurled *Snakebite* into the top of the wall with all her might. She reached out and tried to pull back the weapon. Instead, the physics worked in favor since the spear was really anchored in, and Isabella was shot towards it. She grabbed the handle with two hands and used the momentum from the pull to fling herself out of the hole, with the agility of a practiced gymnast.

A large man with a bushy, red beard, waited for her at the edge.

"Can't say I love the new look," Isabella said to her old friend.

He grunted and swung a greatsword that appeared small in his hands. *Seaslayer.* Isabella ducked under the perpendicular swing and spat just a bit of mercury fulminate between them. The blast sent her flying over the side of the hole. She cried out in pain as hundreds of tiny pieces of gravel embedded themselves into her flesh.

But the small explosion released *Snakebite* from where it was stuck and just in time as a heavy battle axe swung down on her. It clanged against the steel shaft—just returned to her hands—breaking it into two pieces. Only the spearhead was made of the enchanted, indestructible meteorite. It was strong enough, however, that the blade didn't rip her in half, only leaving a shallow cut beneath her chest.

As the man brought his weapon back up, Isabella pushed the remnants of *Snakebite* into his shoulder. He fell to the ground and she stood up, prepared to finish the job but then a bird attacked her, clawing at her face. Isabella ripped it off and doused it an aqua regia, melting even the bones of the falcon.

A girl screamed and an arrow took Isabella's ear. She spun *Snakebite* in the air and sought out the person who did it while seething with rage. Instead, she found Eoin manipulating water from a barrel on his back. He shot it to where she was standing as the gravel was suddenly lifted and pushed to the side, exposing the dirt underneath. Soil became mud and her feet sunk into it. Before she could react, it solidified, trapping her feet into the ground. She bent down to attempt to free herself but then an arrow ripped away her index finger, eliciting a cry more of frustration than pain.

"Stop Elise!" she heard Eoin say. Isabella brought her head up to see the Irishman grabbing the girl in overalls, who was wailing about something called Horus.

"You're on the wrong side of the battle," the man with the battle axe said with a French accent, walking up to her. "In time, I hope you will see this. But for now, all I can say is sorry."

He swung the blunt end of the axe at her and then everything went black.

Savannah knelt beside Isabella as she came to consciousness. She was no longer stuck in the earth and the sun had begun to rise.

"Are you okay?" the American asked as if she actually looked okay.

Isabella ignored the question and sat up, grunting from the pain. Knights may have been able to heal, but that didn't stop the pain or soreness. "Where the fuck are they?"

"I don't know. They knocked me out after interrogating me."

For all Isabella knew, Savannah could've been lying and had went with Eoin and his team on her own volition. She would keep that in mind, but Merlin had assigned her a job so that could wait later.

"What did you tell them?" Isabella asked, knowing Savannah didn't know anything they already didn't know.

"Everything, I guess." The American didn't seem very concerned. "Where Camelot is. Where we're going. Who I am. Stuff like that. I don't care enough to argue with three Knights."

Isabella nodded and then checked the area where her ear had been. It still bled and would continue to bleed until she patched it. The same went for her finger and chest. She was pissed off but fortunate she hadn't bled completely out, though she had a pounding headache from the blood loss. Isabella had gone so long without any major injuries and now she lost an ear and a finger to a little girl. It almost made her want to go after them herself, but Isabella knew alone she would be destroyed. And she had a job to do.

She went to work creating the compound known as octyl cyanoacrylate within her stomach, using the natural ingredients it contained. Once it was finished, she spat a glob of the medical superglue into her hand and massaged it into the right side of her head—gritting her teeth through the sting—until it hardened. She repeated the process for her other wounds, rolling her eyes when Savannah averted her eyes while she lifted her shirt for the chest cut.

"They're the ones that Merlin was talking about," Isabella said. "The ones who chose a darker path. Eoin—the giant—used to be with us. He was there longer than me."

"If they're the enemy, then why did they not kill us?"

"Because they think they are good but believe me when I say they are not." Isabella picked up what was left of *Snakebite*, gazing at it with despair. The steel shaft could be replaced but she didn't know when or if it could be the same as the enchanted one she had before. "Merlin will explain."

"Nathan is what they said his name was."

Isabella looked up quickly at this. Merlin never told her his real name.

"I have to call him," Isabella said. "And tell him what happened."

Savannah acted as if she wanted to say something,

thought wisely, and kept her mouth shut.

Isabella wished she had brought some grass as she pulled out her phone and hit the most recent number. It rang for only a second before it was answered. There was no "hello" or anything on the other just silence as he waited for the emergency she had to detail.

"We have a problem," Isabella said and again there was no answer.

"I just got in a fight with Eoin. He made some friends."

A shimmering in the air caught her eye and Merlin appeared in a green robe.

He nodded at the American. "Good day, Guinevere, I hope all is well."

Savannah sputtered for a second—rightly so taken back at the man's calmness—before returning the nod.

"How long?" Merlin asked, turning back to Isabella.

"I'm not sure—we were both knocked unconscious—but judging by the time, four hours at least."

"Who was with Sir Lancelot?"

"The Earth and Life Knight."

"Sir Gawain and Sir Gareth," Merlin said to himself. "A powerful duo. How experienced were they?"

"The Life Knight was only a young girl, yet she took my ear and finger." The words stung to Isabella, but she made sure her face didn't show any signs of embarrassment. Merlin found feelings to be a sign of weakness. "The other one was even more powerful. And we both know how Eoin was. More importantly, they could work together, using their abilities in unison."

Merlin rubbed at his peach fuzz. Isabella still found it odd that the man in front of her couldn't even legally drink in his native country.

"I will deal with them," he said. "Any other problems to be had on this adventure?"

Isabella thought back to the situation with the French police. She considered not telling the wizard boy, but she figured he'd find out eventually, if he didn't know already. There was also the notion that he could read minds.

"We had a . . . complication with some police in Strasbourg."

"I know. Thank you for thy honesty, but it was dealt with poorly."

Isabella raised her eyes in question.

"You should have dispatched of all who witnessed thy 'resurrection' rather than just incapacitate them."

"You know how I feel about killing."

"And I am sure quite a few of thy friends would disagree with that statement."

She didn't respond but instead focused on maintaining eye contact with her mentor and keeping a straight face.

"Anyhow," Merlin turned and smiled in an unnatural manner at Savannah. "I wish you good luck and great health on the rest of thy quest. Farewell."

And with that, he was gone. Silence followed his leave where Savannah stared pointedly at her, and Isabella tried to recover from the encounter.

"Let's go," she finally said. "We have to go back and get our shit and then return to the road."

# Chapter Forty

**Purple was all** there was. An endless sea that drifted before and after time. An expanse that will never be fully understood by the minds of man. The Next connected everything and that's where Merlin currently resided. He meditated with legs crossed in the classical sense. He neither floated nor sat; he was just present. Physics did not exist in that realm.

Being omnipresent, the Next could be used to search out any person in existence. It was difficult work to narrow down a single person out of the nearly eight billion on Earth. And that was just for this world. The Next stretched across an infinite number of universes, plenty with different versions of the same person. So, it indeed was a difficult task.

Ector was more experienced in the Next and would have a much easier time searching for the treacherous knights, but he had a more important assignment to complete. Merlin was more powerful, anyway. He was omniscient enough to realize he was no god; the Next was a humbling domain. However, no individual could stand against him in his own world. He had met the old gods and they lay trapped in their lunacy.

Lancelot and his friends would be found. It was only a

matter of time.

He allowed his mind to relax, focusing only on the extreme quiet of his purple surroundings. Then he let it slowly stretch in every direction, poking around for any sign of a knight. Thousands appeared before him, few from his universe, many more from others. He sorted through the faces that blurred as his enhanced consciousness rejected one after the other. Soon, he found Tristan with Guinevere where he left them. Bors in Germany. But that is where it ended. Kay and Ector were in the Next, so they couldn't be detected. Someone was blocking him, and there were only a handful of beings who could do that. It could've been the old gods, but they never cared about their universe throughout the past eras. There was Ector, but Merlin knew with great confidence that the man would never betray him. And Bors knew not to mess with him. So, it could only be one person. Arthur. The one person who could rival him in power. He was out there somewhere. They would find him—Ector was working on it now.

But for now, Merlin pushed. Pushed his mind to its limit like he had only done two other times. Millions of faces flashed past his third eye. He wiped blood from his nose yet still pushed as his body deteriorated and rebuilt itself in a painful process. He didn't know how long he stayed that way, but finally, he found something. It wasn't Arthur but it may have been just as sweet.

A rare, genuine smile crossed his face.

# Chapter Forty-One

**Santos typically tended** to stay away from large crowds of people. Too many hands that could be carrying a knife to kill him. But after much meditation into the future, he found that the odds of death were slim—only twenty-three out of the thousand scenarios he studied. It was Oktoberfest in Munich; he would attend as he did every year.

Pushing his way through the crowd in his beige trench coat, he kept a careful eye out for the person that had stabbed him in fourteen of the scenarios. A Caucasian male 6'2, 6'3 in height and about 210 pounds. He wore a gray turtleneck with some lettering that was blocked by the swarming crowd. A clean-shaven face and brown eyes didn't help separate him from the thousands of other tourists. Then there was the brunette in the vibrant blue dress, inappropriate for the cool weather, but perfect to match her eyes. Both passed and no knife found itself in his back.

He found a stand with not too long of a line and waited with his back to a neighboring tent. Fifteen minutes later, he faced a woman dressed in a dirndl that showed her large breasts. She smiled brightly at him between rosy cheeks.

"*Weissbier und obatzda und brezn, bitte,*" Santos asked kindly but not hiding where his gaze landed.

A moment later, he ventured around the tents, carrying a frothy, overfilling beer and a thick pretzel with Bavarian cheese dip. He sat down in the grass, well away from a couple of drunks passed out behind the tent. Santos checked his watch given to him by the girl he met here forty-two years ago.

It didn't seem that long ago. Santos had found evidence that there was a girl here in Munich with the beautiful gift of life. Everton had joined him in his search. Back then they had wanted to rescue knights from themselves and teach them how to control their powers and use them for good. There were no politics. No impending war. No Merlin.

Oktoberfest was in full go, making it extremely difficult to pinpoint the girl. For days, they searched for her, leaving the festival with bellies full of beer, pretzels, and sausages. One afternoon, an elderly man dropped to the floor in one of the tents, going into cardiac arrest. Just moments later, a girl appeared beside the man. She was in her mid-twenties with dark hair and a slim figure. Santos had felt himself pulled to her, an oasis in the desert a knight must trek. He was in love and didn't even know her name.

The girl had pressed her hands on the man—one on his chest, the other on his temple. Her eyes glowed green like that of a summer pine and a minute later the man sat up. They had found the Life Knight.

Santos checked his watch and finished his beer, throwing away the remainder of the pretzel. He walked to the edge of the festival and called taxi services and had one come pick him up. Soon, a cream-colored vehicle pulled up in front of him and he got in.

"*Der bahnhof, bitte*," he told the driver.

At the train station, he scanned his pre-purchased ticket and boarded. It would take approximately four hours to reach Berlin. To pass the time, he sipped from a glass of Fernet Branca mixed with orange juice—they tragically did not have his preferred choice of Amargo Obrero and grapefruit juice—and read from a book called *Your Next Five Moves: Master the Art of Business Strategy*. He didn't have plans to start a business, but Santos fully believed in the old adage: knowledge is power. It was a goal of his to learn something new every day. One never knew when they might need the information.

The miles of clustered trees with leaves changing from green to yellow, red, and orange ended and the history-rich city of Berlin began. The train came to a stop and he exited, leaving for the terminal where a woman held a sign with his name on it. She was skinny with cheekbones that jutted angrily out at him. The only greeting from her was a slight nod. No more words were exchanged as she led him outside to a jet-black Mercedes with windows of an even darker tent. He sat in the back and soon they were at the capitol building: the Reichstag.

It was a similar, three-section design to other European capital buildings with an unpainted, stone masonry and pillars that ran across the entirety of the anterior end. The greatest distinction was the glass dome over the center.

Santos followed the woman across the recently trimmed lawn and over the, fortunately, few-in-number stairs. She led him to the domed room lit up in a way only sunlight could do. Empty blue seats surrounded a podium. Well, empty except for one. He approached the man who seemed of similar age to him.

"Herr Santos," the man said in a harsh, German accent without turning. "*Willkommen im Reichstagsdom.*"

Santos had reached the man and took a seat next to him. "*Abend, Kanzler Baur.*"

"They think we did it," Chancellor Baur said, foregoing

pleasantries as he stared straight ahead.

"There are whispers," Santos agreed. "But no declarations. I've been doing what I can to ease your neighbors' grievances against Germany."

Baur nodded, not appearing to be much relieved.

"I had expected to be speaking with President Schneider."

"President Schneider has unfortunately been bed-stricken for the past month. The stress of the situation has been a bit too much, I'm afraid."

*What a leader they have here.*

"It is indeed a difficult situation we are all in," was all Santos said.

"Who did it?" The chancellor asked as he rapidly tapped his foot into the floor, anger finally appearing in his voice. "Who set off a nuclear bomb on our border, killing seventy thousand of our people."

A profile of Baur had shown a paranoid tendency. Santos tapped into it now. He let out a sigh and his shoulders sunk down as if he was giving away some top-secret information. "Spies in Russia told us there has been talk of a return of the USSR. We're not sure if the bombing is related to them. But we're doing everything we can to find out.

Baur finally turned to Santos, eyes like saucers. "It was them wasn't it? I should've known."

"Now we can't jump to any conclusions," Santos said but knew the chancellor already had.

"What should we do?"

*Tell Schneider to get his fat ass out of bed and meet with the neighboring leaders himself to make amends. Suck their unused cocks if that's what it takes.*

"Nothing for now. I have everything in control," Santos said instead and leaned in close. "But between you and me, prepare in secret for war."

# Chapter FortyTwo

## Savannah

**A large cloud** of smoke was captured by the surrounding, temperate air of Serbia as the Alfa Romeo sped with the top down past a pastel of reds, oranges, and yellows. Isabella and Savannah had left immediately once Merlin had disappeared, stopping only to pick up their baggage from the hotel.

The Brit let go of the wheel for a terrifying moment to relight the blunt with a Bic and then took a heavy drag before returning her injured hand to the wheel. This was her second one—though the first was only half—since they had been on the road and Savannah was worried. Behind those crazed, hazel eyes, Savannah saw a million thoughts being processed. She wanted to ask her about what Elise had said on her Naval experience but feared the answer. So, she went with her second question.

"You knew him," Savannah said. "Eoin McGowan."

Isabella glanced over at her and took another hit, seemingly contemplating whether to say anything. "Yes," she said eventually. "He used to be one of us. When I was first . .

. brought to Camelot, he, Immanuel, and Everton were the only ones there."

Isabella touched the places where her ear and finger had been. She had been doing this here and there for the entirety of the drive, apparently, hoping they'd be there next time she went for them.

"Everton was the boss and Immanuel was . . . never really there. They were both at least a decade older than me. Eoin had joined not much earlier and soon we had become good friends."

"Did he take you on your 'quest?' "

"Back then we didn't do quests. Immanuel would drop us off at the portal where we would do our trial with the old gods. Merlin created the quests."

"The old gods?"

"You'll see." Isabella swerved past a white Camry. "When he kidnapped Sabine, I felt lost. He was my best friend. My only friend."

"He said he was just protecting her," Savannah said, defending a man she barely knew.

"He lied," Isabella said without giving any reasoning.

The rest of the drive out of Serbia was in silence, crossing the border two hours later. They had to stop at a check-in to show an official their passports, something they only had to do one other time—when entering Serbia from Hungary—due to something called the Schengen Agreement. Savannah had been surprised to see Isabella remove a passport with her name and face on it from the middle compartment. She had never left the country so had no need for one. The Brit explained it was forged like that's a perfectly normal thing to do.

## Rajeev

Eighteen hours—even with Rajeev and Dmitri switching

off—were all they could do. Rajeev kept nodding off seventeen hours in with Dmitri passed out and beyond resuscitation, but he saw a sign for Damascus and pushed himself to get there. Once there, he didn't bother to find a place to stay the night and just laid back and closed his eyes under the lights of a random grocery store parking lot.

Sun penetrated Rajeev's eyes through a red lens, feeling as if he had only closed them moments ago. He rolled his head to the right and saw to no surprise that Dmitri was still asleep, snoring at his normal high octave.

With a great amount of will, he pulled himself out of the BMW and entered the store, returning with a couple of energy drinks and a large bag of honey-spiced nuts, which he would try to consume before the Russian arose from his slumber and took the open bag as an offering.

Today was the day the other knights were to be entering Turkey, though he didn't know what time. There were sixteen hours left—or at least until Istanbul—and he didn't even know how he would find them. Maybe Dmitri could make a call to that Fernando character when they got into the country.

Fifteen minutes later, when the stolen car found its way back on the interstate, Rajeev woke the Russian to ask. Dmitri bestirred with a grumble but the extra sleep seemed to put him in a better mood than yesterday.

"If my old friend wants you to meet those two—or more—knights then you will meet those two—or more—knights," Dmitri said and then closed his eyes.

"Why?"

With eyes still shut, he said, "I don't know. He's resourceful that's all. I've found it best not to question him."

That seemed to be all he would get out of the Russian and again the radio became his only company.

And his thoughts.

What would he do when he found the knights? Would they be able to help him take Halgarth? Would they even be enough? Could that thing—another daegaryn or something worse?—that disrupted his metal-vision be able to temporarily "turn off" his powers?

The dastardly twins known as stress and anxiety accompanied him out of Syria and into Turkey, whispering their buffoonery in both ears all the way to the historical city of Istanbul.

## Savannah

Now in Bulgaria, they continued on for another four hours—stopping once for gas and a smoke break for Savannah since she never felt comfortable lighting up in the convertible—until they get to Sliven.

Appearing like a city from Middle-Earth, the Bulgarian city lay within the Balkan Mountains' embrace. A fog welcomed the girls as they drove down into the valley. They passed buildings with red-clay roofs as they moved slowly through empty streets, on the search for a café—Isabella could never just settle for a McDonald's; she needed a taste of the culture.

They found one on the corner of a block. There were five tables out front but only one was occupied by a group of twenty-something year olds.

It appeared the fear of war stretched all the way to the end of Europe.

They seated themselves at a table covered with a thin layer of grease and were waited on by a dejected old woman. After rapidly tapping into her phone, Isabella pointed at a couple of items on the menu and the woman left without a word. She returned not much later with two plates of presumably pre-made food. The first dish some kind of pastry that the Brit called a *banitsa*. The unexpected combination of eggs and cheese within a sweet, airy bread greeted Savannah's tongue and she went in for another bite. The second platter, *sarmi*, contained what appeared to be dumplings. She took a less hesitant bite than she did with the banitsa, this time, however, her taste buds did not approve of the Bulgarian food. The wrapping was cabbage that was somehow made to look like dough. Inside, there was rice and meat that was chewier than it probably should have been. The cabbage reminded her of Cormac and his Reuben wraps that she threw up over the side of *Merlin's Breath*. Savannah had some more of the banitsa and let Isabella finish the sarmi.

## Rajeev

Istanbul didn't do much to impress him. There were no skyscrapers or buildings of marvelous, modern architecture. Only a mosque—identified by its domed ceilings and prominence in the Islamic city—with six minarets rising above it did much to draw his awe.

They found a small café along the Sea of Marmara to eat for the first time all day—those nuts did not last long as Dmitri found the time to wake up and eat the majority of it before falling back to sleep. Rajeev had wanted to continue on to the Bulgarian-Turkish border, but Dmitri insisted they'd be able to still catch the knights after a quick dinner.

A waiter greeted them almost immediately after they had sat down with cups of water and Dmitri ordered first, surprising the man with his fluency in Arabic to the point he actually started clapping. He got the lamb *inegol kofte* and a bowl of *ezogelin corba*. Rajeev took the waiter's suggestion and went with the *manti*.

"What will we do after we meet up with the knights?" Rajeev asked once the waiter had left with their orders.

"Hmm, so Fernando, my friend on the phone, said I needed to stay with you to make sure you don't do something stupid. Going after the daegaryns, for example."

"What!" Rajeev said a little too loudly, drawing looks from the nearby customers. He lowered his voice. "You've been leading me on about getting my revenge and now you tell me to throw it all out?"

"Rajeev!" Dmitri covered his heart with a sun-spotted hand. "You keep hearing what you want to hear. I never once supported your mad quest for vengeance. Actually, it was quite the opposite. I convinced you to leave that cave. I pushed you all the way to Turkey. For all you know, there might not be another knight in the entire Middle East. It was my word against, well . . . nobody's."

"Don't you want to go after them?" Rajeev asked. "They took your eye for goodness sake."

"It's not that I don't want." Dmitri held his hands out. "It's just that I'd have a better chance of storming into Halgarth and returning with a hundred pairs of daegaryn eyes than to go against Fernando's will."

The idea that he was now working for somebody else—except this time it's his own life on the line, not Yasmin's—didn't do much to settle his worries. "If I am not shaking the hand of another one of me by the end of the day, I will take your other eye."

"Oh, the knights will be there. Don't get your skivvies in a twist."

Rajeev opened his mouth to further berate Dmitri, but the waiter returned with their dinner.

With their bellies finally full, the pair continued through Istanbul in the BMW. Thirty minutes later, the great city had disappeared from the rearview mirror.

## Savannah

Their night would not end in Europe, and they left Sliven as soon as the check was paid with Isabella's credit card that seemingly had no limit. And it was only two hours until they were at the Turkey border. The wait to cross was longer than any for the other countries they went to, but eventually they were through.

The plan was to reach Istanbul and find a hotel for the night. And so that was where they drove when a small humming in the back of Savannah's head distracted her from the foreign scenery. She almost dismissed it as her imagination, but with how her life was now she thought it might be worth mentioning.

Isabella nodded at the inquiry, another blunt between the fingers of her complete hand—Savannah wasn't sure where she found the time to roll them. "It means we are—"

A large mass slammed into the Romeo. She heard something pop in her shoulder and then a sharp, more painful crack in her neck. And even before the car had stopped rolling, she felt her bones and joints moving uncomfortably under her skin. The convertible came to a halt on its passenger side. The pain from the crash was already diminishing and she hurriedly unfastened her seat belt to fall onto dry grass that caught immediately on fire. It wasn't until then that she realized she too was inflamed. And naked.

"Savannah!" Isabella called and Savannah saw to her surprise that the Brit was *behind* her and struggling to her feet. Her femur was edging its way back into her leg. Savannah vomited at the sight. "Behind you!"

Savannah turned around, not even trying to extinguish herself. A massive human being with a dragon tattoo wrapped around his bulging, olive forearm walked around the remains of the Alfa Romeo. *A daegaryn.*

Thinking of James burnt in her arms, she didn't freeze,

instead pointing her hands at the monster, and fully opened her furnace, barely comprehending that she was screaming at the top of her lungs. Flames roared out of her, engulfing the daegaryn. But it just smiled at her and continued moving towards her.

Something whistled by her ear and flew at it. The thing caught it with dizzying speed and twirled it between its fingers. *Snakebite*. Looking over her shoulder, Savannah saw Isabella pulling at it with an invisible force, but instead the daegaryn used that force to pull *her*. The Brit flew over her like a ragdoll into the monster's grasp, whose smile never wavered through the altercation.

The daegaryn's head then exploded into a thousand pieces. Isabella fell to a knee and looked around with what was left of *Snakebite* in her normal hand. Standing in the middle of the road beside a truck, stood a Middle Eastern man. He approached them, wearing only a tank top and shorts, eyes fading from a dull gray to an earthy brown. In his hand, he held a hilt where shards of metal reformed upon.

Isabella still stood in a defensive position, but Savannah let fire dwindle back into her furnace. Someone who kills a daegaryn is a friend to her.

"Hello." He smiled up at them—he was probably five-foot-seven. A goatee below a sensible mustache decorated his face. "My name is Rajeev Patel, and I am here to help."

# Part 3

---

# A Trial by Fire

*When you walk through the fire you will not be burned; the flames will not set you ablaze.*

Isaiah 43:2 (NIV)

# Chapter FortyThree

**The man calling** himself Rajeev, focused his gaze on Isabella, seemingly embarrassed at Savannah's nakedness.

"I'm Savannah Hamlin," she introduced herself.

"Isabella Knowles," the Brit said, eyes narrowed as she tried to get a read on the stranger.

"Uh, very nice to meet you two," he ripped off his tank top, revealing a wiry, cut frame with the mark of a shield on his chest, and held it out for her. "Here. Do you two speak Arabic?"

"No," Savannah said, slipping it on. The height difference between them caused it to only barely cover her belly button. "But it seems you speak English."

He gave her a puzzled look. "No, I…how do you understand what I'm saying?"

"Knights unconsciously translate each other," Isabella said. "I guess it was something the first Merlin had built into our marks."

"*First* Merlin?' Rajeev asked. "There's another?" His face reddened as he noticed how loosely the shirt covered Savannah and spun quickly around. "Dmitri! Get out and give her your shirt."

Savannah was so transfixed on the man, that she never noticed the black BMW. An old, fat man with a disheveled beard and an eyepatch exited it.

"What, I was enjoying the show," the newcomer said in a Russian accent, letting out a heavy guffaw.

Isabella actually let out a growl in reply.

"I'm just kidding, okay, okay." He removed his shirt, showing off an entirely different type of physique with no mark. "Anyway, I prefer sword fighting if you know what I mean."

Seeing the sweat pooling down the Russian's face, Savannah almost denied the offering and Donald Duck it, but she figured she wouldn't be able to get a proper conversation out of Rajeev if her cooter was hanging out.

Wearing a tiny tank top and a t-shirt wrapped awkwardly around her waist, she felt even more uncomfortable than when she was naked.

"That's Dmitri Smirnov," Rajeev said of the Russian. He was much more comfortable now that she was semi-clothed. "He's a pain in the ass but has information and contacts that I need."

"You have powers, don't you?" Savannah asked.

"Yes. Some have called me the Iron Knight." Rajeev let a small smile touch his face. "And I assume you are the Fire Knight."

"Ember, and the Brit, here who is sizing you up, is the Poison Knight."

"Alchemy, actually," Isabella said with narrowed hazel eyes. "Why are you here?"

"Not that we aren't thankful for your help," Savannah added.

"Fernando told us where to find you," Rajeev answered.

Savannah turned to the Brit who had an equal look of confusion on her face. She could tell that the Middle Eastern man had expected a different response.

"Uh, so Fernando doesn't really make contact with knights," Dmitri said. "He only interferes when it's absolutely necessary. It prevents any, er, conflicts of interest."

"Conflicts of interest?" Isabella asked.

"He plays all sides of the field, so needs to appear un-aligned with any possible opposition."

"So, we're just a part of his chess game?"

"Well." Dmitri seemed very uncomfortable around three disagreeable knights. "Yes, actually. But, for the most part, you are kings that he protects. He moves others around and only your kind when he absolutely needs to, which is rare. Fernando's a great chess player."

Rajeev's eyes scrunched as he attempted to follow the conversation. Savannah thought it was because this informa-tion was all new to him until Dmitri translated for him in what she could only assume was Arabic. But the confusion only grew thicker on his diminutive facial features.

"And I guess you're the pawn that brought Rajeev here," Isabella said after the Middle Eastern was caught up—this language barrier would get annoying pretty quick. "Why?"

"Ah . . . yes. I've always been a foot soldier even before I worked with—or perhaps for—Fernando. It's who I am." he cleared his throat. "Now for the 'why;' I don't know. I have learned to not ask questions."

"Then . . . wait here, I got to make a call." Without taking her eyes off the odd duo, she removed her phone and hit a single button. Savannah presumed she was calling Merlin, but Isabella put it down almost immediately. "Straight to voice-mail, dammit." She fixated on Dmitri. "We have somewhere to be. And you're not coming with us."

The Russian opened his mouth to say something, but Rajeev cut him off. "At least let us take you to Istanbul. You, uh . . . seem to be lacking in transportation."

Isabella became somehow even more tense at that but didn't say no.

"Then it's settled," Dmitri clapped his hands together. "I call shotgun, as you Americans call it." He winked at Savannah.

The back seats of the BMW were sticky with God knows what. *At least it's not my clothes I'm sitting on it with,* Savannah thought. Isabella didn't appear to notice the state of the seats, instead she kept a careful hand on *Snakebite* and stared holes into the back of their saviors' heads.

"Where are you two heading?" Rajeev asked once they were all settled and on their way.

"Turkmenistan," Savannah blurted out, eliciting an elbow in the side by the Brit.

"Why there?"

"None of your business," Isabella answered quickly, giving Savannah a dirty look.

"Hmm." He glanced into the rearview mirror and nodded. It was silent for a few moments with only the sound of Arabic music coming from the radio, before he spoke again. "Is this your first run-in with daegaryns?"

Savannah glanced at Isabella before answering. "No, they . . . they killed someone close to me."

There was sympathy in his eyes when he again peered at her through the rearview. "They killed my wife." Rajeev raised his left hand to show her his wedding ring. "The daegaryn who attacked you, Balthasar, had kidnapped me and taken me to their lair. They wanted me to get the Grail for them, instead I found my sword and killed one of them. In retaliation, they killed my wife. Yasmin. That was three days ago." He turned down the radio, playing some song in Arabic. "I know where they live—just outside Mecca—come with me, and we can get our revenge together."

"Rajeev," Dmitri started but was cut off.

"No. I can't beat them myself but with you two—perhaps more if we can find others—we can. What waits for you in Turkmenistan couldn't possibly be more important than that."

"We're going to Turkmenistan to get a sword," Savannah said and was stared down by Isabella. "A magical one—like yours, I guess—one that can kill daegaryns. After that, there are three others with powers from the group Isabella is in. One of them took on three daegaryns at once, killing two of them. They can help."

Beside her, Isabella shifted in her sticky seat and Savannah asked her a question with her eyes. She shook her head but didn't say anything.

"Then we'll go to Turkmenistan together and get our revenge soon after," Rajeev said.

Savannah knew she should feel glad but judging by the unsettled Isabella and the satisfied Dmitri, she felt something was amiss.

# Chapter Forty Four

**A pair of** shadows inspected a car wreck after a squad of false-facing police officers and hazard workers cordoned off this section of E80 due to the turnover of a vehicle carrying a highly toxic substance. The headless daegaryn rested in the middle of the road with a halo of pieces of his brain and skull.

"Want a smoke?" one asked the other.

Eyes from under the hood he wore penetrated hers.

"Ah, yes. Scared of fire," she flicked open a lighter. "Such an irrational fear for your age. How old are you again? Like fifteen hundred years old?"

The other phantom raised the warhammer by his side.

"Fine, I'll put it out, but not because I think you'd beat me in a fight."

There was a silence where the woman kept tapping her feet to the annoyance of her companion.

"So, what have you been up to?" she asked.

He gave her another unspoken answer.

"Of course, but do you, like, have any hobbies other than cleaning up messes? No? Well, maybe you should start crocheting; it helps me unwind from this work stress." She slapped a hand to her face. "Ohmygod. We could be crochet buddies." She waved at their black, drab clothing. "We even both have the same great taste in fashion."

A nasally sound came out of the man's ruined mouth. She leaned close.

"What? Bors, don't be silly. We can both shadow them, at least until Santos tells us otherwise. It'd be nice to have some company. Sometimes I feel like all this loneliness is making me *insane*." Her eyes became saucers at this last part.

Another whisper.

"I don't know, he should be here soon." She put her hands on her hips and stuck out her bottom lip. "Wait, don't tell me you aren't enjoying our conversation."

"Miss me?" a voice called from above and landed before them, flashing his easy-going smile. He was young with olive skin and curly hair.

"Ilcaeus," She gave him a hug and a full kiss on the lips. "Where have you been? I feel like I haven't seen you in *forever*."

"If I told you, I'd have to kill you." There was a glint in his reptilian eyes.

Bors whispered something.

"It will be my pleasure, Sir Bors!" he said good-humored-ly, then lifted the Alfa Romeo as if it was its Hot Wheels version. He launched himself back into the sky, sending a minor sonic wave into the shadows that caused them to stagger a bit backwards.

Ilcaeus returned a few moments later and hovered over the remains of the daegaryn. "Whenever one of these guys turn up dead, I always wonder if they're a relative. Daegaryns have been inbreeding for centuries, so it's very possible. Like I think maybe that's Cousin John. For all I know, that could be my dad lying there."

"That's Balthasar," she said. "And, unless he felt the need

for a change, he takes his pleasure with his sister."

He nodded and took off with the body, coming back with a pressure washer from God knows where. The three of them went to work, cleaning up the scene and soon it seemed like nothing ever happened on this section of European Route 80. It would be up to others to plant the traces of a wreck and radiation leak expected from the crash of the supposed hazard vehicle.

"It's been too long, Tess," Ilcaeus said as they prepared to part ways.

"Yes, it has," Tess agreed. "You need to stop by my place sometime. Have ourselves a good time."

"You don't have 'a place' and you know that won't happen. Bors, it was good to see you again." Without waiting for a response, Ilcaeus jetted off to wherever next he was needed.

"So . . . now what, Bors?" Tess asked of her silent partner, but at that moment, her phone decided to buzz. She answered it and listened to the calm, yet commanding, voice on the other end.

"Yes sir," she said eventually then heard a click. Tess turned to Bors. "Well, it seems I'm needed in Guatemala."

The mostly emotionless assassin almost brightened at the statement.

Tess frowned. "Well, it's been a pleasure as always, Bors." She looked down at herself. "Do I have much blood on me? I'm going to try to get an Uber and I'd hate for them to think that I might kill them."

# Chapter Forty-Five

**"Light your hand,"** Isabella commanded of her tutor. "No, your hand, HAND!"

They had stayed the night in Istanbul—Savannah doubted the Brit had slept a wink—then drove for eight-plus hours—after Isabella had gotten Rajeev to scrub the seats—before taking a break in the Amasya. First, they had stopped for food, allowing the newcomers to order their dishes. When Isabella's Middle Eastern meal was sat before her, she brought it to her nose and inhaled deeply to the oddity of all those around her. Savannah had a feeling the Brit would never trust Rajeev and Dmitri.

But now that their stomachs were full, Isabella wanted to train some, apparently not impressed with Savannah's display against the daegaryn. She found an isolated place on the other side of the Yeşilırmak River. The focus today was control. Starting out easy, Savannah was just trying to enflame her hand, though even that simple task had become difficult; the fire just kept creeping up her arm.

"Concentrate!" Isabella yelled in her face. She had been

even more of a bitch lately, Savannah didn't know if it was because of the strangers or something else.

"I can't concentrate when you're screaming in my face," Savannah said with the same intensity.

"Your little fire show yesterday could've killed anybody in close proximity."

"It's not like you did much to help," Savannah said, the arguing didn't do anything to assist her control of the fire. "Without Rajeev saving us, we'd both be dead."

"And wouldn't he like you to think that?" Isabella's face had gone beet red. "Why don't you quit praising him and fill your gob with his knob. Yeah, I see the way you look at him. At least then you'd shut the fuck up."

"Why don't I intercede," Rajeev started. He appeared a lot more timid now for someone who had killed a daegaryn without barely any effort yesterday.

Isabella marched up to the Qatari—he had shared much of his earlier life with them during the drive—until she was eye-to-eye with him. He was visibly worried. "The only reason I let you come with us was because I rather you try to attack me from the front than from behind. I don't trust you and will *never* trust you. You understand?"

Before he could answer, Dmitri spoke up, grinning madly as he chomped on Twizzlers. "You do remember that it's our car, so technically you came with us."

"You fat, powerless twat." Now she turned to him. "Even with all that lard around your bearded neck, I could still strangle you with one hand. And also, I'm really sure that a Qatari and a Russian got a BMW with a Saudi Arabia license plate legally."

Instead of answering and perhaps risking his life, he pulled from his shirt pocket a tightly rolled blunt.

"Is that . . ."

"If you were going to say Purple Paradise, you'd be

wrong," Dmitri said. "It's a strand known as *Rahmat Allah*. Or in your most ugly language, God's Mercy. It's surprisingly difficult to get the stuff in this country. I've never been fond of this stinky cigarette, but I heard you love the stuff."

"Heard from this Fernando character?"

"No, from your tall friend there." He nodded at Savannah, who couldn't decide if she should feel proud or scared.

"Hmm, well I do enjoy smoking." She was trying really hard to keep the smile off her face as she took the blunt. "But this doesn't mean I trust you. And remember I can detect poisons within seconds of inhaling it, then create an antidote to combat it."

"Oh, I wouldn't dare to attempt to poison the Alchemy Knight." He seemed very pleased with himself.

"You didn't happen to buy a lighter too, did you?"

"I didn't think you needed one." Dmitri gestured at Savannah.

Isabella scowled. "You're lucky I'm now in a good mood."

She walked over to Savannah and held out God's Mercy. "Don't burn me, bitch."

Savannah returned the Brit's angsty expression and allowed a small flame to unfurl from her index finger. She touched the tip of the blunt. Isabella quickly stuck it between her lips and took a couple of short hits. Instantly, it seemed like a great weight had left her body.

"Control," she said at last, her voice calmest it's been in days. "Sometimes requires less thought. See how you lit your finger and only your finger? You have to both concentrate and not overthink. Fire only acts at your command, so keep a steady mind. Now remember, use your anchor and enflame your hand."

The skin under the burning heart on her chest heated up as she activated her furnace and allowed the flames to course through her arteries, rising to her shoulder then down her arm, and finally to her waiting hand. Fire erupted in the center of her palm and stayed there. She could feel it trying to spread but it took only moments before it became autonomic.

"Very good," Isabella said, the weed taking its blissful effect on her. She was a lot more manageable to be around when high. "Now do your other hand, but faster."

For thirty minutes, she practiced control under the Brit's calm gaze, while Rajeev and Dmitri watched from the side, both obviously bored, before taking a short break. Savannah was sweating profusely and took a heavy drag from a cigarette that she had picked up in Istanbul.

"Once you finish that ciggie," Isabella said, her blunt long gone but her high only growing. "We'll work on control *outside* of the body. My powers don't go to that extent, so this will be new territory for both of us. But thankfully, we have Rajeev here who does have experience with that."

Rajeev sat up from where he lounged on the grass by the river, having denied the offer of a cigarette from Savannah. Dmitri was fast asleep beside him. "I'm not a good teacher," he said. "And can't really explain how I do what I do. It's just instinct."

"Just try, at least."

He stood up, leaving his sword behind. "Metal is a lot different than fire. For the most part, it's stable, while fire has a mind of its own. But I'll do what I can."

Reaching into his pocket, he removed a handful of coins. Speaking absently, he said, "Keeping change handy was an old habit before I got that," he motioned to his sword. "It was an easy way to defend myself. It was also something simple that I could practice my powers on." The coins floated and whirled around his hand at lightning speed. "I could push it away and pull it back to me, but it took me a while before I had any sense of control outside of that. It wasn't until I turned to other forces rather than just the item I wanted to move that I became proficient in the art." The coins dropped back in his palm. "If you took any high school physics class, you'd know we live within a magnetic field. It appears to me only when I clear my mind and *really* concentrate. Even then it's only barely visible as tiny ripples—almost like the squiggles you get when you look at the sun for too long. Through some experimentation, I found I can use the field as leverage, pushing it at the coins from every side." Rajeev demonstrated this, hovering the change out in front of him. "I could lessen pressure from one end to move them to the opposite end. With much practice, I stopped needing to rely on the magnetic field." He squinted at her. "Do you have something like that?"

Savannah thought hard about whether or not she had ever seen any "ripples" or "squiggles" appear in her vision. At last, she shook her head, sheepishly.

"Oxygen," Dmitri said from where he had been supposedly sleeping. His one eye stared at her. Savannah had a feeling that cold, blue eye would haunt her dreams. "is what fire needs to survive, not much different from us. You may be able to picture it as a grid and only ignite what you want to ignite. As your angry friend says, much of your powers are psychological. Try it."

Isabella opened her mouth—to criticize or thank, Savannah didn't know—but was cut off by the Russian. "I've worked with knights since before you were born."

"I'll try it." Savannah closed her eyes and instead of relying on her furnace, she solely used her mind. And there, red balls—a remnant of high school chemistry—floated all around her. When she opened her eyes, she could still kind of visualize it.

They had bought a couple of six-packs of some Turkish soda to use as target practice. She now turned to them— the bottles having been previously spread out on the ground some distance away—and enflamed her hand, where it stayed.

Focusing on the leftmost soda and the line of oversized oxygen molecules before it—highlighted in her mind's eye—she ejected a stream of flames, trying to keep them within the trajectory. It exploded into a million shards.

Applause erupted from the audience, disrupting her zin.

"Well done," Isabella said, seemingly impressed for the first time Savannah had known her. She turned to Dmitri and gave him a nod. Respect for her and the Russian, another first. *What was in that blunt?* "Very well done."

"Now destroy a bottle without releasing fire from yourself," Dmitri said, now standing next to Isabella. "Spontaneous creation."

"Is that even possible?" the Brit asked. "My experience has shown that our powers are anchored to the source of it," she tapped her breast—hidden for once; revealing clothing was hard to find around here.

"I've seen it happen," he said. "It's difficult to achieve but possible."

Savannah nodded then faced the bottles with a fiery hand out. She highlighted the grid where one of the sodas was. Flames spewed out of her palm, exploding the targeted bottle. She sighed but was still happy with the results; it was a light-and-day difference from a week ago.

After a couple of more failed attempts—though, still successful in their own rights—she gave up for the time being. Sweat had soaked through her clothes, and she had a pounding headache.

"Let's call it a day," Isabella said. "You've improved enough today and may actually not burn all your clothes next time a daegaryn decides to stop by."

That was about as good as a compliment Savannah would get from the Brit. She'd take it.

# Chapter Forty-Six

**With brown eyes** that took in everything, Santos pushed his way through the crowded streets of Jerusalem, fully aware of the hundreds of sleeves that could hide the tool of his demise. A look into the future hadn't given him as much reassurance as he would like, so on both sides of him walked two men, both with opposing statures. To his left, was an Israeli officer with a mustache that only soldiers seemed to pull off. On the other side, a shadow towered over the sea of humanity.

Glinting with the Arabian sun that turned his armpits into a swamp was a golden lid covering an octagonal building. The Dome of the Rock, they called it, an apt name considering the surrounding topography. Past meetings had been in the Knesset but after recent circumstances, the president preferred meeting somewhere a bit more holy.

The officer radioed somebody and two soldiers materialized out the front door. Being in constant dispute with Gaza led to a large security presence, especially in regard to a person in such a high government position as Santos.

The trio was herded inside the building where even more members of the military stood sentry. And at the center of the rotunda was Prime Minister Caleb Yisrael, sitting in presumably his office chair. He was young with curly hair and round glasses that didn't make him appear any older. Hovering over him stood the unofficial Secretary of Yahweh—a position established several decades hence and occupied at a variable manner—Shai Klein.

The rabbi stood in contrast against his better, an old man with a hunched back and a floppy jowl. Having a rabbi on the government payroll is typically unsanctioned but when money passes into the right hands, eyes tend to look the other way. When questioned about his rabbi, Yisrael said he was only there for the lightening of his soul.

Santos had his ear in enough places to know that was not the case, where actually the Prime Minister didn't do anything without Klein's say-so. Yisrael believed that a nation founded by God should be ruled by him.

"Fernando!" Yisrael said in English and, taking to his feet, hurried over to the alarm of the soldiers around. "It has been too long, my friend. I've been thinking about what you said about that Leviticus passage and really have some interesting thoughts to propose to you."

"Unfortunately, I'm not here to discuss theology." Santos shook the offered hand.

"Yes," the Prime Minister's face dropped. "Yes, indeed. Grievous times we are in. But let us pray first. Rabbi Klein, will you lead us?"

Everyone bowed their heads, and Santos joined them respectfully, though not a practitioner of the Jewish religion. It didn't really matter, however. Even if he could have heard the elderly man—his voice was whispery and barely audible in this acoustic room—the prayer was spoken in Hebrew, one of the few languages he wasn't fluent in.

Once the prayer had been concluded, Yisrael led him to a chair—not nearly as nice as his own—and they sat down to discuss business.

"Could you kindly explain what happened—let's see here—five days ago?" Santos asked. "One of your men had explained it over the phone, but I'd like to hear about it in your own words."

"Well, I was hoping you would be able to arrive earlier," Yisrael started in a manner that illustrated his fear of upsetting others.

"As you know, Prime Minster—"

"Please, Caleb."

"Caleb," he sat down and removed his fedora, combing one hand through short, white hair. "as you know, there has been much trouble going around God's dominion." Dropping the lord's name always gave him a few points from the Israeli.

"Do you believe that Strasbourg is connected with what happened at the Church of the Holy Sepulchre?" Klein stared at Santos over Yisrael's shoulder.

"I cannot be of a hundred percent certainty, but sources have placed a known terrorist working out of the Indian government at the scene of the crimes. A man of the name Tej Vayida."

"India." Yisrael became flabbergasted and frantically searched for words. "How…wh…what reason could they possibly have for…for destroying Strasbourg? For desecrating the tomb of Joseph of Arimathea?"

The rabbi and soldiers didn't have any verbal reactions to the alarming news, but it seemed they were holding their breath.

Santos let out a sigh as if what he was about to say brought great weight to his soul. "Can these men be trusted?"

"With my life."

"What about theirs?"

The Prime Minister tilted his head slightly, making him appear even more boyish. "I'm afraid I don't understand."

"Have one of them take their own life."

"Fer—Mr. Santos! That's extremely inappropriate." He began to rise to his feet but stopped when he noticed the look on Santo's face. His voice dropped to that of a mouse, more appropriate for his youthful appearance. "I can't do that. This is a holy place. *They have families.*"

Santos calmly held his right hand up and his shadowy friend stepped forward, raising the brutal warhammer.

Yisrael's jaw worked as he contemplated his choices. His life or another's. In the end, the decision was not that difficult to make. "Rabbi Klein, would you please pray for *Rav Turai* Weiss."

"*Sɜr, plēz!*" the poor officer pleaded.

"No, foreplay," Santos said. "Proceed in your command."

"Do as what needs to be done," Yisrael said. "And may God forgive our souls."

With tears, in the grown man's eyes, he removed his side-arm and jabbed it into his temple.

"And that will be enough," Santo said. "You have demonstrated that these men can indeed be trusted.

The soldier quickly returned his handgun and straightened his soldiers. He seemed more ashamed of his tears than scared of how close he came to dying.

Yisrael opened his mouth but wisely thought better of it.

"I am an ancestor of Bors the Younger of Arthurian lore," Santos announced to the occupants of the Dome. "Long ago Merlin gave him and all the other knights certain powers that are passed down by one way or the other. Mine is Time. And if any of this sounds foolish to you just remember how your Prime Minister was this close to having that young man take his own life because I told him so. Anyone have anything to say?"

Not a single person blinked in defiance. If he said he shit gold, they would be waiting outside the bathroom to collect it.

"Now, *Caleb*, there are others like me and several are not nearly as likable as I. India has been studying us for decades. In Strasbourg, Vayida had been tracking a certain knight with abilities similar to a nuclear bomb. She was startled and a hundred thousand people died because of it. Here, there was no knight, instead Vayida looted the tomb of the man you believe to be Joseph of Arimathea but really belongs to the Arthurian knight, Galahad. The Holy Grail is not a myth and resided with Galahad. It contains very powerful magic that could be used to incapacitate a knight, perhaps even kill one."

"What…what should we do?" Yisrael asked.

Santos always took a sick satisfaction when leaders of entire countries asked him of a poor Argentinian family what to do.

"I can tell you with certainty that knights were never a problem before India became involved." Santos leaned forward. "And if you ever decide to make a move against one of my own, I will come after you."

With other leaders, Santos may have avoided any direct threats, but he knew Yisrael would crumble under his own fear. In regard to the others in the room, they've seen his power and wouldn't lift a finger against him. To think that was from abilities he fought to obtain; they would piss their pants if they were ever to witness his God given ones.

"A war is coming," Santos continued. "It's inescapable. If you want your little stubborn nation to survive it, you will obey my every command and *only* my command. Understand?"

Even the zealous rabbi found it would be best to nod his sun-spotted head.

# Chapter FortySeven

**"Hello, uh, Rajeev,"** Dmitri's voice barely penetrated the sturdy, oak door of the hotel, which rattled on its less-than-sturdy hinges from his frantic knocking. "I have a bit of an issue."

Rajeev groaned from his uncomfortably firm bed. It couldn't have been later than six in the morning, though it was difficult to tell with the heavy curtains that let no light in. They had driven another six hours after Amaysa before finding a hotel in Ezurum. "What is it?"

"My eye—or the place it used to be—is burning." Maybe Rajeev was just hearing things, but it sounded like there was a tremble in the back of his throat. "There's puss coming out of it, too."

With a sigh, Rajeev clambered out of bed and heaved the door open. He vomited immediately at the sight, turning his head at the last minute to spray the wall next to the door with last night's dinner. The eyepatch was off, exposing the empty socket that had cream cheese mixed with blood oozing from it.

"You would've never survived in the military," Dmitri

said but his normal humor had left his voice.

"How long has it been like that?"

"I just woke up like this," the Russian said. "After years, in the Russian ops, the thing that scared me the most was infection. It's a difficult beast to fight in the field."

Moving with urgency, Rajeev put on some fresh clothes he had picked up in Amaysa. "It's been, what, eight days since they took it out, yeah?"

"Nine, I believe. But they had applied some sort of salve over it. It has been three days since I've been without it. I guess it never fully healed during that time."

"I'll tell the women about it, then we'll go to the nearest hospital."

"Ugh, okay, just hurry."

Rajeev would've enjoyed this tone of desperation out of the normally overconfident Russian under different circumstances. Instead, he knocked on Savannah's door—he would need her backup when confronting Isabella—just slightly less vivaciously than Dmitri. She opened the door, rubbing the sleep out of eyes that were an even deeper blue than the Arabian Sea. She wore an oversized sweatshirt that fell down to her upper thigh. Rajeev prayed he wasn't blushing.

"Morning, Rajeev." Savannah said in her thick American accent that left off the "g's" from the end of words. She gave a small smile that quickly dissipated when she saw the look on his face. "What's going on?"

"Dmitri's eye socket got infected."

"Isabella may be able to do something. She can make… stuff."

The Brit was in the next room and just after one knock she appeared in the door frame fully dressed. It didn't seem as if she had just woken up.

"What do you want?"

Rajeev explained what happened.

She let out an exaggerated sigh. "Well, I guess I can't let my drug dealer die, can I?"

"We're taking him to the hospital."

"Why do that when you have a walking medicine bag right here." She grinned. Rajeev was starting to realize that her natural smile had a little snark in it. "I don't think our insurance covers torture."

Dmitri spoke something in English that was *surely* apt and appropriate for the conversation.

Isabella didn't even winch at the atrocious wound, while Savannah found something interesting on the wall. "Come to my room and I'll clean out the wound. I'll create a poultice and some antibiotics for you to take."

She led him to her bathroom, while Rajeev and Savannah were more than happy to wait in the bedroom.

"Your wife," Savannah said almost immediately. If he knew one thing about her it was that she despised the quiet. "What was her name?"

He glanced over at her. This was not something Rajeev really wanted to talk about, but he humored her anyway. "Yasmin."

"A beautiful name, how long were you together?"

"And she was even more beautiful." He smiled even though his heart panged. "Unfortunately, we were only married eight months. We had been dating for well over a year, however."

"Did you have any kids?"

Rajeev shook his head.

"I had one," she nodded her head, and her eyes went somewhere else. "Her name was Paige. She was adopted," Savannah acted like she was going to add to that but decided not to. "She died in a fire. My fire."

Tears brimmed her eyelids, and she hastily swiped them away.

"I'm sorry," was all Rajeev could think to say.

"She's oversharing, isn't she?" Isabella called from the bathroom. "It's a damned habit of hers. She needs to understand we don't want to hear her whole life story after knowing her for all of a week."

Savannah's face turned several shades more red than her hair. "Maybe if you opened up more, you wouldn't be such a morose bitch, who needs weed to get through every day."

Dmitri yelled something out in English, followed by a nervous laugh.

"Quit being a whiny, little wanker," Isabella said.

"*I believe that's his only setting,*" a snake-like whisper filled the Turkish hotel room. A tall and muscular woman drifted through the nearly soundproof door, shirtless and with a dragon tattoo on her forearm. Glanderos had found him.

Rajeev and Savannah both stood up quickly just as Isabella burst out of the bathroom, reflexively taking a defensive position in front of them. The broken spear almost seemed to materialize into her hand.

"How did you find us?" the Brit asked.

"*I've been tracking knights since before your parents were born.*"

"Then why did it take you so long? I've been around for twenty-nine years."

"*I didn't have a reason.*" She smiled in the cruel way of daegaryns. "*We're not monsters, no matter what you may think. But you killed my brother.*"

Rajeev remembered the tattoo on Balthasar's forearm. It was the same as hers. He wondered if it was idiotic to think they came out of the womb with their ink.

"Your brother." Isabella returned the smile. "Let me guess, he also kept you company on those cold nights in whatever hole you call home."

"*You jape as if I have emotions,*" Glanderos said. "*Rajeev, you have taken something from me and for that I must take your life. It's the daegaryn code.*"

"I beat you before," he held his hand out to the side. "I can do it again."

"Stop!" Isabella demanded once she realized what he was about to do. "There are occupied rooms between us and your sword. Summoning it here could hurt them."

"I can detect metals in the body. There's nobody alive between us and it." He found *Irontruth* and pulled it to him. A moment later it cut through the wall into his waiting hand.

"*You didn't beat me, fool. I could've ripped you to pieces if you didn't blindside Catharsis and force me to take her to safety.*"

"I thought daegaryns didn't have feelings," Rajeev said.

"*We have loyalty,*" Glanderos said. "*Come easy and I'll spare your friends.*"

"No," Isabella said to both Rajeev's and Savannah's very visible surprise. "We have loyalty, too."

"*So be it.*" She brought her shoulders together and grimaced. Seconds later, an object of horror from a *Hellraiser* movie appeared over her head. Marble white shined from the hellish construction that dripped blood onto her head. A tail, thin as a blade and Rajeev guessed as sharp as it. Glanderos smiled at their revolted expressions as it bounced well over her—seemingly with a mind of its own.

"Bloody, fracking hell," Isabella mumbled under her breath and then yelled at Savannah. "Grab Dmitri and get the hell out of here."

"No, I can help," she said, though she looked terrified, and steam was already boiling out of her pores.

Glanderos just smiled, perfectly content to let them make the first move.

"Fine, just don't die," Isabella said, fuming but helpless to do much else. "Both of you cover me." She ran over to her bag at the foot of the bed.

"She's intangible," Rajeev told Savannah. "Which means

when she's phasing we can't harm her. But that goes both ways. Keep a steady stream of fire on her."

Savannah stuck both hands out and flames erupted at the daegaryn. Using the shards of *Irontruth*, Rajeev created a tornado where Glanderos was.

Her smile didn't waver as she stood within the whirlwind of fire and metal.

"Don't let up," Rajeev hissed under his breath.

With the composure of a yoga instructor, she stepped into the wall on Rajeev's side.

Olmerion returned to its homes and flames consumed a cabinet as two knights waited, not sure which direction the daegaryn would attack. Rajeev concentrated on the natural metals in Glanderos, but the phasing must've hidden it.

He felt a subtle tremble in the framework under him and pushed Savannah out of the way just before Glanderos arose to the surface like a phantom. His reflexive arc triggered *Irontruth* to raise in front of him and narrowly parry the tail, though losing his feet in the process. She attacked again but right at the moment as daegaryn bone collided with enchanted olmerion, a small object pierced Glanderos between the shoulder blades. She cried out more in annoyance than in pain.

From where he laid on the ground with Savannah not far from him—having tripped over her own feet—Rajeev saw Isabella with her hand outstretched and several glass vials at her feet. *Snakebite* was the culprit of the daegaryn's misery.

"*What did you do?*" Glanderos asked. For the first time, Rajeev heard something under that neutral hiss. Fear. He realized that with her ability she should be able to phase through the spearhead, yet it still stuck there, a thorn in her abnormally large body.

"I created a cement paste and mixed it with osmium," Isabella explained. "Osmium is the densest element. Phasing through it is possible but will cause you to sink uncontrollably. You'll be a hundred feet underground in less than five minutes."

"*So be it,*" the daegaryn said. "*It'll cause this quarrel to be just a little more fair. Give you more of a chance than you gave my brother.*"

"Yeah, the wanker who rammed into the side of my Alfa Romeo 4C Spider," Isabella said. "Gave us a real good chance."

Rajeev looked to Savannah during this exchange and could tell she was shaky as she should've been, but hadn't completely combusted, only her right hand was smoldering.

Glanderos hissed and lunged at Rajeev, her tail flaring in an arc to take off his head. As he raised *Irontruth* to save himself, she was thrown off balance and the tail just scraped off the top of the sword, creating a sheer, jarring sound.

Sparing a glance over his shoulder, Rajeev saw the veins in Isabella's forehead pop as she strained with the pull of an invisible force. Glanderos resisted the Brit for just a second before using Isabella's pull as momentum to propel herself toward the Alchemy knight. Isabella barely dodged the arching tail by diving to the side.

Rajeev quickly took to his feet and charged the daegaryn, who hovered over the fallen Brit. He struck at Glanderos with intent to sever her spine. Instead, *Irontruth* swung around in a one-eighty, nearly causing him to lose his balance. The osmium must've not affected her ability to become completely intangible.

Glanderos let out a cruel, reptilian laugh at the effort and attacked with her tail. Isabella pulled at *Snakebite* again, allowing Rajeev time to weakly deflect it. With the daegaryn off balance, Isabella pushed her into the wall, which she unconsciously phased through. The Brit hurried to her feet and pulled Rajeev to where Savannah watched with hands enflamed, waiting for an opening.

"When she comes back," Isabella said to Savannah. "Blast her."

The daegaryn entered the hotel room in the same fashion she left it and Savannah launched flames at her. With no warning, Glanderos exploded, bits of brain, skull, and guts painting the dull gray wallpaper as well as the shocked knights.

"Well, that was a much more potent concoction than I expected," Isabella said, lifting up the bottom of her shirt to wipe up some of the gore from her eyes.

Rajeev and Savannah both numbly turned to the Brit, who gave them a pride-filled grin.

"Osmium is not the only thing I mixed into the cement. Ammonium perchlorate is a compound commonly used as rocket propellant. Extremely reactive especially with fire. But I thought her impenetrable skin would contain the explosion."

Russian stammering of surely artful language came from the bathroom. Dmitri peered out, single eye widening at the sight. He turned to them. Fortunately, puss no longer oozed out of his empty socket. "Can I not leave you three alone for five minutes?" The Russian shook his head, speaking first in Arabic then English as he's made the habit of since Isabella and Savannah joined them. "The maids are not going like this. No, they will not."

# Chapter Forty-Eight

**How the mighty** have fallen.

Sir Bors the Younger, son of a king and a knight of the round table. Who led battles and fought demons. Now a maid to fools who could barely slay a daegaryn with the three of them. Oaths spoken too long to remember bound him to this demeaning task.

Sitting down his massive warhammer onto the ground with a thud, he removed a rag. Bors was no stranger to blood and went to work on his grisly job, scrubbing the wooden floor of the hotel room. His pace was slow but with an anticipatory vigor.

It didn't take long until the towel was soaked dripping red. Bringing over the bucket he had left by the door, Bors squeezed the blood into it. He repeated the process several more times until the bucket was a quarter of the way full. At that point he couldn't wait any longer and brought the iron rim to his lips and drank heavily, not allowing his greed to push the blood to the sides of his scarred mouth.

Little known to many—as would be expected—daegaryn blood did not have that nasty copper taste to it like human's, instead it contained the tang of something citrusy only a bit more acidic. That was not the reason Bors supped on the blood of the alien creatures. It was for the nourishment it gave to those brave enough to obtain it. There was power in daegaryn blood. And those fools left it to waste. Fortunately, he had a voracious appetite.

The job took him an hour to complete. There was no need to rush through a delicacy he might not have for some time.

"Why don't you treat me as highly as that daegaryn," Ilcaeus had snuck up behind. Bors was also amazed how one so large could go unnoticed by someone like himself. "I might not be as good looking but at least my personality is…existent."

Speech had all for the most part left the old knight. Even if he had his tongue, few words would escape his scarred lips. Daegaryn blood had its price. Instead, he walked out of the room, staring into Ilcaeus' unnatural eyes with as much malice as he could spare.

The boy followed him out and reached for the fire alarm. Bors spun around and grabbed his wrist in a lightning quick move.

"Nobody could've possibly seen what happened," Ilcaeus said, ripped away from Bors. "I'm not killing innocent people based on a minuscule chance they glimpsed something. What if they did, anyway? Who would believe them."

Bors had a good idea who but let the kid pull the alarm. He only lived this long by choosing his battles wisely.

Outside, Bors moved in the direction of a car he would take to follow the fools, while frantic tourists wormed around him. Ilcaeus camouflaged himself against the Turkish scenery and flew above the hotel. Fire soon erupted from a hidden source in the sky, consuming the hotel in minutes. Bors winched at the sight and slipped into the Prius.

# Chapter Forty Nin

**An American, Brit,** Qatari, and Russian walk into a ba
Though maybe a better joke would be an alcoholic, pothea
recent widower, and possible former drug lord escaped from
KGB-ran asylum walk into a bar would be a better one. Wh
could go wrong?

It was the last night of their two-week quest. Tomorro
morning, they would be leaving the capital of Azerbaijan, Bak
via a boat across the Caspian Sea into Turkmenistan. But t
night, Isabella had the idea to celebrate the end of her impriso
ment with Savannah by hitting the local bars. The Brit must'
forgotten about her alcoholism. Or just didn't care.

She wore red leather pants and a tiny black crop top th
showed off some under-boob. Savannah couldn't believe s
had packed going-out clothes. After driving most of the day, e
erybody else was exhausted except for Isabella. The blunt fill
with God's Mercy that sat between her puffed-up, shining li
was probably the reason.

On Savannah's part, she wore a nicer-looking blouse she h
already worn once or twice, plus her best pair of jeans. The bo
were even worse off, each donning a plain T-shirt and shor

Though that fashion statement would be the most comfortable in the heat of Azerbaijan.

Isabella called an Uber and fifteen minutes later they were driving through the populous Baku. Savannah could tell cities they had stopped in during their travels through the Middle East were in the Middle East. Baku, on the other hand, had a completely different air to it. Domes and their protective minarets—tell-tale signs of a mosque—were a more rare occurrence. Instead, buildings scraped the sky—three specifically, constructed next to each other with the tops tilted like the flame of a candle. Those defining details that separated foreign cities and those from her home probably showed the American in her.

"You know, we could've gone there," Isabella was saying as they passed a nightclub with a line that stretched forever. "But Dmitri's wrinkly bum would get us thrown right out."

"Hey!" the Russian said. "The name Dmitri Smirnov sends shivers down the spines of men across the country. If the clubs weren't run by high school dropouts who suckled on their mother's teat until they were six, I would be *paid* to enter and then drowned in the vodka of my ancestors, hehe."

"Yeah, I don't care," Isabella said. "I just want to get rat-arshed."

"I've always loved you Brits and your colorful slang," Dmitri said, letting out a loud fart that sent everybody—including the Uber driver—reeling to roll down the windows.

They were gladly let off in front of a bar, with a line of millennials waiting outside. Young eyes turned to the odd group. They poked and prodded each other. Laughed and whispered into friends' ears.

"Ah, that must be about me," Dmitri said. "They recognize *the* Dmitri Smirnov. An intelligent bunch, those kids are."

Before any of his unwilling comrades could say anything, he spoke to his audience. "Hello, young people of Azerbaijan.

Please, no pictures or autographs; I am with my friends."

"Fracking hell," Isabella said, face growing red. With anger or embarrassment, Savannah couldn't tell. She scowled at the onlookers until most turned away, then dragged her group to the back of the line.

The bouncers were efficient and soon they had made their way to the front. They were smaller than Savannah had expected with her limited bar experience but their twin, pointed beards gave them a strong intimidation factor. Both eyed Dmitri with suspicion.

"*Heç bir problem yaratmayacaqsan, elə deyil?*" The bulkier one asked Dmitri.

"*Xeyr, uşaqlarım istəyirdilər ki, o zaman şənlik etməyi öyrətim,*" the Russian said, speaking the foreign language with ease.

"Hmm." The bouncer seemed to accept the answer, then addressed the whole group, holding up the universal sign of an ID.

Isabella gave him hers and scrutinized it heavily before taking it inside. He returned a minute later and waved her in. The same process happened with Savannah—she felt worry build up inside her, knowing that it was a fake acquired by Isabella, but it checked out too. Weird that she would care about something like that after everything that had happened. Rajeev was next.

"It was stolen," Rajeev said, displaying confidence that gave Savannah an idea this wasn't his first rodeo. "I got mugged picking up coffee this morning."

The bouncer seemed to know enough Arabic to understand what was said. Rajeev, on the other hand, didn't know any Azerbaijani, but it wasn't hard to figure out that the man didn't buy it.

Dmitri went to his aid. "Rajeev, *bu mənim oğlumdur, qanla deyil. Mən əmin ola bilərəm ki, o…yaşlıdır.*"

The bouncer seemed to lighten up a bit, but his tone

of voice and hand gestures seemed to Savannah that Rajeev wasn't getting through.

"Okay," he said. "You guys go ahead. I'll take a walk around the block and see what I find."

"Is that safe?" Savannah asked. "We're in a country none of us have been in. There could be terrorists on every block."

"Speak for yourself," the Russian said. "Dmitri Smirnov has been everywhere."

"I think I'll be fine," Rajeev said, giving her a knowing look.

"Oh, right."

Rajeev parted from the group and the rest entered the dim confines of the bar. Shoulder-to-shoulder, butt-to-butt, young adults danced to Azerbaijani rap. TVs in every corner played a soccer game that no one seemed to care about or was too drunk to notice. The bars Savannah was used to had no more than twenty patrons on a Friday night and you could get a burger with your beer, then finish up the night with some pull tab investments.

"How do you know Azerbaijani?" Isabella asked into Dmitri's ear as she dragged them to the bar.

"The Soviet Union required its special ops to know all the languages of its sovereignty."

"You were in the special ops of a communist party?" Isabella asked with her familiar suspicion.

"Many years ago."

They had reached the bar and Isabella stared daggers at one of the bartenders until he turned to them.

"Dmitri," she snapped at the Russian. "A gin and tonic."

He relayed the order and his own to the impatient bartender then raised an eyebrow back at Savannah. She slashed her hand in front of her throat.

"Oh, hell. You're an alcoholic, aren't you?" Isabella said.

"Yup," Savannah said.

"Then why didn't you stay back?"

"Because we just nearly got killed by a monster."

"Technically daegaryns are aliens," Dmitri butted in.

Their drinks were set down, and Isabella paid with the card that seemed to have no limit.

Isabella and Dmitri dove into a conversation that Savannah found hard to follow with the noise of the bar. Instead, her attention was fixated on her surroundings. It was enough that she was worried about a daegaryn sneaking up on her but being stuck in the middle of a crowd of drunk millennials was another thing. Savannah had never gone to parties in high school—and the one time she had, she got pregnant—but even being in any type of social event that didn't include solely her inner circle gave her anxiety. This was worse than those occasions. All she had was a Brit who may hate her and a Russian who probably had said all of ten words to her. It didn't help that booze was just a hand wave away. Only the thought of James' blistered face and glossy eyes kept her from doing so.

At least nobody tried to hit on her.

Thirty minutes had gone by painstakingly slowly, and Isabella and Dmitri were just finishing their second drink when a fight broke out. Savannah couldn't tell who started it and had a feeling she wouldn't have been able to even if she was fluent in Azerbaijani. There were no words of hostility or even a guttural shout, only the two shoving each other for whatever reason and some onlookers deciding to join in.

"Should we do something?" Savannah asked, standing up.

"Nooo," Isabella slurred. "It's just a bar kerfuffle. We can't stop every fight, even those more serious. There are powers above us that'll notice. More people will be in trouble. Including us."

"Savannaaah," Dmitri said. "Have a drink; it will help mellow you out a bit."

Her vision became blurry as her agoraphobia increased to a debilitating number.

"I'm going to go find Rajeev," Savannah said and left before either could respond.

She found him sitting on a curb, head up and eyes closed.

"Hey," she said, taking a seat next to him.

"If only you could see what I could see," Rajeev said, not at all startled by her presence. "Each metal appears as a different color in my mind. In a city like this, it's a kaleidoscope."

"I feel like the last two weeks have been a kaleidoscope," Savannah said. "So many things have happened that I am unable to fully process."

He opened his eyes and turned to her. "Do you think we could ever live normal lives?"

Savannah tried to imagine a future where all daegaryns had been killed and her powers were under control. It never came to fruition.

She shook her head.

"Yeah, me neither."

Silence followed while many questions flooded Savannah's brain and Rajeev gazed out into Baku, lost in his own world.

"Why did you leave?" Rajeev finally asked.

"What, the US?"

"No," he smiled in good humor. "You already told me why you left there. I meant the bar."

"Oh." Savannah found, to her embarrassment, that she was blushing. "It's not really my type of crowd."

Rajeev laughed. "I wish I could say the same."

"I'm going to be honest, you don't seem much like a partier to me."

"That's because the past year has matured me more than that length of time should've. But up until Yasmin got cancer, I went out two or three times a week since I was seventeen. I never was a great kid."

When Rajeev talked about his wife, Savannah could tell he was wrecked over her death. The Qatari tried to hide it, but some emotions are just too powerful to mask. She almost asked about her before remembering his reaction to that yesterday. Savannah had done enough therapy to know that some people just needed time.

There was a commotion behind them. Isabella ran out of the bar with Dmitri close at her heels. Savannah wondered if she should be more surprised by the fact that she was being chased out by two bouncers or that she was giggling.

*Giggling. Yeah, definitely giggling.*

"You should've *seen* Dmitri," the Brit said to them, barely able to contain herself. "Some guy started to hit on me, then had the *nerve* to *fondle* one of my *tits*. Dmitri reached over the bar to grab a bottle of vodka and *shattered* it over the wanker's head."

"He hit on her, and I hit on him, hehe," the Russian added.

Savannah glanced at Rajeev, and they both broke out in laughter. It felt good to laugh. It had been too long.

"Let's get out of here," Isabella said, pretending to be worried as she peered over her shoulder, but the smile wouldn't leave her face. "They said they would call the police."

No sirens sounded, though, by the time their Uber got there. And only laughter filled the air of the run-down Santa Fe as they zoomed through the very much alive capital of Azerbaijan.

# Chapter Fifty

**The overbooking of** Tessa's flight left her stranded at the Lisbon airport for an extended layover. She had naturally tried to bribe people for their ticket but with a cacophony of finance types that had "important" business in the States, the attempts were futile.

It was no matter. It had been a while since she had gone clubbing and had stumbled upon a nice one not far from the airport. It was a blurry night and the next morning she found herself in the bed of a man whose name she didn't know, whose language she pretended not to understand.

Ah, how she missed those kinds of nights.

Her hangover only followed her to the airport and was gone by the time she boarded her plane. There was another layover in Miami, where she sidled up to a bar and flirted with some kid who was probably still in high school.

The final flight took her to La Aurora airport in Guatemala City, about twenty miles from where she had been sent. A quick taxi ride took her to the edge of Antigua, where the scenery could be taken straight out of a Feeding America advertisement. Worn-down buildings, downtrodden individuals, and naked, bloated children greeted her at the requested drop-off.

The first part of the mission meant human contact rather than elimination, so she wore civilian clothes with a bag slung over her back. Without a hood, any passerby could tell she was stunning with brown hair that stopped just above her shoulder and blue eyes that could capture any man. Those who knew her in any minor way, however, would question if that was really her true features.

The Guatemalans must've had more important things to worry about than a *gringo* tramping around their neighborhood. But finally, someone took the bait. He was shirtless with a sizable belly that probably would've defined him as obese here but fit in Canada. A scraggly beard which had probably never been treated sprouted from his face that already sported some wrinkles, surprising for a man of his supposed younger age.

"Hello, beautiful," he said in poor English. "Come inside. I make you coffee."

"*Usted es demasiado amable, señor*," Tessa said. *No puedo negarme.*"

"Ah, beautiful and gifted." He went back to Spanish and had that glint in his eye that all creeps seemed to share. "What a treat. Come, come."

She followed him into the disgruntled tenement home with yellowed windows and peeling paint that smelled like a mix of rotten eggs and the underarm of a pubescent boy. The interior decor consisted of a table with one chair and several kitchen appliances that probably didn't work. The man moved over to a coffee pot that was almost opaque with the grit built up within.

"I'll pass on the coffee," Tessa said, continuing in Spanish. "But I'd like to know about a little girl that disappeared from this…*village.*"

"How about you give me *something*, and then I'll give you *something*, eh."

"Nope." Tessa shook a knife out of her sleeve and brought it to the man's neck. Patience was never her greatest strength. "What happened to her?"

"Okay, okay." He reeled back and tripped over a bottle, landing butt-first on the dusty floor. "Ow. I didn't know her but when a *gringo* comes here, everybody finds out. Easy to steal from. Hey, please, don't kill me!" he exclaimed when Tessa advanced on him. "She had just been born, not six months ago."

"What did he look like?"

"People said he wore a cloak like the, uh…wizard from that hobbit movie—Gandalf or something of the sorts. I also heard he was young."

"What happened?"

He sat up against the wall. "The *gringo* took her. Apparently, there wasn't even a fight, the mother just gave her to him. That's all I know, I swear."

"I believe you."

The sigh of relief from the Guatemalan was cut short by a knife buried deep in his throat.

# Chapter FiftyOne

**After many hours** of swirling clouds—broken up by the phenomenon resembling shining fairies playing among the cumulus—a great island of light surrounded by a sea of darkness came into view of the airplane window. Beijing. One of few cities at the top in technological industrialization while also holding on to its historical mainframe. Tonight, though, it would need to let go of its communist past and instead be subjected to a greater power. Him.

No driver waited for Santos at the airport, so he had to hail his own taxi. The Great Hall of the People was a foreboding place enough, and the thousand soldiers standing at attention before it only supported the fact. He exited the cab after tipping generously and approached the Chinese capital building. Not wanting Zhao's imposing attempts to make him appear callow, Santos stood tall and walked between two columns of militants—with his guard close behind—as if *he* was the dictator of China.

"*Zhuā zhú,*" one soldier—a general judging by his stars and demeanor—said, holding out an open hand. He was clean-shaven like the rest but much older, with gray hair peeking under his cap. However, his most jarring feature was the scar, starting from above his right eyebrows and ending below the drooping sack of the other eye.

"Do you know who I am?" Santos said in Mandarin, speaking in a cool manner but with a tone that it could heat up any minute.

"Fernando Gabriel-Alejandro Santos," the man said. "Secret advisor to the nations on all things." He narrowed his eyes and lowered his voice. *"Fantastical."*

From the corner of his eye, Santos saw his shadowy friend take a step forward and raised his hand just an inch to stop him.

"I assume you are in close companionship with President Zhao," Santos said calmly.

"No one is in close companionship to the President," the officer said. "But, yes, I am the supreme commander of his military."

"Ah, forgive me but I am blanking on your name."

"That's because you have never heard of it. Being nameless makes it more difficult for my enemies to locate me or my family. But perhaps you have heard of the Red Fist?"

"Indeed, I have. A pleasure to meet you," Santos said with no inclination in his voice that it was a pleasure. "Your exploits are very…*well known.*"

"At least only the ones I want to be," the Red Fist said. "Even though I have enjoyed our parley to the utmost extent, I must digress and initiate a full body cavity search of your person."

"Very well, proceed."

In so many years, Santos had never been subjected to such humiliation as what happened at that moment, being fondled in front of thousands by a soldier he could incapacitate with a swift blow.

"And your bodyguard," the general said after he was finished. "Must stay out here with my men."

"I can assure you, sir, that Binh here is as harmless as a puppy," Santos said. "With that being said, don't try to eat him; he has a killer bite."

"And it's because of that killer bite that I must insist that he stay away from President Zhao. Surely, you can understand."

A curt nod at the shadow and then he was following the Red Fist through the crowd of soldiers, any of which could have a knife tucked up their sleeve.

Santos didn't look into the future this morning. He feared the outcome of the meeting, but it needed to be done. The future of his kind depended on it.

The Red Fist led him through corridors that twisted and turned to a dizzying extent that even with his sharp mind, he would find it difficult to egress the Great Hall by himself.

Finally, they stopped before two large double doors the color of blood and communists. The general gave a series of coded raps on the oak and just seconds later it opened to the dictator of China.

Haitao Zhao had the countenance of a man who rarely smiled. High cheekbones, bold eyebrows, and a lack of crows feet would steer any man or woman to the other side of the street in the unfortunate circumstances they ever came across him. Even at this hour, he appeared to have been hard at work as seen by the scattering of papers on his desk.

"Señor Santos," Zhao said, his version of a smile barely moving pursed lips. "I have been looking forward to your arrival."

"And it is my greatest pleasure to be here," Santos returned. "But where might be, President Farooqi?"

Santos had asked—or demanded—that the president of Pakistan be here for this meeting to save him a trip with time winding down.

"He is on his way; they had to move around a storm."

"Weird that I came the same way and didn't experience even the slightest bit of turbulence."

"Weather is a difficult phenomenon to predict," Zhao moved back behind his cluttered desk. "Please, have a seat. We have much to discuss."

The Red Fist closed the door and let them be. Santos took a seat in a purposely uncomfortable chair. The dictator waved for him to begin.

"Shall we wait for Farooqi?" Santos asked.

"We can fill him in later."

There was obviously some trickery going on—a coup perhaps—but he was in the lion's den and would rely on his greatest strength. Discourse. "A war is coming."

"That's what my father said during the Cold War," Zhao countered. "What makes you so sure?"

"We both know about my influence in every single major country on Earth."

"In some more than others."

"If you'll forgive my language, I stirred up shit in a boiling pot and soon that stink will permeate every corner of the world."

Zhao, for his part, only raised his heavy eyebrows. "Is that so? And why, please tell, would you do such an *abominable* thing?"

Santos had already decided he would reveal all of his cards to the dictator. He could bullshit or intimidate other leaders but not Zhao. Now, he would need that information to reverse Zhao's decision to betray him.

"For the last century, or so, there has been a most volatile game involving my kind. I was only a player then, fresh to the new world I found myself in. Now, I am the game master and there are two dangerous players in this dance. One of them is a kid with powers twelve times as great as my own. A lot of responsibility for one so young, especially for one not so sane.

"The other is India. For as long as I've been alive, they have been experimenting on ways to eliminate knights. If they succeed there will be war like none other.

"This war I commence will knock them both off track from fulfilling their disastrous plans."

"Start a war to prevent a war," Zhao mused.

"A necessary means to save all of humanity."

"Hmm."

Santos interlaced his fingers in front of him. "Farooqi isn't coming, is he?"

"He actually arrived last night and is most likely asleep at the lovely Wangfujing."

"I assume Arole has spoken with you?"

"A representative, yes." Zhao attempted another smile. "He said you were planning on starting World War III. A ridiculous notion but one he supported with much evidence. And here you're saying the same thing."

"How much were you paid?" Santos asked.

"Not in yuan, if that's what you're asking. Instead, we were supplied with resources that are much more valuable."

"Is this the part where you detain me in one of your *renown* prisons?"

"That's too much paperwork." He stood to where he and the portrait of him behind the desk merged into one. "Your disappearance will be much easier."

Santos took to his feet as well. "That's going to be difficult to do."

"I'm pretty sure your man said the same thing."

"A weak bluff, you should know better; he doesn't talk much."

Zhao's lip twitched into a smile as he reached under the desk. Two secret panels on each side of the office slid open, revealing soldiers holding machine guns that fired without hesitation.

Time slowed down at his command to where only he could move between its ebb and flow. Bullets made their way to him like bogged-down mosquitos. With his usual composure, Santos moved around them, reaching under his beige coat for twin hatchets that should've been discovered by the Red Fist during his frisking. No time to consider what that could mean. Instead, all eight soldiers fell easily under his thirsty blades with a quick slit of the throat. For Zhao, he had a different plan. Slice after slice, he chopped the dictator's thick neck—knowing he would be feeling the pain in real time—until his head drifted towards the floor.

With not a drop of blood spilled on him, he opened the heavy, red door but the general was not there. In his periphery, though, the light was fading. He turned around to find shadows creeping up along the walls and misting across the floor like a fog from hell.

"You're Arole's pet, aren't you?"

No response came from the darkness of the office, instead a large figure stepped into the fading light, immune to the slowed time. From head-to-toe, the foe was donned in dark armor, which Santos could only assume was olmerion—how else could they resist his powers? In their hand was a sickle of similar origin.

Santos had heard some chirps from his birds about India's experiments to create their own knight. It seemed to have worked.

"With whom do I have the pleasure of being acquainted?" he asked but again received nothing but very faint sounds of gunshots. *Good.* That meant Bihn was still alive. "Well then." He brought his hatchets up to a fighting stance. Words were his strength, not arms—especially in fair contests. He would lose this battle.

With that pessimistic thought, he struck out, swinging the right hatchet down to the gap between the helm and breastplate and the left level with the abdomen. With the ease of an experienced arms man, the knight side-swept the left hatchet to disarm him of his right with the sickle, perfectly shaped for the job.

Santos churned the gears in his mind, trying to find some way to figure out how to pierce that armor with his powers. Just seconds ago, he heard the subtle ring of a machine gun as it hit the ground, so that meant time was still slowed down within his radius; the knight was the only one immune to it.

He made a couple of jabs at the knight, hoping to spot some weakness in their defense. There were none.

"What did they do to you?" Santos asked.

Their answer was a swipe at his neck with the sickle, but it was just a feint made to disarm him of his last hatchet.

But it didn't matter; his stalling had paid off. Bihn appeared over the knight's shoulder—a shadow of a shadow. His hood had been torn off, revealing his bloodied, but prominent, Vietnamese features. The knight started to turn around, noticing where Santos's eyes were, but slammed through the wall with the strength of *Hourglass*.

Wasting not a minute, Santos scrambled out of the office while maintaining his sphere of slowed-time. Multiple times he ran into dead ends and each time he thought he would meet his end. But the red and white corridors were empty all the way to the front of the Hall of People. He was met on the outside, but not by living souls. Thousands of bodies littered the lawn of the capitol building.

That gave Santos some hope for Bihn's success against the knight. But not enough for him to slow down his pace as he ran through the dark towards safety.

# Chapter FiftyTwo

**Savannah had expected** she would need to babysit Isabella and Dmitri the next morning, but somehow, they seemed unaffected by the large quantities of alcohol they consumed. Dmitri was singing some Russian ditty as they walked down the dock and Isabella appeared as cherry as her negative countenance would allow.

Turkmenistan was just across the Caspian Sea, an eight-hour trip by ferry. It would've been much longer if they had gone with Merlin's original plan to use some decommissioned pirate ship, but Isabella had said he wanted them back at Camelot as soon as possible. There seemed to be a lot of inconsistencies in Merlin's thinking, but Savannah wasn't complaining. It was an absolutely perfect fall day.

With that being said, the ferry waiting for them at the end of the dock was smaller and more worn down compared to its neighbors, though that dismal state allowed them to privately rent it.

Waiting for them on the ramp were two men. The captain and his interpreter. The captain was a dark-skinned man from Cyprus who came here when a job opportunity landed at his doorstep. Though Isabella predicted it had more to do with a recent surge in the distribution of a new drug there. The hobble in his step balanced by the offset of a cane, may have supported the notion. The interpreter, from Azerbaijan, was of lighter skin and almost as short as Rajeev but with a much larger belly. They both stared at the odd quartet unabashedly.

The captain greeted them in a reluctant manner followed shortly by the translation from the interpreter. "Hello, I am Captain Lambrou."

"And I am Zaur," the interpreter said. "Captain Lambrou's personal translator. I presume English is common among you."

Rajeev opened his mouth to object, but Dmitri shoved an elbow into his side. The Russian spoke something in Azerbaijani to Zaur and they both laughed, one nervously, the other boisterously. Nobody else seemed amused at their secret gib.

"This is an eight-hour journey," Lambrou said through Zaur. "There will be no food offered and you may have one water bottle each, so I hope you ate this morning. There will be no pegging; this is not a love boat. Also, the head has been broken for years, so if you need to piss all I have is a bucket. Do any of you have any bowel issues?"

"I think your brother may have cleaned it out this morning," Dmitri said to the poorly receptive audience.

Everyone else shook their heads at both comments.

"Good, there will be no shitting on my boat. Hold it or dangle your ass over the side. I'll give you the opportunity to use the portable bathrooms available on the dock before we leave."

There was a mass rush to the nearest porty john with a confused Rajeev following behind.


A long period of time had passed by since they had left the

Port of Baku, but it was impossible to know exactly since Lambrou had taken away Isabella's and Rajeev's phones. The reason was that he didn't want them to take any pictures of the poor conditions of the ferry and try to get his license revoked. And poor conditions there were. Mold dominated every corner, and the odor of mildew followed them even out on deck. The once white, leather seats were now yellow and cracked and somehow slightly damp at every spot. Most concerning was the bleached area on the deck at the front of the ferry. It was a deliberate way to get rid of some substance, one too big to be vomit or urine.

Savannah really missed the jovial, Irish captain, Cormac.

To her left, Isabella dragged herself to sit a couple of feet from Savannah. She had been away for at least an hour. Her face was pale, eyes puffy, and a sigh sent a whiff of the sick mixture of weed and bile to Savannah. Considering her placid demeanor on *Merlin's Breath*, it seemed she was having a delayed hangover and attempting to fight it off with some of God's Mercy.

"Any idea how long we have?" Isabella asked, somehow even more surly than usual.

"Can't be too much longer."

"I should've killed that wanker for taking my bloody phone."

They were silent for several moments and let her thoughts drift in sync with the waves below them.

"You shagged, yet?" Isabella asked.

Savannah realized her empty gaze had fallen on Rajeev, taking a nap on the bench on the opposite side of the ferry. She sputtered for a second as she tried to grasp for a comeback, but only caught a reddened face. "His wife just died," was what she finally landed on.

Isabella shrugged. "I've shagged against wilder excuses."

"Have you shagged him," Savannah rebutted, pointing at

the back of the boat where Dmitri's voice could be heard as he conversed with Zaur in Azerbaijani.

"Ah, piss off," Isabella sat back and closed her eyes, and it seemed like that was that.

"What are you going to do after you *retrieve the ancient sword from the Door to Hell and complete your epic quest?*" The Brit spoke without opening an eye, saying the last part with the dramatic emphasis of an old-timey movie narrator.

"What do you mean?" After nine days of being virtually handcuffed to Isabella, it felt weird to think she had a choice in anything.

"Will you join Rajeev and that Russian fool on your boyfriend's suicide mission of revenge? Or will you come back with me and join up with Merlin to save other knights? Or will you go about your merry way and burn another hubby, perhaps even seeking out your old friends from Belgrade?"

Savannah knotted her brows. "I thought you agreed that we would go back to Camelot, get Merlin and the others and attack the daegaryn cave in Mecca."

"I didn't agree on anything," Isabella said. "And I'd think you'd find it bloody-damned impossible to convince Merlin."

"But I saw him take on three daegaryns with ease. Why play defense when we have the pieces to take the battle to them?"

"Because nobody leaves Halgarth alive," Isabella said with steel in her voice.

"But-but," Savannah stuttered, not wanting to believe what Isabella was implying. "Rajeev did."

The Brit sat up and let out another odorous sigh as she gave Savannah a hard look. "Do you really believe that? He abruptly appears out of nowhere to save us at the last second. Then just days later another daegaryn arrives at the exact hotel we were at."

Savannah gazed over at Rajeev and massaged her temple

# Chapter FiftyThree

**While Turkey, Armenia,** and Azerbaijan were all fairly industrialized, Turkmenistan matched Savannah's idea of what the Middle East was. Past the port city of Turkmenbashi—where a gold man greeted them upon a tall pedestal—it was arid as could be. There was nothing but sand, rocks, and the potholed road below them for hundreds of miles. In regard to the road, there was only one, forcing them to drive southeast for five hours until they reached the capital, Ashgabat, and then drive another two due north.

The Darvaza gas crater was a tourist trap for only the most fervent of explorers and those with an occult ideology, allowing a glimpse into Hell. In reality, the crater was formed not by Satan, but by a Soviet crew drilling for natural gas. The drilling ground had collapsed, so they lit the gas on fire to prevent its spread, and it remained enflame to that day.

According to the lady who worked the front desk of the Doorway to Hell tourist center, the slowest time at the crater is just after sunrise. And so, they would need to find a place to stay for the night.

Just miles from the crater, small mobile homes were for

sale. The proximity did, however, create a potential danger. Three houses had their pipes explode in the past decade, killing one resident's dog and removing the third finger of the owner's right hand. A safer and cheaper option was a motel in Derweze, but the cost and risk of the mobile homes promoted isolation.

The homes were actually almost eight miles from the crater according to Isabella's phone, which hung onto a single bar, but close enough to where the humming in Savannah's skull had turned shrill. There were six homes, though two of them had yellow police tape strung over the green, aluminum front doors. Considering the money they—or more aptly Merlin—were forking over, Savannah expected some sort of luxury. Instead, the lot resembled much the state of trailer parks that she, her husband, and adopted daughter had lived in. Dirt and grime coated the once white exterior and rust covered every inch of visible metal. The windows were ashy and drapes stained.

If any bed bugs lived in this hell hole, they would be in one of those death traps.

One of the ugly, green doors opened and out exited the skinniest man, Savannah had ever seen. Bones protruded out of his face and his eyes lay deep within their sockets. That with the gray hair that barely clung to his head made him appear as the personification of Death.

"Hello, you must be Elizabeth," he said in a wispy voice, but speaking fluent English.

"Uh, no, Isabella, actually." The Brit allowed no insult to penetrate her tone.

"Yes. Elizabeth was…er, never mind." He shook his head. "My name is Batyr and welcome to Batyr's Lot. Your *öÿ* is *dördünji*." Batyr waved four fingers with one hand and gave them a key with the other.

Upon entering the home, they were hit with a powerful

fragrance of flowers and some type of spice, but underneath they could still smell mildew and other potentially harmful odors—*does natural gas smell?*

"What's so bad with a little less isolation at the motel?" Savannah asked as she peered at the smoke-stained walls.

"You should've seen the places I slept while in the Navy," Isabella countered.

Savannah looked to Rajeev and Dmitri for help.

"I've slept with my ass in the air and cock in the snow during my stay in Petak Island," Dmitri said. "I can pass out anywhere."

"Every Friday, I would go to Yasmin's house," Rajeev said. "Those are the nights that my father would be most drunk and be more likely to beat me. When her parents got tired of me, I would sleep on the street."

"I'm sorry," Savannah said and, without thinking, reached over and squeezed his hand. He gave her a small smile.

"Oh hell," Isabella said with a sigh. "You two are perfect for each other."

"Where is everyone going to sleep, anyway?" Savannah asked, quickly removing her hand from Rajeev's. There wasn't much room in the cramped mobile home.

"Well, you two certainly aren't sleeping together; you need your rest for tomorrow. Rajeev has the couch," Isabella said. "Dmitri the twin bed. And you and I will share the queen. And no," she said when Savannah started to open her mouth. "We will not be shagging."

"I was going to ask what will happen tomorrow," Savannah said. "I mean, the sword is not just going to appear out of nowhere, will it?"

She had spent so much time thinking about what she would do after this was all over, but barely even considered what would actually happen at the crater.

"It's different for everybody," Isabella said. "I had to go

deep into the Amazon to find a tree with toxic amber that I consumed. I'm not sure if it was physically or mentally, but I was teleported to a small cottage where Sir Tristan and his wife, Iseult, waited for me. They asked me many questions—none of which I will repeat. Then, without much warning, I was back in Peru and *Snakebite* was sticking from the tree."

"For me, it was Galahad's shield," Rajeev said. "It lies with his body in a tomb under the Church of the Holy Sepulchre in Jerusalem. Right when I touched it, I was transported to a brothel where Galahad was naked and surrounded by whores. He tried to get me to stay for a while but eventually, *Irontruth* materialized into his hand. and he gave it to me."

"It sounds like you got the fun knight," Isabella said.

"So, what, I just jump into the Doorway to Hell and hope I'm teleported into whatever dimension Guinevere is?" Savannah asked.

"Pretty much," Isabella said. "You'll know when you get there. By now, I'm sure your humming is almost unbearable. Once at the crater, it will tell you what to do."

Rajeev nodded in agreement.

"Well, if you *blyats* are done talking, I'm going to bed," Dmitri said, heading over to his room. "I forgot how much traveling makes me tired."

The others soon joined him in retreating to their sleeping arrangements, but it was a long while before Savannah could fall asleep. Her humming reminded her of what tomorrow would bring.

# Chapter Fifty-Four

**Just as promised,** an hour after the sun had clambered over the horizon, the area surrounding the crater was empty beside the four of them. They leaned against the unsettling, rickety fence, and peered down into the Darvaza Gas Crater. Instead of the bottomless pit they half-expected, tendrils of flames intertwined themselves through crevices leading to a bonfire in the middle, thirty feet deep. No wonder nobody came after sunrise; it was both impressive and underwhelming at the same time.

The humming was pulsing within her brain, making it difficult to conjure even a single thought. So, when she brought one leg over the fence, there was no realization of the action. And when she shrugged off Rajeev's hand, it was autonomic.

The sides of the crater were uneven with loose rocks, yet Savannah descended it without one slip. The hem of her jeans caught fire first, spreading up to through her t-shirt, then turned her hair into an auburn inferno.

Like a lighthouse in a storm, the central flame called to her. And when she reached it, the tendrils of fire pulled her to its burning grasp of desire.

It was as if she was thrown from a burning house to Hell's deepest pits. Out of the frying pan, into the fire. Her trance was abruptly let go, giving room for a dizzying, sensory-overloaded confusion. Her surroundings became clear then distorted, then clear again as she found herself within a large cavern, standing on stone that was warm to her bare feet. Torches were lined up along the walls leading to a pit of fire behind a throne placed on a high platform. Seated on it was somebody who could've been Savannah's twin. Except, instead of her wiry arms and legs, muscles rippled throughout the woman's body. And her eyes were tilted with experience and animosity.

"Savannah," she said in a commanding voice. "'Tis nice to finally meet thee."

"Lady Guin—"

"IT IS SIR GUINEVERE," the queen boomed, sparks shooting from her fiery hair. She slowly regained her composure and spoke more calmly this time. "I apologize for my outburst; it has been so long since I have had guests. Men had never taken seriously my knighthood and it really writhed under my skin."

"It…it's fine," Savannah stammered.

"Hmm. And why is it that thee found it appropriate to appear before a queen the same way as the day thee was born?" Guinevere asked.

Her nipples hardened as she realized for the first time that she was naked. Face the color of her hair, she covered herself.

"Here," Guinevere waved a hand and suddenly she was covered with a jet black, skin-tight, one-piece suit. " 'Tis non-flammable. Makes for less fire-induced accidents. Try it."

Savannah allowed her furnace to grow out of control and soon she was engulfed in flames. And as promised, the clothing did not burn away. She let the flames disperse and thanked the queen.

" 'Tis nothing. I can't have you embarrassing me out there."

Her cheeks reddened again. "Uh, can I just have my sword? Please?" She just wanted to get this over with as quickly as possible.

"*Your sword?*" Guinevere questioned. "I believe what thee meant was if thee could borrow *my sword* until you inevitably die as all mortals do."

"Er, yes. Please."

"Thou hast the chance to meet the queen of Camelot. A knight of the Round Table, and thou just want to get *Ash* and leave?" Guinevere seemed actually offended at Savannah's impatience.

"My friends are waiting for me."

"'Friends' is a bit of a strong word for thy relationship to those three. Anyhow, time works differently here. Hours spent with me will feel like minutes to those outside of my home."

Guinevere stood up and walked to the fire that blazed behind the iron throne. She reached within and retrieved a sword identical to Rajeev's except this one was whole.

"Kneel!" the queen commanded as Savannah approached her.

There was no hesitation in Savannah's movement.

"*Ash* is not like other weapons. "'Tis not even equivalent to nuclear warheads. It can, and has, wiped out entire civilizations," she said. "The wielder needs to be of a rational mind. Thou art too emotional. That will change."

Guinevere laid the edge of the blade on Savannah's shoulder, and suddenly she was back in the halls of Lynchwood Middle School. Young kids milled around, some conversing with their peers, others rushing to their next classes—their oversized backpacks bouncing around and instilling future lumbar issues.

And there she was, ten or eleven—sometime before her powers had emerged—with her auburn hair tied into braids her mother had done the night before. She had braces then but they never seemed to be cumbersome like it was for others. Mollie was one of those girls. Even before she had undergone the dental work, she had a severe speech impediment where she would slur all her 'S's.'

That day—the memory was as clear as if it happened that morning—Mollie's impediment was accompanied by a stutter when she was asked to read a passage from *Where the Red Fern Grows* in class. Laughs were stifled and some of the cheerleaders whispered to each other. The teacher, obviously hungover, acted like he didn't hear anything, but Mollie did.

After class, the cheerleaders followed Mollie through the hallway into the bathroom and Savannah followed them, knowing something was up. Now, Savannah watched her younger self as she stood before the girl's room while kids swarmed around her. Both versions took a deep breath before entering.

"M-M-M-Mollie," the shorter one, Miranda, said while her tall friend, Olivia, banged on the graffiti-ruined stall. "C-C-C-Come on out. W-W-We just want to talk to you."

They snickered at their mockery as if it was the most hilarious thing in the world.

Young Savannah turned to where she had entered, then straightened up and said, "Guys, can you just let her be? What has she done to y'all?"

"Savannah," Olivia said, smiling as if they were close friends. "C'mon we're just having some fun."

Miranda pouted at her with the same good humor. "We were just teasing her."

Young Savannah stood taller than both of them and they have had front row seats to what she does to opponents.

"Please, just leave," Savannah said, taking a step toward them.

They looked at each other, laughed and shook their heads as if this was one large joke, then moved past the Savannahs out of the restroom.

"For too long," Guinevere's voice reverberated through the peeling ceiling. "Thee have ideated on the most painful pieces of thy past rather than on the good thee have done. That is where thy strength cometh from."

The room swirled around her and Lynchwood's restroom became a street corner outside of the diner she served at while living in Georgia. A batty, old woman sat beneath a road sign and held up a sign: **Let off from job. Homeless. God Bless.**

The woman gave Savannah a wan smile and Savannah invited her back to her tiny apartment. It had only been months since she had killed her own parents. Pregnant for that same amount of time, she felt a need to repay her sins and reverse the karma for her baby.

The next morning, all of her valuable possessions— the few she had—were gone with the woman, as well as the sparse tips she had received the night before.

"And a fortnight later you did the same thing," Guinevere spoke from the sky. "*Ash* and self-control can only do so much to harness thy powers. Thou must love thyself."

"That's easier said than done," Savannah said as she watched her past self, leading the woman to her worn-down Corolla.

Guinevere sighed and in a blink of an eye, they were back in the empty castle. "When we were given these powers, Merlin also promised us a personal heaven of our choosing, a place to go once we died and where we could be gatekeepers for his weapons. Arthur had cheated on me more times than I could count, with both women *and* men, including some of his own knights. I soon fell in love with Lancelot but when Arthur found out, he placed me on a pyre. Only Lancelot fought for me. And then even he cheated on me with some queen from Scotland.

"Soon after, I made my heaven to be an empty castle where only I ruled. But Merlin was tricky, and he trapped me here to never see my theoretical subjects.

"My point is that life is cruel. Sometimes the only person who will ever love thee is yourself. If thou can't do that, thou will be sucked into a void of insanity."

"I…I'll try," Savannah eventually said.

"I believe that is the most I will get out of thee," Guinevere said. "Leave me, but do not forget me. This portal will always be open for thee."

And with that Guinevere flipped the sword into Savannah's unconsciously open hand. She caught it with ease and was transported in the same vertigo-like manner back to the other side of the Doorway to Hell.

# Chapter Fifty Five

**Seconds after Savannah** disappeared from the crater, the air next to Rajeev rippled, then a person stood there, holding an intimidating staff with blades on both ends, facing opposite directions. They wore a forest green cloak with the hood up. But the stranger's visage was not hidden for long as he removed the hood with the drama of a *The Lord of the Rings* character. It was a man, though, one perhaps even younger than himself, with peach fuzz and expressionless, blue eyes.

"Sir Galahad 'tis my greatest pleasure to finally meet thee," he said in an American accent and even gave a slight bow. "I am Merlin."

Rajeev glanced over at Isabella, saw a warning glare, and decided not to question the man's identity or correct his own. "Likewise." He held out his hand and after a moment it was taken and lightly shaken.

"And thee must be Dmitri," Merlin turned to the Russian and said with some level of malice in his voice. "I have heard much of thee."

Dmitri for his own part did not come up with some corny retort but instead just nodded respectfully and said,

"And I you."

"Sir Tristan," Merlin said to the Brit. "Well done traversing some complicated *distractions* thrown thy way."

All she gave was a curt nod.

He looked from Rajeev to Isabella, with just a hint of scorn. "Where are thy weapons?"

Isabella was quick to react, pulling out the spear tip from the back of her pants. "I forgot to mention earlier that Eoin had broken the staff."

"We will need to fix that," he said coldly and eyed Rajeev.

"I left mine in the mobile home we rented," he said, nervous but knowing why.

"*Irontruth* is not a toy," Merlin scolded him like a child even though he appeared to be younger. "It should be on thy person at all times. I will lend thee a scabbard. Summon it now."

Rajeev sought out the sword and anybody in between him and it. The tell-tell sign of a human, perhaps two overlapped, appeared near the path. That also meant they'd be discovered soon. Hopefully, Savannh was almost finishd with whatever she was doing in the crater. He related this to Merlin.

"It was not a request, Galahad," the man said.

They stared each other down for several moments, but eventually, Merlin's cold eyes forced Rajeev to drop his and hold a hand out. *Irontruth* slapped his palm a minute later. Rajeev slowly moved his head towards it and breathed a large sigh of relief when no blood was found on it.

There was movement out of the corner of Rajeev's eye, and he swiveled to see Savannah emerging from the central fire like a phantom, now wearing a tight, black unitard-like thing; red hair and blue eyes the only color on her.

Merlin leaned over the edge of the crater, twitching his lips in what must be his version of a smile. He reached down to give her a hand as she scrambled up the side, not so light on her feet as she was on the way down.

"Congratulations, Guinevere, on the success of thy quest," he said monotone. "How does it feel to hold *Ash*?"

She held the sword up before her and waved it in front of herself as if she forgot she had it. "Like a lightning rod, a path in which I can direct my powers. Also, it feels…feels—"

"Godlike," Merlin said.

Savannah nodded, running her hand against the dark blade.

"That is enough small talk," Merlin said as if anything he had said resembled any bit of a normal conversation. "There is a pressing agenda that needeth to be attended to immediately."

Merlin waved his hand and the rippling prior to his arrival again appeared. He gestured at Rajeev, who stared at the man as if he was crazy before realizing that expression had already been on his face. Merlin wrinkled his eyes in frustration and suddenly Rajeev felt a force push him into the ripple. Then in a blink of an eye, he was on a beach, staring at a sapphire ocean while his shoes sunk into white sand. Two people waited for him.

One was a teenager of some Asian descent, who wore only shorts and seemed like he'd rather be anywhere else. His scrawny body did not hide the great sword sheathed over his back. The other was a tall black man dressed in a dark suit with a receding hairline and a goatee. Rajeev was so transfixed on his unseeing, glazed eyes that he at first didn't notice the baby held in his arms.

"What's going on, man?" the Asian kid said. "I'm Masaru Kato and Death here besides me goes by Ector, though I don't know his real name. Welcome to Ibiza."

"Rajeev Patel," he said went to shake Masaru's waiting hand. Instead, the teen dapped him up. "Why am I here?"

"You'll see."

"Immanuel," Dmitri boomed. The others had joined Rajeev on the beach. "You appear well, my friend."

The hint of a smile crossed Ector/Immanuel's face. "Dmitri." He spoke in a low octave. "I wish I could say the same for you."

"Well, now I feel hurt," Masaru murmured to nobody.

"Follow me," Merlin said, obviously annoyed at the fellowship between the two.

He led them to two dark tables that stood out among the white sand. Something was on one of them and when they got close, Rajeev heard Savannah gasp. He also stopped abruptly, causing Masaru to run right into him.

"What?" the kid asked. "You've never seen a dead body before?"

It wasn't just a dead body. The naked girl lying on the table had to have been seventeen or eighteen. But most jarring was the crude stitch across the diameter of her neck. The head had been sewn on.

"Her name was Sabine," Merlin explained to Rajeev. "Though she was knighted as Sir Bedivere. Three years ago, my mentor, Sir Percival, got wind of a young knight—he had a way with that—in Munich, Germany. I wasn't much older than Kay, but he took me along with another, Lancelot."

Immanuel laid the baby down on the empty table and then went to stand behind Savannah as if he suspected her run. Rajeev glanced to his left at the ocean. *Where would she go?*

"Her gift was radiation, however, 'twas more a curse than anything else. A chaotic power that should have never been given to a human being. And 'twas her downfall. When we fell asleep that night, Lancelot snuck her out with the help of an accomplice—Gawain, I hast assumed, but cannot be certain. The next day, there was an explosion. A nuclear one.

"Not long after, Sabine was killed in her prison cell." Beheaded by none other than the ones who stole her from me.

# Chapter Fifty‑Six

**The sacrifice of** *a loyal servant is a disheartening act, indeed. Perhaps what's worse is the knowledge that his death would only bring destruction to the world. It's ironic that such great of weight is lighter for a man with a heart of stone.*

Snowflakes melted on Santos's face as he again stood before the Élysée Palace. Its etymology as the final resting place of the mythical Greek heroes seemed ever more present in mind. Winter had come early for northern Europe, and it would only get colder after today.

He looked up into the gray sky, knowing Ilcaeus was somewhere up there. France had always felt like a safe place for him but after his encounter with India's bastard, he decided it would be a good idea to bring the half-breed along with him.

The heavy double doors were opened up for him by two Republican Guards. They were expecting him.

He was led past the gold, priceless painting and all the privileges of the royal family's oppression of those less than them, to Biron's office. With a quick rap on the mahogany, one of the Guards pulled open the so apt French Doors. President Jean Biron sat behind his gold desk, normally neatly gelled hair a shaggy mess. Minister of the Armed Forces Jules Bernard stood next to him almost as tall as the seated president, her countenance proper and stern as usual, not a hair out of place.

"It's time, isn't it?" Biron asked, his voice quaking.

Santos nodded solemnly. "Since we've last spoken, Stromberg has allied with Spain and moved nuclear missiles from England to Ibiza. They're pointed at Israel and my contact says he could fire them any second or never. Stromberg is more paranoid than ever."

"I thought it was Malory and the UK."

"Things changed."

"I can't believe this is happening." Biron gulped, the anxious president nothing like the portrait behind him, while Bernard didn't even flinch. "What do you want us to do?"

Santos paused with a very real expression of great sorrow and reluctance. There was no need to fake his countenance; he'd seen what the next few words would bring. "Send a squadron of fighter pilots in Dassault Rafales. Place a nuclear warhead in a random one unbeknownst to the pilot. Let them know they most likely won't return."

"I'm guessing we won't have time to evacuate everyone?"

Santos shook his head.

Biron nodded but didn't do anything.

"This requires immediate attention."

Aimless nodding.

"Now, Jean," Santos demanded and this time the president reached for the phone on the desk but didn't pick it up.

"You'll be preventing a nuclear war," Santos said.

"Or starting it," Biron countered weakly.

"Do it!" Santos raised his voice, an extremely rare thing.

The French president stared at the phone for an eternity

but then looked up with a newfound rigidity. "No. No, I will not take the lives of innocents and risk war all because one man—no matter how spectacular he is—said there are nukes primed to rain down on Israel."

"Fine then," Santos said and in one fluid motion, a hatchet was buried into his face, blood splattering all over his portrait and the Minister of the Armed Forces. He casually wiped off the blade with a handkerchief removed as smoothly from the beige coat as the hatchet.

"President Bernard," Santos asked of the former Minister. "Can I expect you to put forth my plans?"

She wiped the blood from her face with the sleeve of her expensive, black suit. "*Oui, monsieur.*"

The phone was picked up and the war had begun.

# Chapter Fifty-Seven

**Emerging from the** mostly sparse greenery behind the beach, were three figures. Savannah didn't need them to get close for her to realize them as Pierre, Elise, and Eoin. They were bridging the gap surprisingly quick while appearing to maintain a normal pace. She realized as they got closer that the unnatural shifting of the sand beneath their feet may have had something to do with it.

Still some distance away, Eoin bellowed against the Mediterranean wind. "Nathan! Hasn't enough blood been shed already? Spare the lad whose only sin is the yearning for his mother's teat."

Merlin released the arrow and it returned to its owner. "Speaks the one who murdered Sabine."

They had finally reached the group and they could see the grievance on the Irishman's bearded face. "It was a mistake we wish we could take back. After Strasbourg, we panicked. There are other ways to control her powers that we were blind to. Don't take out what we did to Sabine on the lad."

"Oh, but I will," Merlin said in the manner of somebody discussing wine with a waiter.

"How about a duel?" Pierre offered, a breeze rustled his already messy hair. "Me versus you. If I win, you leave the baby with us. If you win, you get my head and Sabine."

"Fair enough," Merlin said. "But a duel between thee and I is anything but that. It will be Kay versus Lancelot."

"He's just a kid," Eoin said.

"One of mine is worth two of thine."

"So be it."

Isabella guided the others to become a large circle around Masaru and Eoin. The Japanese teen had already drawn his sword from the sheathe on his back. It was as long as his legs, yet it did not waver between his hands. Eoin's sword was probably just as great but within the giant's grip, it seemed like a child's toy.

"Hey, Savannah!" Elise had snuck up next to her. The French girl seemed completely out of place on this impending battlefield in her bright pink sundress. "Are you not excited? I've only seen these kinds of things on television. Eoin is going to kill that kid."

Savannah shivered at the brusque remark and turned away. Merlin meant to murder that baby as part of some ritual to resurrect Sabine. She didn't think any outcome of the battle would change it.

Merlin had decided to float over the makeshift arena. The crisscrossing of his legs and hanging robes gave off the impression of an anime character.

"Begin," he said and without a moment to think, Masaru swung his sword at Eoin with all his strength behind it. The Irishman blocked it with ease and then twisted the blade, so it was on the other side of Masaru's. With one hand on his sword, he pushed Masaru's towards the ground and landed a hard fist into the teen's face. And just like that, the duel was over.

"Well, that was boring," Elise said to Savannah and even

faked a yawn.

"Finish him," Merlin said to Eoin.

"Cut his head off, Eoin!" Elise added.

Even from where she stood, Savannah could see the fear in Masaru's eyes as Eoin stood over him.

"No," the Irish giant said and walked away.

"I was counting on that," Merlin said and reached a hand out to Eoin, who immediately fell to the ground in sudden paralysis.

"I thought you believed in fairness," Pierre hissed and removed his massive battle axe from behind his back.

"Is that what thee calls what thee did to Sab—" Merlin was knocked out of the sky by a volley of sand.

Within seconds, Pierre had transformed into a giant sand monster, towering over the distant palm trees. Another sand fist struck Merlin as he spun through the air and tried to regain equilibrium.

Elise cried out in what could've been glee or strife then raised her hands as her eyes turned solid green. Behind them, birds of all kinds swarmed out of the woods and tore at the spinning wizard. The French girl's laughter at Merlin bleeding in the artificial sandstorm was quickly cut off by a hard jab by Isabella.

"Savannah!" Isabella yelled, her golden-streaked hair blowing in the makeshift storm. "I'm going to send an explosive at the little froggie. Direct your flames at it to trigger the explosion."

*Merlin's going to kill the baby,* Savannah realized, barely hearing the Brit as she unconsciously burned. She remembered her baby, still scalding from her traumatic labor. She remembered Paige as she cried out her name through the smoke and the flames. *He's the enemy. Not Pierre, nor Eoin, nor Elise.*

"I can't," Savannah said and blasted fire at Merlin. "I will not watch another baby die."

"You stupid, self-righteous bitch," Isabella said and slashed Savannah's arm with her spearhead as quickly as a snake's bite. But before she could attack again, a halo of shards wrapped around her neck. Behind her, Rajeev held a hand out, red-faced with a large, central vein bulging on his forehead from his concentration.

Masaru stood above Eoin waving his great sword around in all directions, not sure where he should throw his assistance.

**"Thou believeth that thee can stop me!"** Merlin's voice boomed such as thunder, while he still remained hidden in a vortex of sand. Clouds blocked the sun and the smell of ozone touched everyone's noses. Lighting flashed out of the sky without the clap of its cousin and struck Pierre's sand monster. Sand exploded everywhere and the Frenchman lay unmoving in the middle of the newly formed petrified glass.

"No!" Elise screamed from the ground and reached out her hands but was picked up and held by Ector. He whispered something in her ear which seemed to calm the French girl. The agent of Merlin gave Savannah a look with his unseeing eyes that was enough for her to quench her flames.

Merlin settled down onto the white sand of Ibiza, brown hair whipping around his young and already calm face. A hundred different cuts and burns healed at a stunning rate. "Sir Galahad, please release Sir Tristan from thy wicked device."

Rajeev glanced over at Savannah for a second but returned the shards back to the handle.

"Now that we are finished with these theatrics, we may commence with the ritual," Merlin said, then held out a hand and lifted Eoin to the table with the baby so that the Irishman stood over it. "The infant is the latest of the line of Bedivere. Her blood mixed with that of a mature knight will bring back Sabine. King Arthur had suspected betrayal and requested a way to resurrect one of his own. My ancestor had obliged."

With two swift swipes of his double-bladed spear, Eoin fell headless over the equally decapitated baby, both their blood spurting in an arc onto the lifeless girl.

Savannah felt tears burst out of her eyes at the sudden slaughter, while Elise screamed into her ear and struggled in Ector's grasp.

Merlin, unfazed by his actions, bent over Sabine and placed a kiss on her bloody forehead. And just like in a fairytale of the Grim Brothers variety, her eyes opened. But there was no realization that she was woken by her Prince Charming. Instead, she spazzed off the table in a panic.

"I'm sorry!" She screamed. "I didn't mean to do it. Please help me!"

"Sabine, 'tis okay, I am here." Merlin tried to hug her but in her frenzy, she couldn't be corralled. "Nathan is here."

"Nathan?" She finally let herself be held. "What happened? Where am I?"

"Thou were murdered by enemies," he said, the rare sign of emotion being heard in his voice. "But I brought thee back. Here in Ibiza. Remember how thee talked about wanting to come here."

"I…" She noticed the headless corpses, leading to another spout of hysteria.

"Do not behold them," Merlin said, turning her around to the ocean that had sparkled like a thousand sapphires in the sun, but now in the darkness he created it was just the color of stone. "One had murdered you, the other had replaced you. They had to die for you to live."

That did nothing to calm her, but instead of convulsing, she began to glow yellow. Merlin tapped her forehead with two fingers then caught her as she fell unconscious.

"Savannah," he said as he laid the girl back on the blood-soaked table. "I am disappointed in thee. I saved thy life and in return thee attempted to smite me."

"I cannot witness another baby die," Savannah said, the heat of Guinevere becoming present in her voice. "I'd rather be the one to die."

"Oh, I will not kill thee if that is what thee art suggests. Thou art too important for that."

He grabbed the air to his side as if it was a sliding door and pulled, this realm splitting apart to reveal James Cox in a dark room, tired but unharmed.

"James!" Savannah couldn't believe what she was seeing. *He's alive. James is alive.* He appeared just as he did the morning before the daegaryns came. Fresh tears touched her cheeks as she took a step towards him.

"That is enough for now," Merlin said, then closed the portal. "Thou see the hold I have on thee? Obey me and thee can see more of thy love."

"But for thee, my dear," Merlin said to Elise. "I have no such bargaining chips and since you just tried to take my life, I possess little trust in thee."

"Fuck you, you ugly bastard," the French girl blurted out.

"Kay, bring her to me."

Savannah wanted to say something. Defend this little girl. But her love for James kept her quiet.

Kay picked Elise up as she kicked and wailed but apparently whatever he had whispered to her kept Elise from using her powers.

Then chaos erupted.

Everyone had been so distracted to not see the squadron of jets appear in the distance. So, when one released a missile the only person to react quickly enough was Merlin. He shot up and met the weapon head-on. Gripping it between his hands with too much ease, he flung it into the jet that had sent it. Then without hesitating, he rammed another jet, punching through the steel and sending it into the Mediterranean.

Savannah dropped her gaze from the aerial demolition

to try to find a way to avoid the falling debris and saw Ector disappear with Elise. He then reappeared by Pierce—still unmoving on top of the petrified glass—and took him.

Rajeev was slightly behind Savannah, hands held up to divert debris around her and Dmitri—who throughout the whole ordeal had ducked down on his side in a fetal position as if that would protect him. Isabella fended for herself and Masaru while the kid moved on a swivel, looking for something to attack.

Isabella was taken next, then Masaru.

A sudden wind sent Savannah reeling backward and when she had recovered Rajeev was gone. There was not much time to consider what had happened since she had to start clearing the debris herself with well-placed blasts of fire.

Dmitri and Sabine were now teleported off one-by-one to wherever Ector was bringing them.

A jarring explosion rocketed her ears. She tilted her neck up to see another jet be obliterated. But this one was different. The burst was blinding to where she had to turn her head and immediately after the sound of metal tearing, there was an unnerving silence.

What happened next would be a mystery as she felt Ector's hand on her shoulder and was led into a purple infinity.

# Epilogue

**A woman in** an evergreen dress the same color as her eyes walked through a field of periwinkle, a single flower tucked in golden hair behind one ear. She hummed through pink lips while she strolled underneath the warmth of the summer sun and continued to when she knelt down, folding the hem of her dress underneath her slender, tan legs.

She picked up one of the purple flowers and gazed through it.

"How sad it is for a man so young to die in such a brusque and violent manner," the woman said in a sing-song tone. "To lose his life due to a deed done by a friend. He will be remembered by some and grieved by less. How bitter is the life of a hero?"

The periwinkle darkened and the petals withered then folded upon themselves until it was a black tulip. The woman released the dead flower into the air and quit humming as she watched it float away.

Once it had disappeared from sight, she stood and walked a quarter mile before again gently falling to her knees.

"Not even old enough to know its own name," she said

in the same voice to another periwinkle, this one significantly smaller than the last. "His only sin the urge to suckle at his mother's teat as the recently deceased had said. Too young to know the significance of his death. Peace be with…" Her voice trailed off as the purple around her turned gray and then black. Death tulips took to the air at a quicker rate than she could keep track of.

Death had arrived at the realm she so much endeared. And the woman was sorrowful, knowing there was nothing she could do.

The collapse of Terrene 43 was nigh, and its people were on their own.

# Acknowledgements

As I like to say, you guys are my inspiration. So, to every person who read this, thank you, I truly couldn't have done this without you.

First and always foremost I must give thanks to God, who I wouldn't be able to do any of this without. Life has been crazy, so it's nice to know he has a plan for me (Jeremiah 29:11).

I dedicated this book to Better Blend because the people there mean so much to me and have forever changed me. So, thank you Madi Adkins, Joseph Berger, Tori Gilman, Riley Hopkins, Jack Manis, Tess Parks, Kris Phillips, Alex Vogelpohl, and Elizabeth Wintersheimer More specifically, I would like to thank Isaac Hamlin for inspiring me to aim high and succeed in a business setting. Casey Cox for being a major role model and showing me how a proper leader isn't someone who commands from the sidelines but is right in the mud with everyone else. Zoe Miller for taking the reins in a sudden change of powers and doing an excellent job. Tessa Gastright for being the first (other than my parents) to read my first book, Shadow of Fear, and believing in me before anyone else. Ben Elstun for truly being the better Ben and my best friend, always there even in my worst moments. Gabby Adkins for always bringing me Starbies and being the most compassionate person ever. Layla Bitchdorfer—I mean Beiersdorfer—for being the silly person she is and someone easy to talk to. Riley Tompos for being a super caring person despite her chronic RBF. Isaac Yoakum for getting me back into a community of Christians. And finally to Logan Graham for bringing me much more insight than a seventeen-year-old ever should.

I can't forget to mention my kids: Eva Vallandingham, Aliza Sanchez, Anna Quinn, Annie Davis, and Kaedence McGuire, who I love more than they ever will know.

MAJOR thanks to Paula McPeake—my unofficial agent—for all she done in support for my book, finding me my first book signing and being a beta reader (while also linking me with others). I don't think I would've sold as many books as I have if it wasn't for her help.

Xavier Comas and his team at Cover Kitchen did another amazing at the cover design, arguably the most important selling feature of a book. He took what was in my head and made it ten times better, creating a cover that is both bold and eerie.

When writing a book, it is easy to make mistakes especially in a multiple-POV novel like Molten Iron. So, thanks to Belle Manuel for taking the editing reigns and pointing out my many, many errors. Also, I have to thank my beta-readers: Paula McPeake, Luke Italiano, and Amanda Chism. It really means a lot that you guys took time out of your busy days to critique my work.

Luke and Adam, thank you for being the best brothers anyone could have. Seeing you guys, I know I did a good job at being your big brother.

And finally, but most importantly I have to thank my parents. Mom and Dad, I can't tell you how many times I've looked at my high school graduation card that I'm sure you don't even remember writing. You said you were proud of me and of all that I have accomplished in my young life. With the struggling start to my writing career and being waitlisted for many PT schools, I didn't really feel like I had. I would wallow in my self-pity but then read that card and think why the hell am I doing this? You and so many others believe in me, so why can't I?

Thank you all for believing in me.

# About the Author

**Ben Naas** is also the author of Shadow of Fear. He lives in Verona, Kentucky and just recently graduated from Northern Kentucky University with a Bachelor of Science in Neuroscience. He will begin his pursuit for a Doctorate in Physical Therapy this summer at Western Kentucky University. For now, you can catch him slinging blends at his "job," Better Blend, or trying to shoot under a hundred on the golf course. He welcomes you to his website (bennaas.com) and his social media (@ bnaas30).